PRAISE FOR

Black Cat Crossing

"*Black Cat Crossing* has everything a cozy mystery could want—intrigue, memorable characters, a small-town setting, and even a few mouthwatering recipes . . . A purr-fectly cozy read."

—Ellery Adams, *New York Times* bestselling author of
Breach of Crust

"If Charlie and Diesel ever make it to Texas, they'll be heading straight to Lavender to meet Sabrina and Hitchcock to talk about solving mysteries. I loved every page of *Black Cat Crossing*, and I can't wait for a return visit to Lavender."

—Miranda James, *New York Times* bestselling author of
the Cat in the Stacks Mysteries

THE BLACK CAT KNOCKS ON WOOD

KAY FINCH

BERKLEY PRIME CRIME, NEW YORK

BERKLEY PRIME CRIME

An imprint of Penguin Random House LLC
375 Hudson Street, New York, New York 10014

THE BLACK CAT KNOCKS ON WOOD

A Berkley Prime Crime Book / published by arrangement with the author

ISBN: 9780425275252

PUBLISHING HISTORY
Berkley Prime Crime mass-market edition / June 2016

PRINTED IN THE UNITED STATES OF AMERICA

10 9 8 7 6 5 4 3 2 1

Cover illustration by Brandon Dorman (Lott Reps).
Cover design by Daniela Medina.

Penguin
Random
House

For Audrey, our sweet little candy lover

ACKNOWLEDGMENTS

Heartfelt thanks go out to the entire cozy mystery community—the talented and gracious authors, the readers and reviewers, and everyone who takes the time to send kind words to those of us who spend so many hours sitting alone at a keyboard.

Thanks to my delightful editor, Michelle Vega, for her cheerful guidance. I'm grateful to Penguin Random House and all of the Berkley folks for their support of my work and for continuing to bring all of us so many great books. Special thanks to my agent, Jessica Faust, for bringing me to this party.

Hugs to my fabulous critique group. Without y'all I'd be lost. Thanks Amy, Bob, Dean, Julie, Kay 2, and Laura. Thanks also to Susie and family for opening your home to our group every week. We appreciate you so much.

Last but never least, thanks to my Texas and my Pennsylvania families for tons of support, especially to my husband, Benton, who endures a lot of crazy fictional questions.

1

M Y TALL BLACK cat perched atop the ink-jet printer like a misplaced hood ornament and supervised as I worked.

"Hitchcock," I said. "Get down from there. You're too heavy. Aunt Rowe won't appreciate it if you break her printer."

His long tail swished across the paper tray. A couple of months had passed since the cat and I adopted each other. Without a doubt, he understood what I wanted him to do. I was already accustomed to him ignoring me.

I turned to look directly into the cat's green eyes. "*Please* get down," I said.

Hitchcock jumped to the floor and promptly began cleaning a paw.

"Thank you." I grinned and returned my attention to the flyer I'd designed for the Love-a-Black-Cat adoption weekend that Magnolia Jensen, our local vet, and I had planned together. The event was scheduled for late August, well in advance of Halloween, which could be a dangerous holiday for black felines. Rescue groups from three surrounding counties had opted in, and the event would be held at the Lawton County fairgrounds. We hoped to set a record for bringing homeless cats together with their new forever families. Now was the time to gear up advertising and donation collecting for the big weekend.

My own printer didn't do color, so I'd come to use Aunt Rowe's for the flyer. I clicked the button and waited for the page to spit out, then showed the flyer to Hitchcock. "I couldn't have found a more handsome model for this flyer than you."

He looked up as if inspecting the page and gave me one of his kitty smirks.

The flyer featured a picture of Hitchcock sprawled on the windowsill of my cottage, one of his favorite lounging spots. "We'll find a place to make copies so we don't use up all of Aunt Rowe's ink."

"Mrreow," Hitchcock said, as if he agreed with the plan.

An outburst of laughter drifted into Aunt Rowe's office from the screened porch. Some of her friends had gathered for brunch, and it sounded like they were having a grand time. I was happy to see her back in her usual routine now that the cast had finally come off the leg she'd broken last spring. She was exercising like a demon—doing Zumba and lifting weights—and looked great. I felt like a slug around her. Devoting long hours to writing at the laptop could do that to a person.

Louder noise that I could only describe as hootin' and hollerin' came my way. Hitchcock and I looked at each other.

"Jeez, they're getting rowdy out there. Let's go investigate."

I closed the computer program I'd been using, picked up the flyer, and headed toward the noise. Music began playing, and the laughter grew even louder. No surprise that a group of four women could make a racket, but now they'd piqued my curiosity. What the heck were they up to?

The smell of biscuits and Glenda's delicious ham-and-cheese casserole baking filled the air as I made my way down the hall. Aunt Rowe's tireless housekeeper was an excellent cook, and she kept the house as well as Aunt Rowe's rental cottages spic-and-span.

As I reached the doorway to the porch, I recognized the song—"Save a Horse (Ride a Cowboy)"—at the same moment I saw Aunt Rowe dancing an unusual two-step while flinging one arm in a circular motion above her head. She wore a red cowboy hat with a purple feather plume and a matching purple button-down shirt. Her three friends clapped hands and stomped their feet in time with the music.

Behind me, Hitchcock had opted to stop a few feet shy of the door, where he sat watching me. Smart cat.

"I'm going in," I told him and placed my flyer on a console table in the hallway. "Wish me luck."

Aunt Rowe kept up her performance for a bit, then slowed and took off her hat before wiping her damp forehead with a shirt sleeve. She caught sight of me.

"Turn that off, Helen," she told the woman nearest her, who punched her cell phone. The song cut off. "What d'ya think, Sabrina?"

I shrugged. "I'm speechless, Aunt Rowe. What are you doing?"

"Practicing my lasso skills," she said.

Lasso? What the heck?

"She's gonna need a lot more practice before she's ready," said Pearl Hogan, whom I knew well from frequent visits to her candy store in town, Sweet Stop. "We all will."

"Practice for what?"

"Lavender's Senior Pro Rodeo," Helen said. "Which color shirt do you like better, Sabrina? Purple like Rowe's or this red one?" She picked up a red long-sleeved shirt from the table, stood, and slipped it on over her floral blouse. "I'm partial to the red." She turned to the left, the right, then twirled to show off the shirt.

I prided myself on my cognitive ability, but they had lost me back at "lasso."

"What on God's green earth are you ladies talking about?" I said. "What rodeo?"

The fourth member of the group, quiet until now, spoke up. Adele Davis had attended high school with Aunt Rowe, and they'd been friends ever since. I had only recently met the woman after she returned from touring Europe with her husband. "You've never been to the Lavender rodeo?" she said.

I shook my head. Not only had I never been, but I was generally opposed to any event that mistreated animals in any way, shape, or form. I couldn't imagine a rodeo as an animal-friendly place.

"Sabrina's a writer," Pearl said. "Literary types don't hang out at rodeos. They prefer bookstores, libraries, candy stores." She winked at me.

I turned to my aunt, who was busy unbuttoning the purple shirt she'd tried on over her clothes.

"There's a rodeo for seniors in Lavender?" I said.

"Not exactly," Adele answered. "The rodeo has been going on for twenty years or more—first Friday of the month—but they're holding the first senior night three weeks from now."

"And we're going to perform," Aunt Rowe said. "You're looking at Team Flowers."

Helen, who ran a tailoring business out of her home, said, "I'm going to embroider the team name on the shirt pocket and the name of our sponsor on back. Around-the-World Cottages."

"You're doing this for the publicity, Aunt Rowe?" I said. "Wouldn't it be cheaper, not to mention safer, to buy an ad in the rodeo program?"

"Program schmogram," Aunt Rowe said. "We're in this for the fun and the excitement. Right, girls?"

"Right," her friends said in unison.

I didn't want to be a spoilsport, but these women ranged in age from midsixties to early seventies and would fit in better at the Red Hat Society. I couldn't imagine them performing in any capacity at a rodeo. I glanced at a near-empty pitcher on a side table and surveyed the women's drinking glasses. It was a little early in the day for Aunt Rowe's legendary Texas Tea—a potent beverage containing several types of alcohol. I decided not to ask about their drinking at the moment. I had another question on my mind.

"Are you sure the Senior Pro Rodeo isn't for seniors who performed as rodeo professionals at some point in their lives?" I said.

Pearl said, "I did some barrel racing back in high school." *What was that, like fifty years ago?*

I wanted to say more, but I clamped my mouth shut. Sounded like this senior rodeo fell at the end of July—a scorching-hot Texas July, with temperatures dropping to ninety at night if we were lucky. Who in their right mind would want to ride in a dusty rodeo arena under those circumstances? I'd learned enough about my aunt in the months since moving to Lavender from Houston to realize it was best to ignore the whole thing and hope she came to her senses before the date arrived.

"I need to get back to my writing, ladies," I said. "Good luck with your practice. Oh, and by the way, I'm with Aunt Rowe. I prefer the purple shirt."

I walked out before my true opinion about their crazy plan could slip from my lips. Hitchcock was nowhere in sight as I grabbed my flyer from the table. I went to the kitchen in hopes of finding Glenda, but she wasn't there. The oven timer indicated another ten minutes for the casserole to bake.

I opened the kitchen door and caught a glimpse of black streaking past me. Hitchcock was an expert at slipping out unnoticed, but I was getting better at catching him in the act.

I was halfway out myself when someone said, "Sabrina, wait."

I turned to see Pearl hurrying across the room toward me. Maybe she felt the same way I did about the rodeo and wanted my advice on how to nix the whole deal.

"What is it, Pearl?" I closed the door and stepped back into the kitchen.

The older woman's pale complexion was flushed. She twisted the hem of her shirt into a tight coil. "I need a favor."

"Okay."

"How's your cat doing?"

"Fine," I answered slowly. "Why do you ask?"

"I'd like to borrow him."

I showed her the flyer. "If you'd like to adopt a cat, I can get you fixed up."

"No, I need *your* cat. He's the bad luck cat, and that's the whole point."

I started to laugh, but noted Pearl's dead-serious expression and sobered quickly. "Are you kidding me?"

"Seriously. I need Hitchcock, just for a little while."

"Have you been talking to Thomas?"

She shook her head. "I didn't have to. Everyone knows you have the bad luck cat."

"You're dead wrong," I said. "The fact that there's some ancient legend about a black cat has no relation to my cat. Ask Thomas. Even he doesn't call Hitchcock El Gato Diablo anymore."

At least not in my presence.

Pearl looked over her shoulder as though to make sure we were alone, then continued as if I hadn't spoken. "See, there's a person who deserves a ton of bad luck right about now, and I'm ready to deliver some."

By using my cat? I couldn't believe the sweet candy-store lady would say such a thing.

"What's going on, Pearl?" I said. "This doesn't sound like you."

"Ordinarily, such an idea would never cross my mind." She chewed on her lower lip. "You know I've had my heart set on buying the property next door to expand my store."

"Right," I said. "I met that woman who drew up the blueprints, your designer."

Pearl nodded. "She's just as put out as I am about this. I made a deal to buy the place, signed the earnest money contract, and paid a thousand down. The property should be mine, fair and square."

"What went wrong?"

"Crystal Devlin, that's what. She's a liar and a cheat. Claims she doesn't know what I'm talking about. Says there was no earnest money contract, as if the paper I signed disappeared into thin air. My check hasn't been cashed."

The Devlin woman was the go-to real estate agent in Lavender and surrounding Texas Hill Country towns. "Crystal Devlin has a reputation to uphold. Why would she lie?"

"Rumor has it she's in cahoots with a bigwig investor from Austin, someone who wants to buy up a bunch of properties in town. He has deep pockets, and she thinks she can kick me to the curb. That's why I want to borrow the cat. I wouldn't need him for very long. Maybe a few hours."

"That's ridiculous," I said, my voice rising. "I'm sorry for what happened with Crystal Devlin, but I won't agree to any such thing. Hitchcock is my pet. You can get your own cat if you like."

"He's the *bad luck cat*," she said. "No other cat will do."

"If he *was* bad luck, which he *isn't*, then why would you want to take him anywhere and risk having bad luck yourself? That doesn't make any sense, Pearl."

"Hitchcock's my friend," she said. "He wouldn't let anything bad happen to *me*. Knock on wood."

I rolled my eyes. There she went with another crazy superstition.

Footsteps sounded in the hallway. "Sabrina, Pearl, everything all right?"

"We're good, Rowe," Pearl yelled. "I'm checking on the casserole."

I moved closer to the woman and met her gaze. "I'm not lending you my cat. First of all, I find the suggestion that my sweet boy would cause any sort of bad luck offensive. Second,

I think it's a better idea for you to hire a lawyer to look into this. Either that or turn the other cheek. No good will come out of a plan for vengeance."

"I can't stand that woman flat-out lying, tryin' to cheat me out of the deal I made," Pearl said heatedly. "She's going to pay, cat or no cat."

"I'm sorry, Pearl," I said again. "*No cat*, and that's final."

I turned and left the house. I might never again experience the happy, childlike feeling of purchasing a sack of my favorite malted milk balls at Pearl Hogan's candy store.

2

I HAD PLANNED TO spend the day writing. After learning about the rodeo and listening to Pearl's annoying request to borrow Hitchcock, any hope I could focus on my novel-in-progress vanished. I took the walking trail past the Paris cottage, one of twelve rental units Aunt Rowe had designed to commemorate her travels to foreign cities. Eleven, now that I lived in the Monte Carlo cottage at my aunt's insistence.

Laughter drifted to me from the Glidden River. With the stifling heat, our guests spent more time cooling off in the pleasant water under the shade of overhanging oak trees and barbequing meals over coals on our pits than patronizing the restaurants and shops in town. They didn't have to spend a lot of money for a relaxing vacation in the Hill Country.

Back at my place, I found Hitchcock inside, lapping eagerly from his water bowl. With my aunt's permission, I had installed a pet door for the cat. I would have preferred to keep him locked safely inside, but this cat was not one to give up his freedom, and he voiced that opinion loudly. Once I'd con-

vinced Thomas Cortez, Aunt Rowe's grounds manager, that
Hitchcock had saved my life during a confrontation with a
killer a few months back, he quit obsessing about removing
the black cat from Lavender. I felt reasonably sure my pet was
safe to wander Aunt Rowe's property. The fact that he sometimes hitched a ride into town with unsuspecting drivers still
concerned me, but I had yet to find a workable solution to
curtail his travels.

I smoothed the flyer I'd printed at Aunt Rowe's and in-
serted the page into a crisp new manila folder, then went to
the kitchen for a glass of iced tea. Hitchcock left his bowl and
jumped up on the table to sit beside my laptop.

"Mrreow."

I turned to him. "Yes, I know I should be writing. After
what just happened, I can't think about fiction. Aunt Rowe
intends to perform in a rodeo, for crying out loud. How crazy
is that?"

He looked at me, his eyes wide.

"You're right. I should be used to her craziness by now. I
try to be supportive, really I do, but where does she come up
with such ideas? And how about Pearl's request to borrow
you? That is so *not* going to happen."

I thought about the sweet Pearl Hogan I'd met at her
store. With the woman's permed white hair, round as a snow
globe, and the wire-framed glasses she wore perched on her
nose she resembled Mrs. Santa Claus. During the holiday
season, she delighted children by dressing as Mrs. Claus
and holding readings of favorite Christmas tales.

Pearl had shared her plans with me to expand the store to
make space for a game room and candy-making classes for
tourists with young children. She had a sound business plan
in the works. I was disappointed that her attempt to buy the
property next to her store had failed. Maybe the Austin developer offered a higher price for the property, but that didn't
excuse Crystal's denying Pearl's contract existed in the first
place.

I understood Pearl's animosity toward the woman, but I couldn't excuse her silly idea to use Hitchcock to cause bad luck for the real estate agent. Until today, I didn't realize Pearl was one of Lavender's superstitious citizens. Approaching Crystal myself to question her about Pearl's contract probably wasn't the best idea. I'd give Pearl a day or so to cool off, then encourage her to consult with an attorney.

What I *could* do today, though, was talk to the rodeo people about the upcoming senior event. That seemed like a task better done in person. I didn't even know where to go or whom to talk to, but I knew someone who would.

I grabbed my phone and called my friend Tyanne Clark at her bookstore.

After three rings, her teenage employee answered with a breathless run-on sentence. "It's a great day at Knead to Read this is Ethan may I help you?"

"Hey, Ethan, it's Sabrina," I said. "Tyanne busy?"

"Not very," he said.

"Great, I need to talk to her, please."

Ten seconds later, my friend came on the line. "How's your new book coming?"

Always her first question.

With fingers crossed, I said, "Just fabulous. My word count is growing by leaps and bounds."

Hitchcock, curled into napping position on the tabletop, raised his head and looked at me.

"Uh-huh," Tyanne said.

"Hey, think you could get away from business for a couple of hours?"

"Maybe," she said tentatively. "Why?"

"Because you and I need to go see a man about a rodeo."

"Have you been drinking?"

"No, but after listening to Aunt Rowe this morning, maybe I should have imbibed along with her and her friends."

"What's Rowe up to this time? I assume she's the reason you want to discuss the rodeo."

"She definitely is." I filled her in on Aunt Rowe's latest scheme. "What I'm thinking is that sometimes she embellishes her stories."

"You *think*?" Tyanne laughed.

"Okay, I know so. That's actually what I'm hoping for. Maybe the rodeo organizers planned for Aunt Rowe and her friends to kick off the night by riding in with the Texas flag or some other perfectly safe activity, and she's making it out to be some rip-roaring Wild West extravaganza."

"Hmm," Tyanne said. "Yeah, I can see that."

"The sooner I know the facts, the less energy I'll expend worrying. You *do* know where the Lavender rodeo is located, right?"

"Sure, we take the kids there once or twice a year. It's officially the Hill Country Rodeo, but half the time people say Lavender Rodeo. It's about fifteen miles out of town. Near that winery we went to when we celebrated your moving here."

I smiled, remembering how we'd giggled into the wee hours after the winery tour and the tasting that followed.

"You up for a drive?" I said. "I can swing by in fifteen minutes."

"I'll be ready," she said.

Hitchcock watched as I disconnected the call. He looked at my computer, then back at me, the way a wife might look at a husband who announced he was going to play golf when the lawn needed mowing.

"Tyanne and I are taking a drive," I said. "I'll write later. Want to come along?"

The cat lowered his head to his paws and closed his eyes. Heaven forbid I should interrupt his nap.

T HE early afternoon sun beat down on my Accord as Tyanne and I headed to the rodeo. The drive took us over hills and into ravines with foot markers to measure floodwaters—

a safety precaution to keep drivers from heading unbeknownst into danger during times of pounding rainstorms.

The Gillespie vineyards came into view, and I saw the sign for the tasting room we'd visited several months earlier. I suspected most tourists were inside the air-conditioned stone structure, though I spotted some people outside in the area designated for visitors who wanted to experience the actual harvesting of grapes.

The land flattened, and we passed several gated and land-scaped entrances to ranches. Tyanne pointed to one particu-larly elaborate entrance marked "The Big D."

"The owner of the rodeo lives there," she said.

I slowed down to look. Beyond the gate and down the lengthy drive sat a majestic two-story house with a backdrop of large trees.

The giant scrolled letter *D* on the bronze-colored gate was impressive. "Reminds me of that song," I said. "Goin' through the big D and don't mean Dallas."

"In this case, it means Devlin," Ty said. "Lance and Crystal Devlin."

"Crystal, the real estate agent?"

"That's her," Tyanne said. "I'm not sure who owned more property before they married, husband or wife. Between the two of 'em, they own pretty much everything you can see up to, and probably well into, the next county."

"How do you know so much about them?" I said.

"Chamber of commerce meetings," she said. "Most of the business owners attend. Your aunt knows Crystal. And Ethan knows the Devlins' son, Cody, from school and mentions him from time to time."

"What do you think of Crystal?"

"She's okay, I guess." Tyanne shrugged. "Why are you interested in her?"

I told her about Pearl's issue with the woman and the candy store owner's request to borrow Hitchcock to cause bad luck for the agent.

Tyanne laughed. "It's bad enough Pearl thinks your cat's bad luck, but she thinks she can use him to direct bad luck to a specific person? Sounds like Pearl has a little too much sugar on the brain. Oh, turn right up at that sign."

A simple white board read, "Hill County Rodeo." I steered onto the gravel driveway and, about a mile in, came to a dirt parking lot that held a couple dozen vehicles, mostly pickups. Next to the lot stood a large whitewashed building with a corral off to the right.

"Pearl is a sweetheart," I said, "no pun intended. I hate to think someone's cheating her."

"I agree. The real estate deal sounds like something that bears looking into."

"Later." I parked the car and pulled the key from the ignition. "Today, it's rodeo time."

Ty looked at me. "There's something I never thought I'd hear you say."

"I'm here strictly for information. I don't want to witness anyone mistreating animals." We climbed out and walked over to the corral where onlookers had gathered to watch young women barrel racing. This I could handle. I squinted against the bright sun and dust kicked up by the horses. As grit hit my skin, I realized Tyanne was more appropriately dressed for this place in her slacks and closed UT-orange Crocs than I was in my shorts and flip-flops.

"Ace McKinney manages the rodeo," Tyanne said. "He's that man leaning on the fence over there."

I followed her gaze to a stocky middle-aged man. His tanned face looked weathered by much time in the sun, and long gray sideburns were visible beneath the brim of his dusty cowboy hat. He was totally focused on the barrel racing, and I wondered if he coached the riders.

"What kind of name is Ace?" I said in a low voice. "Sounds like a cardshark."

"That's the writer in you talkin'," Tyanne said. "Probably a nickname for some boring name his parents gave him."

"Cletus," said a voice behind us.

We almost knocked heads turning in unison to see a forty-ish blond man wearing dark sunglasses and standing very close.

"Excuse me?" I said.

"His given name is Cletus," the man said. "Wouldn't *you* rather go by Ace?" He grinned at me, showing off perfect white teeth.

I felt a flush rising up my neck.

He kept his eyes on me and tipped his head toward the barrel racers. "You one of their mothers?"

"Me? No." I laughed, then without thinking added, "I'm a writer."

"Rider?" he said.

"No, a writer, as in novel writer."

Tyanne added, "A darn good one, too, Hayden Birch."

The man turned to Tyanne, snapped his fingers, and pointed at her. "You're the book lady."

"Got it in one try," she said. "Haven't seen you in my store lately. We just got the latest C. J. Box if you're interested."

"I am, but they keep me pretty busy here. Don't know when I'll get into town." He turned back to me. "You doing research or what?"

This guy didn't need to know the book I was working on was set in New England and starred a female FBI agent or my real reason for today's visit.

"Research, yeah," I said. "This is my first time to the rodeo."

Tyanne gave me a look but didn't say anything.

"You from the city?" he said.

"From Houston, but I live here in Lavender now."

He grinned some more. "I can show you around, Miss . . ."

"Sorry," Tyanne said. "My bad. Hayden, this is my good friend Sabrina Tate. Sabrina, Hayden is, believe it or not, the rodeo clown."

I forced myself to keep a straight face. "Wow, that sounds like an interesting job."

"Fun, with a certain amount of danger," he said. "Rambo the wild bull strikes fear in the hearts of most, but I know how to handle that boy. C'mon, I'll show you ladies around."

"I've been here before," Tyanne said, adding a wink behind Hayden's back. "I'd like to stay and watch the barrel racers."

"Okay." I hoped she didn't think I'd have any romantic interest in this guy. A man who bragged about spending time with a wild bull wasn't exactly my type.

I followed Hayden past the whitewashed building. We walked through a side gate to a large paved area with ticket booths on our left, concession stands on our right.

"It's a small operation," Hayden said as we entered an arena lined with bleachers on two sides. "Brings a decent crowd, nothing like the Houston Livestock Show and Rodeo."

The Houston rodeo was a huge moneymaking event that brought in famous singers and snarled traffic for about a month every winter, but I'd never attended.

"To tell the truth," I said, "I'm not really a fan of rodeos. I'm an animal lover."

"Most of us are," he said, "especially Mr. D, the owner."

"I'm glad to hear that."

We walked the circle around the arena, and he pointed out the bull chutes and a barn where animals were kept prior to roping events.

I cringed at the thought and averted my gaze. "What can you tell me about the upcoming senior rodeo?"

Before he could answer, a loud voice hollered. "Birch, stop your lollygagging and get to working those horses."

I spun to see Cletus McKinney—Ace—approaching us.

Hayden said, "On my way, Ace."

"Quit clowning around," Ace said, "when there's work to do."

Hayden looked at me and spoke in a voice too low for Ace to hear. "He loves saying that, but he's just jealous. See you around, Sabrina."

"Thanks for the tour."

As Ace neared me, he said, "Sorry to break that up, ma'am, but this is a working rodeo, and it'd do you good to steer clear of that particular clown. I mean that in more than one sense of the word. He's a bit too fond of the ladies."

My face grew warm. "I assure you, I have no interest in your clown. I came here to do some research."

"'bout what?"

"The Senior Pro Rodeo," I said.

He looked me up and down. "You don't look like a pro or a senior."

"I'll take that as a compliment, but I need to know more about plans for the event."

"A couple champion riders from Dallas are comin'." He rubbed his chin. "We signed up some locals to perform."

"All professionals, right?"

"Mostly," he said. "What's your interest?"

"My aunt and her friends are planning to take part," I said. "I think she must be mistaken about your intentions for the event. Rowena Flowers."

"Yeah." Ace lifted his hat and scratched his head. "I remember her. She signed up for goat tyin'."

"*Goat* tying?"

He smirked. "You have a problem with that?"

"As a matter of fact, yes. There is no good reason to rope a goat."

"All due respect, ma'am, it ain't against the law. If it's your aunt you're worried about, I believe this is her decision. She can sign a waiver same as everybody else who performs here or bow out. Makes no difference to me."

"Surely Mr. Devlin doesn't approve of your endangering the lives of senior citizens. I'll speak with him about this."

Ace laughed. "Good luck with that. Lance came up with the senior rodeo idea, little lady, and I believe I know what he'd do or not do better'n you."

The man didn't stand more than two inches taller than me, and I didn't appreciate the "little lady" tag. And boy oh boy did I ever want to wipe that smug expression off his face.

"Then I'll speak with Crystal," I said. "I'm sure she has more influence over him than you do."

"That woman don't care about nothin' 'cept herself," Ace said. "Never has, never will. You finished with your weak threats now?"

Tyanne came through the gate, walking fast toward us.

I straightened and kept my eyes on Ace. "I'm not finished talking about the cruelty of roping goats."

He threw back his head in a deep laugh, then pinned me with a dark-eyed stare. "You have a problem with goat tyin', ma'am, you got no business livin' in Texas. I have work to do. Good day." He turned and headed for the gate.

Tyanne put a restraining hand on my arm, but I couldn't hold back a retort.

"You haven't heard the last about this."

Ace glanced over his shoulder and kept walking. "Knock yourself out."

3

"THAT MAN COULD ruin the good name of cowboys all over Texas." I had fumed about Ace McKinney the whole way back to Tyanne's bookstore, and I wasn't finished yet. There were no customers in the store, and I was glad for the opportunity to freely speak my mind while I paced the length of the sales counter. "McKinney ought to care about safety. If he doesn't, he should at least be concerned about lawsuits 'cause if one of these senior citizens falls and breaks a hip—"

"He probably makes them sign something." Tyanne arranged and rearranged books in a display by the front door.

I crossed my arms over my chest. "The jerk *did* say something about a waiver, but still. I want Aunt Rowe to be safe, Ty. Her friends, too."

"I know," she said. "I'm a bit surprised the ladies are all on board for such strenuous activity."

"They're blindly following Aunt Rowe, their ringleader. If you ask me, she's too fearless for her own good."

"Better than being a scaredy-cat, isn't it?" Ty grinned.

"I'm not sure. Can you seriously see my aunt dealing with that McKinney yokel?"

"I'm sure Rowe can hold her own with the patronizing cowboy."

"What cowboy?" Ethan came from the storeroom carrying an armload of new paperbacks. The teen knelt to arrange the books on shelves near the checkout counter.

"A man at the rodeo," Tyanne said.

"Mr. Devlin?"

"No," I said, "an unlikeable guy who works for him."

"Oh," Ethan said. "Mr. Devlin is no prize himself, least not according to Cody."

"Lance Devlin's son?" I said.

"Yeah." Ethan placed the last of the books on the shelf and stood. "Cody's not my best friend or anything. Kid has issues, but seems like he also has two sorry excuses for parents."

"What makes you say that?" I walked over to the window seat and perched between the bookstore cats, Zelda and Willis. I ran a hand down each cat's back, and their motors started up.

"Cody had the lead in the school play," Ethan said. "My mom would have had a front-row seat, taken like a thousand pictures, you know."

Ty nodded. "Sounds like me."

"That's a normal mom," Ethan said. "Proud of whatever the kids do."

I thought about my own mother, who didn't fit the normal mom model.

"I'd expect Crystal Devlin to be a very proud mother," Tyanne said.

"Maybe about other stuff," Ethan said. "Not when it comes to acting. That's what Cody wants to do with his life. His parents don't approve, and neither one of them came to see him."

"Maybe they had a prior engagement," Tyanne said.

"The play ran two different weekends," Ethan said.

Tyanne frowned. "Hard to imagine an excuse good enough to miss every performance."

Ethan nodded. "That's what I'm saying."

Willis got up, stretched, and stood on my lap so he could rub his head against my chin. "My mother doesn't approve of my writing, but I'm doing it anyway."

"Without your aunt's encouragement you might still be working at that law firm," Ty said. "Your *fearless* aunt."

We both knew I wouldn't have taken the plunge of quitting my job if not for Aunt Rowe. "Sometimes it's hard to take a chance on a dream."

"Cody says he's moving to L.A. no matter what his parents think. He's almost eighteen." Ethan headed back toward the storeroom.

Tyanne watched him go, not responding to his last statement. Her kids weren't old enough to make drastic moves, but I knew she'd voice her opinion if and when the time came.

"Sounds like Crystal Devlin's priorities are messed up," I said. "She missed her son's big moment. She cheated Pearl, a fellow businesswoman. All in all, I'm thinking these Devlins aren't the nicest people."

"Crystal has a redeeming quality," Tyanne said. "Most people do."

"What's hers?" I said.

"She gives a good amount of money to charity. Got an award at the last chamber of commerce meeting for making a large donation to the Find-a-Cure walkathon."

"Huh." I patted each of the cats and stood. "Maybe this would be a good time for me to solicit a donation for the Love-a-Black-Cat event."

"And ask her why she cheated Pearl?" Tyanne said.

I smiled. "That, too, if I can work it into the conversation. After I get a donation, of course."

My friend nodded. "Smart."

"Could you print a copy of that flyer I e-mailed over here yesterday?"

"Already did." Tyanne walked behind the sales counter to retrieve a copy of my flyer and handed it to me. "I was going to hang this one in the window, but I can print another."

I DROVE the short distance to Bluebonnet Street where Devlin Realty sat four doors down from Sweet Stop. I couldn't quit thinking about the rodeo. I had to try talking rationally with Aunt Rowe about the danger factor. Surely she didn't want to break her leg again. If that didn't work, her friends might come to their senses and talk her out of it before the date came. Which wouldn't save me from worrying until then.

I parked on the street and told myself to set aside my attitude about Crystal Devlin missing her own son's performance in the school play. I'd have to put on a pleasant face if I hoped to get a donation from the woman. As I walked toward the office, I realized the front door, with "Devlin Realty" scrolled in gold on the glass, stood open. I heard a raised voice coming from inside.

"I told you time and again to keep the door shut," a woman screeched. "Clean up the mess. We can't have clients walking into this disaster."

My fist was poised to rap on the door, my flyer in the other hand. I paused, stuck the flyer in my tote, and poked my head into the office.

The bossy woman, in a gray pencil skirt with heels and a blousy red top, stood with her back to me. Her artificially light blond hair was pulled back and held in a large clip. Silver earrings dangled halfway to her shoulders.

Magazines and real estate flyers were strewn on the floor, along with a desk calendar, pens, and unopened mail. In front of the desk, pink Shasta daisies lay in a pool of water and glass shards from a broken vase. The desktop lamp was knocked over but had escaped a fall to the floor. A younger woman in tan slacks and a dingy brown top knelt on the floor with a roll of paper towels in one hand.

"For the love of God, Jordan, pick up those papers before they get wet."

The girl was mopping up water with the paper towels, and pencil-skirt lady was apparently too good to help. Either that or her skirt was too tight for her to bend down to the floor.

I crossed into the room and whisked the pages that weren't even close to the water from the floor. I grabbed the mail, then stood and placed everything on the desk. When I turned around, I recognized Crystal Devlin because her face adorned advertisements all over town.

She pasted on a fake-looking smile. "Thank you so much," she said in a syrupy voice. "I'm sorry you had to witness this little accident. We seem to have had a run-in with a stray black cat this afternoon."

I paused with my hand halfway into my tote to retrieve the flyer.

"There was a cat here in your office?" I said.

Crystal nodded like this was the most tragic event she could have imagined. "I walked in and there he sat, on Jordan's desk. A huge black cat with big green eyes."

Good grief. Had Pearl brought Hitchcock to town after our conversation?

"I don't know how he got in here," Jordan said. "I did *not* leave the door open."

Crystal looked down at the other woman. "Don't use that tone with me, Jordan. I saw the cat, big as life, and it didn't walk in through the wall. Now, Miss . . ."

She turned to me and offered a hand with perfect French-manicured nails. "I'm Crystal Devlin."

We shook, and I introduced myself, well aware of Crystal's discreet inspection of my T-shirt, shorts, and flip-flops.

"Are you in the market to purchase real estate?" she said.

"Um, no," I said, "but about that cat. Where is he now?"

Crystal shrugged. "Anybody's guess. He took off after racing around the room like he was possessed."

"Had you seen him around before?"

Crystal shrugged. "I don't think so."

Jordan looked up from her task and shook her head. "Certainly not in here."

"Were you chasing the cat? Is that how all of this happened?" I swept my arm to indicate the mess.

"All I did was walk in," Crystal said. "I'm between appointments and came by to make some phone calls. Opened the door, and the animal went berserk. I'm not sure what *she* was doing." She looked pointedly at Jordan.

Jordan ignored Crystal and dragged a nearby wastebasket closer to her. She gathered the sopping-wet towels and threw them into the basket, though I had the distinct impression she'd have loved to throw them at Crystal.

"Now, Sabrina," Crystal said, "If you're not buying real estate, do you have something to sell?"

"No, I didn't come about real estate at all." I glanced at my tote. Would these women ID Hitchcock if I showed them the flyer with his picture front and center? I decided to take the chance and pulled out the page.

"This may not be the best day to ask since you've just had a bad experience with a black cat." I showed them the flyer and explained about the upcoming adoption event. "I'm gathering donations to fund the pet food, vaccinations, and spaying and neutering of the future adoptees."

Their expressions didn't change when they glanced at the picture of Hitchcock.

"Of course I'll donate," said Crystal. "Just because one black cat caused me bad luck today doesn't mean I have anything against the species in general. I'll grab my checkbook from my desk."

I bit my lip to keep from responding to her bad luck remark.

Her heels tap-tapped across the tiled floor. She opened a door and went inside.

Jordan was still on her knees, carefully picking up pieces of the broken glass and tossing them in the trash. I stooped to help her and noticed tufts of black cat hair on the floor, too.

I didn't want the cat they saw to be Hitchcock, but what were the odds that a different black cat showed up here?

"Did the cat you saw resemble the cat on my flyer?" I asked.

Jordan glanced up. "Should it?"

"I don't know, just making conversation."

"Black cats look pretty much alike," she said. "All I know is I didn't leave the freakin' door open. Why would I when every little mosquito or gnat that gets in here throws her into a tizzy?"

"Sounds like the cat did the same."

"True." Jordan smirked.

"She difficult to work for?" I whispered.

"Did Davy Crockett die at the Alamo?"

Crystal's heels tapped in our direction, and Jordan shut up.

"Here we go." Crystal reappeared and crossed the room.

I stood and accepted the company check she handed me. *Holy moly. Five hundred dollars.*

I smiled. "Thank you on behalf of black cats everywhere." Crystal Devlin might have other not-so-likeable traits, but she cared about animals, and that said a lot in my book.

"You are most welcome," Crystal said. "Happy to help. I trust there will be a program of some sort and Devlin Realty will be listed as a donor."

"Absolutely," I said.

"Excellent." Crystal nodded. "Now I do need to run to my next appointment."

Given that the woman had just made a generous donation, I decided this was not the time to quiz her about Pearl's real estate deal. I'd come back for that conversation.

Pearl was the woman destined for interrogation this afternoon. Her store was conveniently close by, and no amount of candy could sweeten me up if I learned she'd brought Hitchcock to town against my wishes.

4

HURRIED DOWN THE sidewalk toward the candy store, scanning the street as I went. No sign of a black cat, not that I expected to spot Hitchcock strolling amongst the tourists. Pearl's proposal to bring him to town was even more ridiculous now that I'd met Crystal Devlin, a woman who didn't strike me as particularly superstitious. If the cat in the real estate office was Pearl's doing, she'd wasted a lot of effort.

Unless her goal was to annoy me—because if that cat was Hitchcock, she'd succeeded big-time.

A young mother with two small boys entered Sweet Stop ahead of me. The kids squealed with delight and raced across the wide-plank floor to the Ninja Turtle display in the corner. I stepped over the threshold and was instantly enveloped by the mixed scents of chocolate, peppermint, and vanilla. With the song "It's A Small World" coming through speakers and the chatter of excited children as background, some of the tension left my shoulders.

Two young women standing behind the glass display case

doled out candy to customers, but Pearl was nowhere in sight. I zeroed in on a customer in uniform. Sleek black hair fell to her shoulders.

Deputy Patricia Rosales.

Not my favorite person, and the feeling was mutual. She accepted a brown paper sack from a clerk and turned before I had a chance to move out of her line of vision.

She smirked and walked in my direction.

"Have a little sweet tooth, Deputy?" I said when she neared.

"A surprise for someone special," she said in a singsong tone. "His favorite. Today's his birthday." She held up the paper sack and gave it a little shake.

I didn't know why she offered this information unless the birthday boy was local game warden Luke Griffin. He and I had spent a little time together. Nothing serious, just sharing a cup of coffee here, an ice cream cone there. Rosales had more than a passing interest in the man, and she acted more annoyed each time she spotted us together.

"How thoughtful of you," I said.

Was today Luke Griffin's birthday? I had no idea. If so, I doubted he planned to celebrate the occasion with Rosales. He usually took off in the opposite direction whenever the deputy came into view.

A middle-aged woman clutching her purchases came up behind Rosales. "Excuse me, Deputy. May I have a word with you?"

Glad for a chance to escape, I excused myself just as Pearl came around a shelf carrying an unopened carton marked "Necco." She stopped short when she saw me.

"Sabrina. What are you doing here?"

Was that guilt crossing her features?

"Where's my cat, Pearl?"

Her brows drew together. "Your cat? How would I know? Isn't he at home?"

"I'm not at home, so I can't answer that." I glanced around

at the customers, then urged Pearl back the way she'd come. We stood between shelves filled with every kind of candy bar imaginable.

The upbeat song "My Favorite Things" came over the sound system, but I wasn't feeling it today.

"Did you bring Hitchcock to town with you, Pearl?"

"Absolutely not." She looked away.

"Pearl?"

"I'll be right back."

She began to turn, but I put a hand on her arm. "Do you have my cat here in the store?"

A little boy had wandered into the aisle and stood nearby eyeing the M&M's. He looked up at us. "I want to see the cat."

Pearl frowned at him. "There's no cat."

"Where is he?" I said.

She scowled. "I didn't touch your cat."

"Did you find a different black cat then?"

"Why would I do that?"

"So, you *did* bring Hitchcock to town."

"I did not."

The little boy's mother hurried into the aisle and took his hand, glancing at us worriedly before she moved away.

"I wanted to see the cat," the little boy whined.

"You're disturbing my customers," Pearl said in a low voice. "I didn't touch your cat."

"Where did the black cat that ran through Crystal Devlin's office come from?"

"I don't know anything about any cat." Pearl pushed past me, headed for the candy counter with me on her heels. She set the carton on top of the display case with a thump.

"I'd like to believe you, but after what you said this morning I'm not sure I can."

"How do *you* know what happened at Crystal's office?" She crossed her arms over her chest.

"I was there for reasons unrelated to you. I thought about going to bat for you, Pearl, but now that I've met Crystal—"

A slim grandmotherly woman who'd been checking out the Disney display turned to us and said, "Are you talking about the Devlin woman who cheated poor Pearl out of her property?"

"That's the one, Doris," Pearl said.

"I heard that an Austin developer plans to open a cigar shop next door," Doris said.

"Cigars?" Pearl practically shouted the word. "Who wants to smell stinking cigars? They'll run off all my customers, and it's all Crystal Devlin's fault." She glared at me. "If you think I'm gonna back off on tryin' to cause that woman bad luck, you have another guess comin'."

"Shush," I said. "Think about something nice, like cream-colored ponies and crisp apple strudels." Customers were staring at us, including Deputy Rosales.

"I'm not in a *nice* mood," Pearl said.

"I noticed, but you don't want Crystal hearing about you bad-mouthing her in front of the whole town. She'd probably slap you with a lawsuit."

"She can just try," Pearl said, "I'll sue her back for cheating me out of the property. I made that offer fair and square."

Rosales walked over to us, her expression stern.

"What's the ruckus about, ladies?"

"Sorry, Deputy," Pearl said. "But I tend to get loud when people like Crystal Devlin think they can cheat me out of something, and then others accuse me of lying." Her glare deepened.

Doris said, "We can start a petition to keep the cigar shop out."

"Good idea," Pearl said.

"That's a better idea than using my cat," I said.

Pearl uncrossed her arms and put her hands on her hips. "I *told* you, I *didn't* do that."

"And don't think about doing it either," I said. "Crystal doesn't seem superstitious, so what would be the point?"

"I've heard enough," Rosales said, "and I have better ways to spend my time."

She looked at me with that last line, and I knew she was baiting me. I ignored her and focused my attention on the homemade fudge counter. I was all kinds of annoyed this afternoon, but nothing that a chunk of York Peppermint Pattie fudge wouldn't fix.

On the way home, I licked the sticky fudge remains off my fingers and hoped Pearl was telling me the truth about the cat, that she hadn't taken Hitchcock anywhere. I hoped to find him napping on the deck of my cottage, where he liked to spend the late afternoons.

As for Pearl's other issues, those were her problems, not mine. She'd find a new property to purchase or maybe go on with her store as is. She did a good business out of the cute space, small though it was. If she didn't like the cigar shop coming in next door, she could move. Her choice.

I pulled off the main road onto Traveler's Lane and immediately spotted Thomas. He stood in a landscaped bed trimming an overgrown vine that threatened to crawl up and cover the Around-the-World Cottages sign. He lowered his clippers and flagged me down. I pulled to a stop and opened my window.

Thomas walked to the car and removed his straw hat before leaning over to talk face-to-face. "Case you were missin' your cat today, I took him for a ride."

My heart rate sped up. "What do you mean?"

"He hitched a ride. Just like you warned me, except this time I caught him red-handed."

"Red-handed?"

"Red-pawed?" Thomas grinned. "Whatever. The cat made the trip home with me. Can't honestly say how he got to town in the first place. I didn't see him on the way in. Then clear as day I saw him take off out of the backseat of my Jeep when I parked at Rowena's house."

I swallowed. "How long ago was that?"

"Twenty minutes or so," Thomas said. "Haven't been back

long. I gotta say I wish you could convince that animal to stay put. I'm doin' my best to get past the bad luck thing, but he was too close for comfort."

"He's not bad luck, Thomas," I said, "but I'll try to keep a better eye on him. Sorry about that."

And even sorrier if it turned out that Pearl had actually taken Hitchcock into town, then turned around and lied to my face.

HITCHCOCK was at home, thank goodness, and napping on the deck of the Monte Carlo cottage, where I could usually find him at this time of day. I hadn't eaten anything except the fudge since midmorning and considered joining Aunt Rowe for dinner. I didn't feel like talking about the rodeo or Pearl, though, and couldn't imagine shutting up on either topic if I saw my aunt. A little wine and time spent plotting out the next few chapters of my book sounded like a better idea.

I fixed a plate with leftover grilled chicken, cheese cubes, and a handful of grapes. Poured myself a glass of white wine, then grabbed a pad and pen and got comfortable in a cushioned chair out on the porch.

The early evening air was heavy with humidity. I popped a grape into my mouth and looked past the trees to the deep blue sky.

Think fiction.

A bit hard to do after all that had happened today. I didn't want to dwell on those stresses. I needed to put thoughts of Pearl, Crystal, the cigar shop, and, wait, *was* it Luke Griffin's birthday or wasn't it?

Try to focus, Sabrina.

I could make black bottom cupcakes—Griffin loved chocolate—then just happen to take them into town tomorrow, see if I could "accidentally" run into him.

So sorry I missed your birthday. I made your favorite cupcakes, then got delayed and couldn't bring them to you in time. Happy belated.

I ate some chicken, then took a healthy swig of my wine. If only there were a magic pill I could take to focus. I lowered my head and rubbed my temples. Ideas began to flow, and I jotted them down on my tablet.

Thirty minutes passed, and I'd made quite a bit of progress when I sat back against the chair cushion and reached for my wineglass. Dusk was beginning to fall. I heard snatches of conversation as guests made their way up from the river and headed back to their cottages. Across the lawn, a woman—a new arrival—unloaded luggage from the trunk of a black car parked next to the Paris cottage.

I reread what I'd written and felt a sense of satisfaction over where the story was headed. If I went straight to the computer, I might get a chapter done tonight. I felt a thousand percent more relaxed than I had an hour ago.

I stood and stretched. Watched the woman at the Paris cottage. Something about her seemed familiar, but I was a good distance away and couldn't put my finger on it. In black slacks and a white shirt she looked like she'd come straight from the office. Hair with a reddish tint, pulled back. She rolled a suitcase into the cottage, stayed out of sight for a minute or so, then came out and opened the back car door.

She wasn't our usual type of guest. Businesspeople usually preferred staying in town. I went down the porch steps and walked to the end of my sidewalk to get a better look. I was getting that hair-standing-up-on-the-back-of-my-neck feeling.

What was that about?

The woman pulled a fat black trial briefcase from her car, and realization hit me.

Rita Colletti.

My former boss. The lawyer I hoped I'd never see again in my life.

5

WENT INSIDE SO Rita Colletti wouldn't spot me. Hitchcock came in through the cat door, got a drink of water, and plopped down on the kitchen mat.

"Of all the people in the world, that woman is the last person I'd expect to see here in the Hill Country," I told the cat. "Jetting off to the Riviera is more her style."

I realized what I'd just said and turned to scan my surroundings. The Monte Carlo cottage was chock-full of Aunt Rowe's personal mementoes from *her* Riviera trip.

"Not that there's anything wrong with that," I amended. "I'm just saying this lawyer has a high-and-mighty personality and nothing's ever good enough. Trust me when I say *nothing*."

Hitchcock looked up at me. "Mrreow."

I smiled at him. "I knew you'd understand."

I glanced at my laptop and the sheaf of papers on the table beside the computer—my novel in progress. The real reason I'd left the law firm job behind. My "little hobby," as Rita

Colletti referred to my writing when I'd given my two weeks' notice.

"I'll show her," I muttered. "She'll be the first person to get an invitation to my book signing." I paused. "Never mind, I don't even want her there."

A moot point if I didn't get myself in gear and work harder. But how could I drum up creative thoughts with *her* nearby? And what the heck was she doing here? Honestly, I wouldn't be able to concentrate until I found out why Rita Colletti was staying in Lavender.

I crossed the living room and lifted a panel of the sheer window curtain to peer outside. The doors on Rita's vehicle were closed, and she was nowhere in sight. Her name wasn't on Aunt Rowe's reservations printout I'd scanned the day before. I'd have noticed. I wondered if she made a spur-of-the-moment decision to stay at Around-the-World Cottages and lucked upon a cancellation or if she was staying with someone whose name *was* on the list. I didn't envision Rita sharing the small Paris cottage with anyone. Seriously, who in their right mind would stay in such close quarters with the unlikeable woman?

What I wanted to know most of all was how long she planned to stay. If it was too long, I might have to take an unplanned road trip to somewhere, anywhere.

Don't be a wuss, Sabrina. Colletti isn't your boss anymore.

Still, I wanted answers. I left my cottage and took the steps down to the river, then walked beside the water until I reached Aunt Rowe's house before climbing the riverbank. A round-about route, one that ensured I wouldn't run into my ex-boss. Up ahead, someone was clapping.

And chanting.

"Go. Go. Go. Go."

No, it was, "Rowe. Rowe. Rowe."

Dear Lord, now what?

I spotted Aunt Rowe's friends, Helen and Adele, sitting on the back deck, facing the lawn. I couldn't see what they were watching, though, until I rounded the corner of the deck.

Aunt Rowe stood in the middle of the yard circling a lasso above her head. Several yards away, a three-foot-tall stuffed giraffe straddled a sawhorse. She threw the rope, missed the giraffe, then started when I came up behind her.

"Hey, you distracted me," she said. "I would have had that."

"C'mon, Rowe," yelled Adele. "Give it another go."

"You can do it," Helen added.

"What's up with the giraffe?" I said.

"Helen brought him. He's a stand-in for the goat."

"What goat?"

"The one I'm going to rope at the rodeo."

I rolled my eyes. "Don't get me started on that topic. I came to ask about the new guest in Paris."

Aunt Rowe smiled. "Her name's Rita Colletti. Seems real nice."

"*Seems* is the operative word there." I frowned. "You *do* remember that name, right?"

Aunt Rowe's readied her rope for another try at the giraffe. "Should I?"

"Skip the memory loss routine," I said. "You know good and well who Rita Colletti is."

"How could I forget the condescending queen?" Aunt Rowe said. "You griped about her plenty of times, but a vacancy is a vacancy, Sabrina, and you're a big girl."

"I know, but—"

"No buts," Aunt Rowe said. "Business is business, the customer is always right, and all that jazz."

"I agree, but—"

Aunt Rowe straightened and plastered on a smile. She looked at a spot over my shoulder and said, "How nice of you to join us. Sabrina, you remember Rita."

My shoulders sagged, and I couldn't summon the will to turn around.

"Imagine my surprise," Rita said in the gravelly voice I remembered all too well, "when I learned Sabrina Tate lives here. Tell me, Sabrina, how's your little hobby coming?"

* * *

WOKE early the next morning, headed straight to Hot Stuff, and set up my laptop in my usual corner of the coffee shop. When I'd begged off of Aunt Rowe's dinner invitation the night before, swearing I had to rush back to work on a critical chapter, Rita said she'd catch up with me another time.

Maybe she was just being polite, which I'd consider a first for her, but I didn't plan on sticking around the cottage where she could easily find me.

Sly and the Family Stone's "Dance to the Music" came through the sound system, cheering me despite myself. Max Dieter, the shop owner, bopped over with a steaming mug and placed it on my table.

"A cuppa Lavender's Sunrise, your usual," he said. "How's the book coming?"

"Fine, I guess. Had a rough time with it last night, but I'm feeling the groove today. This will help." I picked up the mug and inhaled deeply, then took a sip.

"Want to talk about it?" he said.

"Talk about what?"

"Whatever's causing those stress lines on your forehead."

I used two fingers to smooth out the indentations between my brows. "Not really."

I'd rather push Rita Colletti to the recesses of my mind— which I'd tried to do while consuming large quantities of wine the night before. All in an attempt to squelch my annoyance that Rita would be my neighbor for the next week while she worked with some new client who lived in the Lavender area.

How lucky was that?

"Did Hitchcock make the trip with you today?" Max said.

I shook my head. "Left him fat and happy, asleep in the middle of my bed."

"Ah, to have the life of a cat." Max sighed.

"Right." I laughed and picked up my mug. "Keep the coffee comin', Max. I plan to write up a storm this morning."

"Will do."

He greeted other customers on his way back to the bar, and I turned to face the laptop screen.

I reread what I'd written the day before, decided it would do for now, and began typing.

Two minutes into the writing, my phone rang.

Shoot. I should have muted that.

An elderly couple at the next table glanced over in annoyance. The phone wasn't all that loud, but I scrambled to pull it from my computer case to turn it down.

I checked the screen and didn't recognize the number. Who would call me before eight in the morning?

Not Rita Colletti, thank goodness. Even though I'd erased her from my contacts, I'd still recognize her number, and this wasn't her. I watched the phone until the ringing stopped. If the call was important, the caller would leave me a message and I'd deal with that later. I placed the phone next to the laptop.

I drank more coffee and focused on the computer screen once more. My FBI agent was doing surveillance on a stormy night. A car pulled into the driveway she'd been watching for hours. A dead body would be discovered in the next few sentences.

My phone vibrated, and the same unknown number appeared on the screen. I tried to ignore it but couldn't keep myself from picking the phone up a minute later. No messages, but the phone almost immediately began ringing a third time. Same number.

Annoyed, I punched the button and answered.

"Sabrina, it's Pearl."

I frowned. "How'd you get my number?"

"From Rowe," she said. "Are you writing at Hot Stuff this morning?"

"Trying to."

"Is Hitchcock with you?"

"No, he's at home."

"Are you sure?"

I pushed my chair back from the table. "Why are you asking me this?"

"I think I saw your cat in town."

"When?" I pressed the phone tighter against my ear to hear her better.

"A few minutes ago."

"You must be mistaken."

At least I hope so.

"You need to come over here," she said.

"I'm busy, Pearl." My cat was a known wanderer, but he sure looked like he was down for a long morning nap when I left the cottage. "Are you looking at a black cat as we speak?"

"No, but I really need your help. Something bad has happened."

"To a cat?" My heart rate sped up.

"No," she said. "I'd rather not say over the phone. *Please*, can't you spare a few minutes to come and see for yourself?"

I blew out a breath. "Where are you? At your store?"

"No, but I'm on Bluebonnet Street. The building that's for sale three doors down from my place."

"The one that used to be a restaurant?" I said.

"Yes."

"If you're wanting another opinion about buying property, I'm not the right person."

"Please," she said again, her voice shaky. "This isn't about the property. It's important, I swear."

"Oh, all right." The woman didn't seem like she'd let this drop, whatever *this* was, and the sooner I went to see what was up, the sooner I could get back to work.

Max agreed to stash my laptop under the counter until I returned, and I set off for Bluebonnet, two streets over. The temperature was already hitting the ninety-degree mark with about a thousand percent humidity. I blew straggly waves of hair off my forehead, then removed the blue elastic and redid my ponytail more tightly as I walked.

The building that used to house Amelia's Cantina was probably eighty years old and had been vacant for a while. Judging from the construction trucks I'd seen there recently, I figured the seller had decided to refurbish in hopes of getting a better price.

A few cars were parked on the street, but the construction trucks hadn't shown up for today's work as of yet. I strode toward the entrance, annoyed that Pearl had dragged me away from my writing, then spotted her standing just inside the open doorway. She looked a mess in a wrinkled plaid blouse over knit slacks. Her curly hair stuck out every which way, and pink splotches stained her cheeks.

"What's going on, Pearl? What are you doing here?"

She heaved a big sigh. "Well, I got up and looked out my window. To check the weather, you know, see if it was going to rain like they said on the weather report." She paused.

"And—" I made a hurry-up-and-spit-it-out hand motion.

"I saw Crystal Devlin. She parked right over there." Pearl pointed to a Cadillac SUV on the street. "Then she rushed into this building. I'm still ticked about that cigar shop coming in next to my candy store, you know, and I felt like she needed to hear about it. Right then."

"Okay. What does all this have to do with a cat?"

"Well, when I saw Crystal I threw on some clothes and came straight over. She'd left the door open, so I came on in, and that's when I saw the black cat. He sure looked like Hitchcock."

"What was this cat doing?" I still didn't understand Pearl's sense of urgency for me to come over.

"Sitting on a pile of two-by-fours when I saw him."

"So you want me to come in and look for the cat?"

"No. There's something much worse. I just wanted you to know the cat was here."

"I'll take a look around to see if I spot Hitchcock inside."

I stepped over the threshold, passing Pearl on my way into the building. A clump of black hair sticking to the rough-edged doorjamb caught my attention like a flashing neon sign. I looked at Pearl. "No denying there was a black cat on the premises."

Good grief, had Hitchcock somehow made his way into town this morning after all? I might have to invest in a kitty GPS gizmo to keep track of the wandering feline.

"See, I'm not imagining things," Pearl said.

"Guess not."

I looked around the two-story entry and didn't spot Hitchcock or any other cat. A row of new windows installed above the entrance allowed sunshine to spill across the floor, lighting stacks of lumber, scaffolding, and debris left behind by the work crew. The place smelled of sawdust and greasy to-go food wrappers. A cat could find a dozen good hiding places, not to mention things to gnaw on.

"What a mess," I said. "Did you talk to Crystal?"

When Pearl didn't respond, I turned to face her and noticed her cheeks had reddened even more. Tears filled her eyes as she shook her head.

"Why not?" I shaded my eyes against the sunlight and scanned the space again, looking all the way up to the top of the scaffolding, where a pile of red bricks sat ready to be added to a partially bricked interior wall. My gaze traveled back to a mute Pearl.

"What's the matter?" I said.

"It's Crystal." Pearl's voice was so low I could barely hear her.

"What about her?" I walked farther into the space and rounded the stack of two-by-fours, nearly stumbling on bricks scattered on the floor. "Where is she?"

But before Pearl could answer, I spotted an arm sticking out from under a heap of fallen bricks. The hand with Crystal Devlin's French-manicured nails, lying in a pool of blood.

6

MY PULSE POUNDED at my throat. "Good Lord, Pearl, what happened? Where are the EMS people?"

"It's too late," Pearl said. "Crystal's dead. I checked."

"You touched her?"

"How else was I gonna know?" Pearl rubbed her neck as if her worst problem was a kink she had to work out. "It's not every day I come across an emergency situation, but I wasn't gonna stand around with my hands in my pockets if she had a chance. I had to stretch, but I managed to reach her neck."

"Okay, okay." Looking at the body, I had no trouble believing that Crystal Devlin was dead. "Jeez, EMS is usually faster than this. What's taking them so long?" I didn't even hear a siren in the distance. "Are you sure you gave them the right address?"

"I had to tell you *he* was here first," Pearl said.

"Who?" I said.

"Hitchcock." Pearl stared at me, all serious. "Who else?"

"Did *you* bring him here, Pearl?" I said, even though I couldn't see how she'd have managed that feat this morning.

"No, I swear I didn't, but this is all my fault. I should *never* have brought up the idea of using him."

"You're right," I said, "but that's the least of our worries."

"If anybody saw your cat, though, it could mean trouble."

"What are you talking about?" I moved closer to Crystal, stooped to get a better look at her, and winced. A lump that felt the size of a golf ball clogged my throat.

Pearl went on, "If people get wind of the fact that the bad luck cat was in this building, they'll say he caused Crystal's death."

"That's ridiculous." I stood too quickly and felt a momentary light-headedness. "I firmly believe my cat is home where he's supposed to be, not here in town, and no one can blame this on him. And on top of everything else, he is *not bad luck*."

Pearl shrugged. "You know how people are, always looking for good gossip."

"Making up lies is not *good*," I said. "Crystal needs our help, so stop it about the cat already."

"I had to warn you," Pearl said. "That's why I called you instead of the sheriff."

I stared at her. "Please tell me you called 911."

Pearl shook her head. "Like I told you, Crystal is already dead. She's beyond help."

"For Pete's sake, Pearl, you *always* call. What were you thinking? This horrible accident, *any* accident, *any* incident, you have to call." I patted my pockets frantically before remembering I'd left my phone in my laptop case.

Dang it.

"Give me a freaking phone."

Pearl pulled hers from a pocket, and I nearly yanked her arm off grabbing the phone from her. Before I could dial, clomping footsteps sounded behind me. Thank goodness, the cavalry was coming after all.

Pearl grabbed my elbow. "We gotta get out of here."

"No, Pearl." I tried to pull my arm from her firm grasp as I turned to the sight of two men the size of linebackers in hard hats coming into the room. The first one took in the scene before him with a swift and sweeping glance.

"Jesus, Mary, and Joseph," he said as he pulled out his own phone. "Chet, keep an eye on these broads. Don't let 'em get away while I call for help."

"It's not like it looks." Panic rose in my chest. "I just got here."

"We didn't kill her," Pearl said. "It was an accident."

"Save it," the man said. Then into the phone: "We got a badly injured woman over here and two suspects. Send help pronto."

HAD never before wished that I could disappear like Samantha of *Bewitched* as fervently as I did in that moment. I slouched in the backseat of a sheriff's department car where Deputy Brent Ainsley had stowed me until he could get around to asking me more questions. Like he thought I'd make a run for it given the chance. The longer he kept me here the hotter I got—both literally and figuratively.

Ainsley had no good reason to lock me in the car. I hadn't refused to talk. He had no evidence to use against me. I wasn't a flight risk. The guy was a big fat bully, which is what I'd heard about him in the past. Which made me worry all the more for Pearl 'cause Ainsley's focus shifted to her the moment he'd spotted blood on her shoes. As far as I could tell, she was still inside with him.

Sweat trickled down my back even though Ainsley had cracked each of the windows about an inch so I could get some air. Didn't do much good on a hot July day. Lucky for me, the car was parked under a tree and there was some cloud cover. Maybe I'd survive.

If only I hadn't listened when Pearl asked me to come over and meet her. I would be happily writing away at Hot Stuff right now, adding to my word count. But no . . . I had to give in to stupid curiosity and get involved in this crime scene. Or accident scene. Which was it? Yesterday Pearl was bad-mouthing Crystal Devlin every chance she got, and today she's standing next to Crystal's dead body. Her luck couldn't get much worse. So why was I the one locked in the back of the cruiser?

Emergency vehicles and gawkers crowded Bluebonnet Street. No surprise that the flashing lights had attracted everyone. Wait till they figured out that Pearl, the sweet candy-store lady, was being held inside for questioning about the death of Lavender's real estate maven. I checked my watch, the only personal possession I had on me besides my clothes and flip-flops. I wondered if Pearl would tell Ainsley about the cat. Or if I would. There had to be another reason I could give for coming when Pearl called, 'cause I sure didn't want people talking about my cat.

Again.

I was obsessing about Hitchcock and whether he was at home sleeping or had actually come into town, when a low voice sounded near my ear.

"You want me to break you out of there?"

I jumped in the seat and turned to see Sheriff Jeb Crawford standing outside the car. His mouth was set in a grim line, but his eyes twinkled in the way that reminded me so much of my late father.

"Please do," I said. "Deputy Ainsley is completely out of line locking me up in here."

The sheriff nodded as he opened the door. "And here I thought Deputy Pat was your favorite of my employees."

I climbed out and smoothed straggly hairs from my sweating forehead. "Ainsley's running a close second."

"I already had a talk with him about this," the sheriff said.

"He made a bad judgment call. You're free to go. We'll call if we need to ask you any further questions."

"What about Pearl?" I said.

The sheriff looked away from me and chewed the inside of his cheek for a second before turning back. "She's a person of interest."

My heart jumped. "That term insinuates something more than an accident. I'd say the construction workers are of more interest than Pearl since their bricks obviously went off like a booby trap when Crystal walked near them."

The sheriff looked at me sharply. "Did you see that happen?"

"No, I didn't see anything. That's how it looked."

"Don't surmise," he said. "Best to keep quiet, actually. It's not your job to solve this."

He thinks Crystal was murdered.

A cry went up from people gathered on the sidewalk. A young man had lifted the crime scene tape and was attempting to cross under it.

"Go on. We have our hands full here." The sheriff turned and took long strides toward the sidewalk. He reached the young man and grabbed his arm, keeping him from stepping inside the building.

I knew I should leave while I had the chance, but my curiosity ruled once again. A teenage girl jogged up to the sheriff and took the young man's other arm. She rested her blond head against him.

Sheriff Crawford leaned in toward them, and I saw his lips moving. From the crowd, I heard the words "Cody" and "son."

Good Lord, the kid was Crystal Devlin's son. No wonder the sheriff had rushed to stop him.

Cody Devlin was tall, a good six feet, and wore knee-length shorts with a T-shirt. Dark bangs nearly hid his eyes, and I was glad for that under these circumstances.

The sheriff instructed the onlookers to stand back and

led Cody down the sidewalk. The girl stuck close to Cody's side, and as they moved away from the crowd, they grew closer to me.

I could hear the girl murmuring, "It's okay, baby, it'll be okay."

Sheriff Crawford said, "Is there someone I can call for you, son?"

Cody Devlin moved down the sidewalk, his gait zombie-like, and didn't appear to hear either one of them.

7

M Y SENSE OF self-preservation kicked in, and I turned away from the sad scene. Better to leave now before Deputy Ainsley came up with a convincing reason I should be held and questioned. As I quick-stepped down the sidewalk, I felt sorrow for Cody Devlin. The kid would have a hard time, losing his mother, even if what Ethan related was true and they hadn't had the best relationship.

I felt a twinge of guilt for leaving Pearl behind, too. In her distressed state of mind, she might blurt out things better left unsaid. Not that the whole town hadn't already heard about her dispute with Crystal Devlin. If Pearl had cooled her jets when she saw Crystal, instead of rushing over to that building for a confrontation, we'd all be having a normal, peaceful morning.

Too late for that.

I'd feel better after I confirmed Hitchcock was at home sleeping the morning away as he usually did. First, I had to retrieve my computer and phone from the coffee shop.

Chances were slim that I'd be able to concentrate on writing today, even though my character was about to find a body and what I'd just experienced could add a ring of authenticity to my chapter. I turned in the direction I'd come, eager to leave the chaos behind, and saw Crystal Devlin's assistant in front of the realty office with a key in her hand. The emergency vehicles had drawn Jordan's attention, and she stood frozen in place.

I didn't want to be the one to tell her the news about her employer, but I couldn't bring myself to pass by the woman without a word.

Jordan smiled and spoke first. "How are you this morning?"

I slowed my pace. "Not too good, to tell the truth."

She frowned. "Why? What's going on down there?"

"You haven't heard?"

She shook her head. "No. I just came from the nursing home across town. I go there every morning before work. Breakfast with my mom."

"That's nice."

She grimaced. "It's not, actually. She acts like she doesn't remember who I am. Spends the time griping at me because her breakfast isn't perfect."

"I'm sorry. Alzheimer's?"

"No, she had a stroke," Jordan said. "Bottom line is she's just mean. Nothing new."

"Oh." I wondered why the woman subjected herself to such treatment every day. I would get poor marks as a daughter if anyone expected me to visit my ornery mother under those circumstances.

Jordan looked past me to the flashing lights. "Was there an accident?"

My train of thought had gone down the mother track, and I jerked back to the present. "Um, you mind if I come in to tell you about it?"

"Okay." She unlocked the door, and we stepped inside.

Jordan flipped a wall switch, and fluorescent lights brightened the office. She walked over to the desk and put her purse down, then leaned over the desk to power up the computer.

"I'm afraid the news is bad," I said slowly. "Crystal—"

Jordan's head popped up, and she turned to face me. "What'd she do this time?"

"It's not what she did, it's what happened to her." I paused and blew out a breath. "Crystal is dead."

Jordan stared at me and slumped against the desk. "Oh no. How did it happen?"

"I'm not exactly sure," I said. "It appears that she was killed by falling bricks."

Jordan's face, usually a rosy shade, had gone pale. "*Where* did it happen?"

"She was in the old restaurant that's up for sale." I described the scene. "Maybe she was meeting a prospective buyer."

Jordan shook her head. "We're not showing that space until the work is completed. Another week, maybe more. She gave me explicit instructions."

I lifted my hands in a beats-me gesture. "Maybe she changed her mind. In any case, she was in the wrong place at the wrong time." I wasn't going to say one word about the possibility of foul play.

Jordan wrapped one arm around her waist and rubbed her forehead with her other hand. "This is just awful. Her poor family. Lance. Cody. Poor Mrs. Morales."

"Who's Mrs. Morales?" I said.

"Crystal's housekeeper, cook, personal assistant. Paloma Morales. She'll be devastated. They were close." Jordan looked toward Crystal's office, at her desk, then back to me. "What happens with all the properties for sale? The closings? Oh no, do I even still have a job? What should I do?" Her eyes filled with tears.

I sensed she was putting on a bit of a show. Jordan hadn't seemed at all fond of Crystal the day before. Of course, they might have simply been out of sorts after the incident with the cat and the broken vase.

"Take it as it comes," I said. "You'll probably hear something from the family or their attorney. Until then I would answer the phone, take messages."

She nodded slowly. "Okay. I can do that."

"Maybe the sheriff will have some advice. I'm sure he'll be by to speak with you."

"Me? Why?"

Oops. Shouldn't have said that.

"You worked together. He'll probably ask you about the property where it happened. Crystal's schedule. That sort of thing."

Jordan frowned. "Sheriff Crawford can ask me all he wants. I don't have any idea what happened to Crystal."

"Of course not," I said.

"I wasn't there," she said. "I was at the nursing home, remember?"

"Right." Why had she assumed the timing of her nursing home visit coincided with Crystal's death?

I turned toward the door. "I have to get going. Sorry to bring you such tragic news."

"Not your fault," Jordan said. "Take care now."

She opened the door, and though she didn't actually give me a push I got the feeling she wanted rid of me in the worst way. I hurried down the sidewalk, wondering all the way why Jordan felt the need to repeat her whereabouts earlier in the morning.

I rounded the corner at the coffee shop quickly and bumped into a man on his way out.

"Hey, Sabrina Tate," he said. "Long time no talk to."

Hayden Birch, the rodeo clown, apparently had excellent balance, because he easily kept his cardboard tray of four tall cups level in spite of our collision.

"Hayden, hi. Sorry, I didn't watch where I was going."

"No harm done," he said. "I'm an indestructible kind of guy. Have to be in my line of work."

"I guess so." I avoided eye contact. He sounded too jolly

to have learned the morning's news, and I didn't want to tell the story again.

"Hey, you okay?" Hayden angled his head to catch my eye.

"I'm fine."

"Been a helluva day so far, huh?" Concern creased his brow.

I looked up. "You know?"

"Course I do."

"About Crystal?"

"Yeah."

"How?"

Hayden waited as the coffee shop door opened and two women walked out. The strains of "Don't Stop 'Til You Get Enough" drifted out. When the door closed and the women had moved a distance from us, he said, "Construction company put in a call straightaway to Mr. D. Guys who walked in and found you and that other woman on-site."

"Pearl."

"Right, Pearl."

"Why did they call Mr. Devlin?" I said. "It's not exactly their job to notify next of kin."

"They're pals of his," he said.

"The good ol' boy network."

"Something like that," Hayden said.

"So Crystal's husband found out she'd died, and then he what? Broadcast the news?"

"He didn't. Ace did. Mr. D told Ace, and Ace sent a text to the staff. Same as he does whenever anything happens that involves us."

"Huh." I looked at the tray Hayden held. "Who's all the coffee for?"

"Ace, me, and a couple of the guys who came in for supplies. I'm going to meet them."

So these guys learned their boss's wife was dead, and they came to town for supplies. Business as usual. That seemed cold, but maybe that's how it was in the ranching business. Couldn't let the livestock go hungry.

"Where are you heading?" he said.

"In there." I nodded toward the coffee shop and noticed Max and a couple of customers looking out the front window at me. "Or maybe not. Last thing I want is to go inside and get caught up in the gossip."

"Want me to go back in and get you some coffee?" he offered.

I looked at him. "No thanks, but if you could retrieve my laptop case from Max and bring it to me, I'd be grateful. I could hold your coffee."

Hayden didn't seem to mind the odd request. He handed me the coffee tray and went back into the shop. After a few seconds, I saw him through the window. Max handed my laptop case to Hayden. When he came back outside, we traded coffee for computer.

"I appreciate that more than you know." I gave Hayden Birch a grateful smile.

"Better watch out," he said. "I may call in a favor."

I thought of Ace McKinney warning me about the clown. "You'd better deliver that coffee now before it gets cold."

He grinned. "I'd rather stay here and while away the morning with you, but duty calls. See you next time around, Sabrina Tate."

I watched for a few seconds as Hayden strode toward a pickup parked at the curb, then slipped the laptop case strap over my shoulder and turned in the direction of my car. My mind raced with the events of the morning. I unzipped a pocket on the case to retrieve my phone and check for messages, hoping for one that said Pearl was released from questioning, but it was too soon for that. When I looked up before crossing the street, I spotted Luke Griffin. He leaned against the front bumper of his pickup, parked next to my car. Griffin looked awfully official in his tan game warden uniform. Aviator sunglasses covered his eyes.

"Hi there," I said when I got closer. "I heard a rumor you're celebrating a birthday."

His eyebrows rose. "You get that from Birch?"

"Birch?" I looked back to where Hayden and I had stood a moment ago, a spot in Griffin's direct line of vision. "No, not from him."

"What were you two so cozy about?" he said in a testy tone of voice I hadn't heard from him before.

"Cozy? You may need to have your eyes checked or take off the dark glasses." I slipped my phone back into the laptop case. "We were anything but cozy, discussing a death."

Griffin's expression told me he hadn't heard about Crystal yet, so I filled him in.

"Man, I'm sorry to hear that." He removed his sunglasses and stuck them in his shirt pocket. "I apologize for making an assumption about that guy."

"Don't worry about it," I said, "but you almost nixed my offer to make your favorite cupcakes. Assuming it really is your birthday."

Griffin smiled. "Yes, ma'am, it is. Want to see my license?"

"That won't be necessary," I said.

"Good. I'd love some of your cupcakes."

He grinned, and I couldn't help smiling back at him.

"I didn't like seeing you with Birch," he said.

"We were talking."

"He was flirting."

"Last I checked, that's not against the law."

"He's a bad influence," Griffin said. "Covers it up with jokes, but I'd steer clear if I were you."

"Bad influence? I'm not twelve anymore, Dad."

"Just saying." Griffin pulled his sunglasses out and unfolded the arms. "Think I'll head over and see if the sheriff needs a hand. Now I know why this street is deserted. Everyone and their cousin is rubbernecking over on Bluebonnet Street."

"You got that right," I said.

"I'll catch up with you later."

"Oh?"

"For those cupcakes."

Griffin climbed in his truck and backed out of the parking space. I stood there for a moment, wondering why he thought Hayden Birch was such a bad influence, then tossed my laptop case on the passenger seat of my own car and climbed inside.

Darn, now I have to add baking cupcakes to my to-do list, along with working on the book and wondering what really happened to Crystal.

The men—Birch and Griffin—had distracted me from checking on my main man.

Hitchcock.

I sure hoped I'd find him at home. Even if I did, though, too much time had passed. With his skills as an escape artist, I'd never know for sure where he'd spent his morning.

8

HEADED HOME, EAGER to see my cat. Before I got there I spotted Glenda on the porch of the Venice cottage. Aunt Rowe's golf cart was parked near the front door with a basket of fresh sheets and towels on the passenger seat. It was late in the day for Glenda to be dealing with linens. She kept a religious schedule, and I knew from the tangle of sheets she held in her arms something wasn't right. I pulled over in front of the cottage and jumped out of my car.

"I suppose we have you to thank for the queen of Sheba staying here," she said as I approached her. "Because of her, my schedule's all whacked out."

"Excuse me?"

"*That woman*," she said. "The lawyer."

"Oh. Her." I had pushed thoughts of Rita Colletti away, like I would block memories of a root canal. "I didn't know she was coming, so don't blame me."

"She said *you* told her about the cottages." Glenda stuffed the ball of sheets under one arm and used her other forearm to brush short dark hair away from her sweaty face. "So I've got you to thank for her highness's special requests. 'I prefer organic Blue Mountain coffee beans,' she says, and 'Do you have any croissants?' and 'I'd love some fresh-squeezed orange juice.'"

"She has those things at work, so she should have stayed in Houston," I said. "We're not buying anything special for her."

"You got that right," Glenda said. "Know what I told her?"

I shook my head. "What?"

"In my most kindly way, I said we are *not* a bed-and-breakfast, and that I'm oh, so sorry, if she prefers a bed-and-breakfast, I could certainly recommend her a nice place in town."

I grinned. "You said that?"

"I did. If you want to report me to Rowe, so be it. Oh, and after I said that, Rita mentioned she likes higher-thread-count sheets. The ones we have on her bed feel a little too scratchy."

"Seriously?" I rolled my eyes. "I'm sorry, Glenda, I didn't make the woman, I just worked for her."

"Bless your heart," Glenda said. "The way she talks grates on me just as much as what she says."

"You're preaching to the choir. Did Rita say what she's doing here in Lavender?"

"Working on a case is all I got. Once she quit griping, I wasn't gonna stand around and chitchat with the woman."

"I hear that," I said. "Let me help you with those." I took the sheets from her, walked them over to the golf cart, and picked up a fresh set. Glenda has a couple of teenagers and doesn't get riled easily. I wasn't one bit surprised that Rita had pushed her over the edge.

We set about prepping the Venice cottage for the next guests to check in. I started making up the bed while she gathered throw rugs and began sweeping the hardwood floors with a broom.

"Have you seen Hitchcock today?" I said as I pulled the fitted sheet onto the mattress.

"Sure," she said, "he came around earlier begging for left-over chicken."

"What a mooch. I didn't know you two were close enough for him to beg you for food."

"That cat leaves no stone unturned," she said. "Came around right after he saw Rowe leave."

"He won't come when she's home?"

"Not since the day she caught him up on the kitchen counter gnawing on her lunch."

"Uh-oh. I need to work on his manners. Where's Aunt Rowe off to today?"

"She's ordering those shirts and hats for the danged rodeo performance," Glenda said.

"Oh, jeez. I'm still hoping that idea will blow over."

"Don't bet on it."

"How long ago was Hitchcock with you?" I said.

"Couple of hours. Why?"

Judging by what Glenda had said so far, I didn't think she knew about Crystal.

"Pearl Hogan claims she saw Hitchcock in town this morning," I said. "I'm afraid he might need an alibi."

"Whatever for?" She lifted a wastebasket to sweep underneath.

I unfolded the flat sheet and swooshed it over the bed. "You haven't heard about Crystal Devlin?"

"No." Glenda stopped sweeping and looked at me. "What about her?"

I stopped fooling with the bedclothes and told her of Crystal's death in the old building.

"Lordy, that poor woman." Glenda set the broom aside. "She sold Lloyd and me our house. Sends us a cute little anniversary card every year. What a horrible accident."

"Sorry to bring the bad news," I said, "but I'm not so sure it was an accident."

Glenda went to a ladder-back chair by the window, sat down, and wiped her palms on her denim capris. "After that last time, I thought she'd have taken precautions. I don't know, a karate class or something."

"What happened last time?" I said.

"She went to show a property and met this guy who knocked her down, grabbed her purse, and drove away in her Mercedes."

"That's awful."

"They caught the guy," Glenda said, "but now this. Some agents wear special alarm bracelets so they can send an alert to the police if they run into trouble. Too bad she didn't have one of those."

A bracelet wouldn't have helped Crystal stop a pile of falling bricks, but I kept the thought to myself.

"And here I was complaining about something that doesn't matter in the grand scheme of things," she said. "How petty. I can put up with Rita Colletti."

"Won't be pleasant."

"It's work." Glenda shrugged. "Do they have any idea who Crystal was meeting this morning?"

I shrugged. "Pearl didn't see anyone else."

Glenda frowned. "How is Pearl involved?"

"She picked a bad time to talk to Crystal. Saw her head into that building and felt like she had to confront her."

Glenda clucked her tongue. "Pearl, Pearl, Pearl."

"I know. Of all the bad decisions."

"She's gonna have a mess of trouble," Glenda said, "'cause it's no secret she's been badgering Crystal. Went to her house a few times, uninvited. Wrote letters. Said she was gonna report Crystal to the state board of Realtors, file a lawsuit against her, whatever she could to make Crystal pay for cheating her out of that deal."

This was the first I'd heard of those things. "All that will come out."

"You'd better believe it," Glenda said.

"Pearl's a wreck." I told Glenda about Pearl's request to borrow my cat and how she was convinced Hitchcock had come to town. "Pearl thinks he crossed Crystal's path this morning, and now she's blaming herself for bringing up the idea of using him to cause Crystal bad luck."

"Like the cat knew the plan and did what she thought in the first place?" Glenda said. "Sounds like Pearl's crazy talk."

"That it is." I sighed. "I'm sure she's not the only one who ever got crossways with Crystal Devlin. Sheriff Crawford will find the truth. Meanwhile, I need to look for Hitchcock. Make sure he's not being held as an accessory to a crime."

Glenda sighed. "I gotta move, too. Rowe will want to take a casserole over to the Devlin ranch. I'm not sure how much time their son spends at home, but the poor boy's gotta eat."

"You know Cody Devlin?" I said.

"He's friends with my neighbor's daughter. I see him over there a lot."

"Small world." I finished making up the bed, then went over to Glenda and gave her a hug. "Stay safe and steer clear of the wicked witch."

"You, too."

I walked back to my car, listening to the laughter and voices drifting up from the river. A perfect place to spend a summer afternoon. The water didn't always bring up peaceful thoughts for me, though. The memory of finding the body of Aunt Rowe's cousin in the river back in spring still caused a chill to run up my spine. Neither Bobby Joe Flowers nor Crystal Devlin would ever again enjoy life's simple pleasures, and that saddened me. I was grateful to be here to enjoy this day, even if the temperature was hot enough to melt a rock.

I'd feel a lot more grateful after I found my cat.

I drove down to the Monte Carlo cottage and scanned the grounds for Hitchcock. I took my laptop inside and looked for the cat, but the only thing I found on my bed was black hair and a cat-shaped indentation in the comforter where I'd last seen him. I checked his favorite spots—the patch of sun on the carpet near my best living room chair, the fireplace hearth, the windowsill overlooking my writing table. The place was small, so I'd exhausted all indoor possibilities in a matter of two minutes.

I opened the door to the back deck and did a double take. Hitchcock sat on the arm of the wooden bench, right next to Rita Colletti. The lawyer looked up at me.

"About time you got home," she said. "I have some work I need you to do. Get your laptop charged up and ready to go."

9

PAUSED, COMPLETELY TAKEN aback by Rita's demand, not to mention her appearance at my home. In this setting, I was accustomed to seeing people in shorts and tank tops or swimsuits. Rita was all business in gray slacks with pumps and a black print shirt. As was her habit, she had an extra pen stuck behind her ear. Her auburn hair looked wild today, frizzed out from the humidity. I looked at the legal pad she held, filled with her loopy handwriting, and the stack of papers and files on the bench next to her. Aside from the hair, she looked every bit the high-powered city attorney. I couldn't believe she'd set up shop on my deck.

Hitchcock gave me a look like, *Can you believe the nerve of this woman?*

The fact that Rita had made herself at home in my personal space annoyed me to no end. She actually expected me to *work* for her?

"You *do* remember I turned in my resignation last year?" I said.

"Right," Rita said. "You quit working at the firm. This is a new day, a new place, and I'm prepared to make a new arrangement with you."

"I'm not interested," I said.

"I'm talking a minimal assignment. Ten hours, tops."

"I don't do legal work anymore." I was curious, though, about what had brought her to Lavender. "What kind of case are you working on?"

"A family partnership. Standard forms need massaging to fit the circumstances." She fanned the pages of the legal pad, and I could see she'd filled a dozen or more of them. "This needs to be input."

Looking at those handwritten pages was a déjà vu moment, and not in a good way. Though Rita was in her midforties, she practiced like an old-school attorney who'd grown up before the invention of computers. More like she thought she was simply too important to type for herself. How many hours, days, weeks of my life had I spent transcribing things for her?

Too many.

I gave her my best forced smile. "I'm sure Aunt Rowe wouldn't mind if you'd like to use her scanner or fax to send your project to the office."

Rita sighed. "That new girl can't read my handwriting to save her life. For this, I need you."

I wasn't agreeing to the work, but I had never before heard anything approaching a compliment from Rita, and I wanted a moment to savor the words.

"Who's the client?" I said.

"Leave the names blank for now. I'll fill them in later."

Like I'd agreed to do the work. I frowned. "Is the client's name a state secret?"

"You know good and well about confidentiality issues," Rita said. "You don't need to bother yourself with the names."

Hitchcock stood, stretched, and leapt gracefully to the windowsill behind Rita.

"I'm not bothering with any of it. I can't do the work. I don't have time."

"I spent all morning grinding out these pages," she said. "This is a time-sensitive project."

"Then I suggest you fax it to the firm right quick. It's after lunch." She could have already done so, unless there was some top-secret reason she didn't want anyone—not even anyone at the firm—to know what she was working on.

Not my problem.

"I'll make it worth your while," Rita said in a last-ditch effort to convince me to help her.

Like I need the money that badly. I have enough in savings to live a good five years in Lavender, thank you very much.

Rita glared at me, like she couldn't believe I wasn't jumping at the opportunity. I smiled sweetly.

"Sorry, but I have an appointment." The woman wouldn't quit hounding me unless I gave her a good excuse for ending the conversation. "Matter of fact, Hitchcock and I are a bit late already."

"Who's Hitchcock?" Rita said.

"My cat. I assumed you'd already met."

Rita eyed me suspiciously.

"We're going to see Doc Jensen."

"Oh, for the love of Pete." Rita stood at the same moment Hitchcock jumped down from the windowsill to land on her files. Papers and folders slid off the bench and scattered over the deck.

I bent to gather the documents around my feet. The name Devlin popped out at me, and I purposely slowed my movements to scan the pages.

"Now look at the mess you've made." Rita knelt beside me and in one fast movement swooshed everything together into a haphazard jumble. She grabbed the papers I had in my hands. Not before I spotted a spreadsheet with the Devlin name on top.

So that's who Rita was working for. I glanced around and didn't see her briefcase or phone anywhere nearby. If she'd sequestered herself on my deck to concentrate on the job, she might not know what had happened to Crystal. Once she learned the news, her project might lose its urgency. Or at least drop from the top-priority spot. I, however, wasn't telling Rita one thing that would keep me tied up with her for a second longer than necessary.

Rita pushed the pages into some semblance of a pile and tamped them on the floor like a deck of cards. She picked up the awkward collection of papers and stood. "This was a wasted trip."

You really thought I would help? In your dreams.

"We must run," I said, directing Rita down the steps. "Don't want to be late for our appointment. Good luck with your project."

I scooped Hitchcock up and watched for a minute as Rita tottered on her heels across the lawn toward the Paris cottage. Then I took the cat inside and grabbed the flyer I wanted to show the vet.

"Don't worry, boy," I told him. "You don't have an appointment. This is a social call."

I made sure I locked the cottage up tight before leaving.

MAGNOLIA Jensen's veterinary clinic was located in a white house on a corner lot a few miles south of Lavender. Maggie and I had discussed getting together about the black cat adoption weekend. If she didn't have time to meet this afternoon, fine. I cared only about getting away from Rita Colletti. If the lawyer didn't want to send the typing assignment off to her office—easy enough to do in this technological age—then why hadn't she typed it on her own danged computer from the start? Involving me didn't make sense.

"Why does her obnoxious behavior continue to surprise me?" I said to Hitchcock. "That doesn't make sense either."

"Mrreow," he said from the passenger seat, where he sat up like a rabbit with his front paws on the door frame.

I parked the car and sweet-talked the cat until he walked across the console and let me pick him up to carry him inside. I had bought a cat carrier, but so far had been unable to maneuver Hitchcock into it. Seeing as I had spent a good bit of time convincing townspeople that he wasn't bad luck and that any efforts to trap him needed to stop, it seemed wrong somehow to force him into something so traplike.

Inside the office, Darla, the young receptionist who barely came up to my chin, was saying good-bye to a woman with a chocolate Lab. The Lab strained at his leash, trying to get closer to us, but his owner yanked him along and they left the building.

Darla turned to us. "Hiya, Miss Sabrina and Hitchcock. You doin' okay? Do y'all have an appointment?" She glanced down at her computer screen.

"We're fine," I told the girl. "No appointment. If Doc Jensen has a few minutes, though, I'd like to talk with her about that adoption event we're working on." I wanted the vet's approval on the flyer before I had copies made.

"She'll be through with her patient soon," Darla said, "and has a little time before the next."

I was about to take a seat, when Hitchcock decided he'd had enough of being restrained and squiggled out of my arms to leap onto the U-shaped counter surrounding the reception-area desk.

"C'mon, Hitchcock," I said. "Don't bother Darla while she's working."

The cat walked to the end of the counter and sat down as if he owned the place.

"Oh, he's not bothering me," Darla said. "Hey, did you hear what happened to Crystal Devlin, that real estate woman?"

She didn't wait for me to answer.

"Miss Pearl from the candy store, you know she and Miss Crystal never did get along. Well, Miss Pearl knocked Miss Crystal upside the head and killed her."

"That's not what—"

"Don't know about you," Darla continued, "but I'd've never thought that sweet little old lady had it in her to murder somebody in cold blood."

Hitchcock let out a long howl, like he was putting in his two cents about her comments.

"Good Lord, Darla," I said. "That's not what happened at all. I hope you haven't been telling everyone you saw today that tall tale."

"She has." A vet tech wearing a lab coat of paw-print fabric walked into the room. "Didn't know what to make of it myself."

"I got the news straight from my friend Nicole," Darla said, "and she's tight with Deputy Rosales."

"This is like a bad game of whisper down the alley," I said, "and I don't think the sheriff would appreciate your passing false information around town." I certainly wasn't going to share anything I knew as fact with this blabbermouth. Did the sheriff's department believe that Pearl had murdered Crystal? Why would they if the falling bricks were what killed the woman?

The tech said, "Ma'am, you need to restrain your cat. Doc's seeing a not-so-cat-friendly Rottweiler, and he'll be out here in a second."

If there was any confrontation between Hitchcock and a Rottweiler, I feared for the dog. Still, I didn't want to take any chances. I approached Hitchcock, and he leapt from the desk to the top of a file cabinet.

The tech pulled a black harness and leash from a wall hook and handed it to me. "Try this."

Easy for her to say.

I took the harness and studied the straps, trying to figure out how to put the thing on a cat. I was still struggling with it when I heard the jingling of a dog's collar and watched as the large brown-and-black dog practically dragged its female owner to the counter. When I looked back to the file cabinet, Hitchcock was nowhere in sight.

"He went thataway." Darla pointed down the hall. "You can go on to Doc's office. I think Hitchcock already did."

Sure enough, I found my cat sitting big as you please on Maggie Jensen's desk with the vet obligingly scratching his head. Doc Jensen wore a pretty turquoise lab coat. Her straight dark hair was streaked with gray, held back in a silver clip that coordinated nicely with her silver-framed eyeglasses.

"Looks like you lost control of your cat," she said with a smile.

"Lost it?" I said. "I never had control of Hitchcock and probably never will."

"You should try. Here, I'll give you some tips on how to use the harness. He'll like it once he gets used to it."

That would never happen, but I watched as the vet handled my cat and made him do things no ordinary person could ever convince him to do. She fastened the harness around him and snapped the leash onto the harness, then handed the other end of the leash to me.

"Simple," she said.

Hitchcock looked like he was smiling at her. Unbelievable.

"That's very impressive, but you know pets don't behave for owners the way they behave for you."

"Maybe not." She laughed. "What brings you here?"

I took my tote off my shoulder and pulled out the flyer I'd printed. "If you approve of this, I'll have copies made to hang up around town and to use to solicit donations. Speaking of which, I already received one." I took out the check Crystal Devlin had written and placed it on the desk. "I'm not sure what to do with this now."

Maggie picked up the check. "Bless her heart," she said. "Crystal was always a supporter of animals in need. I was distressed to hear the bad news about her."

"Maybe we should return the check under the circumstances," I said.

"I'll hold on to it for a bit," Maggie said. "Might ask her husband what to do. I see him quite often." She picked up the flyer and studied it. "This is great. Of course, we had a perfect model."

She turned to Hitchcock, comparing him in person to his likeness on the page. He looked at her through slitted eyes and began purring.

I laughed. "He's such a suck-up, isn't he?"

"You and I think the best of Hitchcock, but not everyone does. I think you should make it a point to keep him restrained as much as you can. He'll get accustomed to the harness with time and practice."

"I want him to be a happy cat. He's lived his life with a sense of freedom. I hate to spoil that."

"I understand," Maggie said, "but you need to protect him from trouble, too."

I frowned. "What sort of trouble are you talking about?"

"Communicable disease, for one. You should keep an eye out for feral cats in your area. Feline AIDS is a problem."

I hadn't seen any feral cats, but Maggie was right. I didn't want to take any chances.

"There's another kind of danger," she said. "The sort where people are blaming Hitchcock for things."

"Uh-oh. What now?"

"Don't get me wrong," Maggie said. "I would never think the worst about this dear cat. That patient who just left, though, the lady with the Rottweiler, said she saw the bad luck cat in town this morning."

I sighed and settled into the chair across the desk from Maggie. "Thomas told me Hitchcock rode home from town with him yesterday. I suppose he could have slipped into town again today without my knowledge."

"That's what I mean," she said. "You need to keep a better eye on him. Lady says that the bad luck cat caused Crystal Devlin's death. The last thing I want to see, and I'm sure you'll agree, is for Hitchcock to get mixed up in a murder investigation."

10

LEFT DOC JENSEN'S office, thoroughly aggravated that anyone would accuse Hitchcock of causing a death. Complaining about the unfairness of people's fears and attitudes about my cat wouldn't solve anything. Better to go home, lock myself in the cottage with Hitchcock, and take out my frustrations on a fictional character. I needed to catch up on my page count. My agent was hopeful about the sales potential for my first novel, and I didn't want to disappoint her by taking forever to write the second.

The afternoon was sunny and hot, nearly a hundred degrees in the shade. We got into my car, Hitchcock still wearing the harness and leash Doc Jensen had generously given us, and I blasted the air-conditioning on high. The cat squirmed on the passenger seat, scratching at the harness. I knew he wanted to pull a Houdini-like act and get free of the thing.

"Hold on, buddy," I said. "We'll go home, and I'll take that contraption off so you can relax."

He cut his eyes to me before folding his legs and settling into his meatloaf position.

I smiled and patted his head. I was about to pull out of the parking lot when my phone rang. Aunt Rowe. I put the car in park and answered, expecting to hear details about the rodeo outfits she'd gone to order.

"Glenda says you're not home," Aunt Rowe said. "Hope you're in town, 'cause I need you now."

My heart rate jumped. "I *am* in town. What's wrong?"

"We're at the sheriff's office, and Pearl's having a spell. I need help getting her home."

"They're releasing her?" That was good news.

"Soon," Aunt Rowe said. "Jeb is finishing with her now. The sooner we get her out of here, the better."

"See you in two minutes."

"Wait by the back door," she said. "You don't want to get in the middle of this. We'll come out."

Sounded ominous.

"Okay." I was already headed their way.

We ended the call without further explanations. Questions ran through my head. What kind of spell was Pearl having? A fainting spell? A panic attack? Something with her heart?

The sheriff's office shared a building with the Lavender Bible Church, which, according to the sign by the road, held services on Sunday mornings and Wednesday and Sunday evenings. That left the rest of the week free for comings and goings related to law and order. During Sunday services, Sheriff Crawford kept a deputy posted outside to keep the church folks separate from those who had business with his office.

A concrete porch with an aluminum awning ran the length of the building. The entrance to the sheriff's office was around back. I found a parking space near the door and pulled in. Hitchcock stood tall and peered out over the dash at the building in front of us.

"We're picking up Aunt Rowe and Pearl," I told him, "so be on your best behavior."

I hoped Pearl wouldn't start in on her nonsense about seeing Hitchcock at the scene of Crystal's death.

I looked around the parking area. Aunt Rowe's car wasn't in sight. I wondered how she'd gotten here. Pearl had likely been brought from the crime scene by a sheriff's deputy. The office door opened. I moved to get out, then relaxed when I saw a blond girl emerging, not Aunt Rowe. I watched the girl pull a cigarette and lighter from a pocket. She headed to a spot a few yards from the door, lit the cigarette, and leaned against the building smoking and staring into space. She wore skinny jeans with turquoise tennis shoes and a white tank top. Her short blond hair was tousled in a cute style that suited her, but her face was pale and her eyes red-rimmed.

After half a minute, I realized she was the girl I'd seen with Cody Devlin earlier in the day. She might be the neighbor Glenda had mentioned. Aside from puffing on her cigarette and casting a worried glance at the door every few seconds, the girl barely moved.

I drummed my fingers on the steering wheel and hoped Aunt Rowe and Pearl hadn't run into an unexpected hitch. Maybe Pearl felt too ill to walk. I checked my tote to make sure I had my spare car key. I could lock the door and leave the motor running so Hitchcock would stay cool, something I'd never have chanced when I lived in Houston. I wasn't overly concerned here, parked at the sheriff's department. Besides, I'd only be gone for a few minutes.

"I'm going to check on them," I told Hitchcock. "You stay here. Don't open the windows."

He made a trilling noise and calmly watched me leave. With the motor running, a cat like Hitchcock could probably push the button to power a window down. I shouldn't have given him any ideas.

I walked up on the porch and stood by the glass entrance. No sign of anyone heading out. The girl and I exchanged a glance.

"Hi," I said. "I'm waiting for someone."

"Me, too." She turned her head and exhaled smoke away from me.

I leaned toward the door and tried to look inside. The glaring sun kept me from seeing anything.

"I wouldn't go in," she said. "Place is a circus."

"Huh," I said. "Sheriff Crawford usually runs an organized office."

She shrugged. "He's juggling a bunch of stressed-out people today."

I paused before mentioning Crystal, then decided to go for it. "Because of Crystal Devlin's death?"

"Yeah. She's my boyfriend's mom." She looked down at her feet. "*Was* his mom."

"I'm so sorry." I introduced myself. "I believe I saw you this morning. Were you with Cody?"

She nodded and blinked rapidly.

"Tough situation," I said. "He'll need a lot of support."

"Right." She gave me a slight smile. "I'm Mimi." She offered her hand and we shook. "Mimi Trevino."

"Sorry we couldn't meet under better circumstances, Mimi. I think you might be a neighbor of my friends, the Kesslers?"

Mimi nodded. "Yeah, I know 'em."

She didn't offer more. After a minute of silence, I said, "Any idea what happened to Crystal?"

"Nope." She shook her head. "Cody and I were having breakfast. Pancakes, at the diner. He got a call."

The door opened again. This time Cody came out. His dark wavy hair fell over his forehead and nearly covered one eye. He came over to Mimi and she tucked an arm through his possessively before introducing us. I offered my condolences to him.

"Thanks, ma'am. Appreciate it." The whites of Cody's crystal blue eyes were streaked with red. I got the impression he was making a Herculean effort to hold his emotions in check.

The teenagers didn't make any move to leave.

"You waiting for someone else?" I said.

"We're catching a ride with my dad," Cody said. "He's in there yelling at some old, uh, ladies."

Uh-oh. I should have headed straight inside when I arrived, no matter what Aunt Rowe said.

"I'd better check on the situation," I said. "My aunt's here."

"Dad's focused on the candy-store woman," Cody said.

"Where's the sheriff?"

"He's in there." The boy shuffled his feet nervously.

My phone vibrated in my pocket, and I pulled it out.

A text from Aunt Rowe simply said, Help.

She was inside with Sheriff Crawford and sending an SOS to me?

"Nice meeting you, Mimi, Cody. I'm being summoned."

Cody dipped his head to acknowledge my words. I darted toward the door, then remembered Hitchcock. I'd take him inside with me, but I didn't want to chance running into any anti-black-cat fanatics. I looked at Mimi and Cody and made a judgment call.

"You kids mind keeping an eye on my car?" I said. "My cat's in there."

"Sure thing," Cody said, and I entered the building.

It took a few seconds for my eyes to adjust from the bright sun as my ears focused on sharp words coming from the back of the space. I knew the office layout well from prior visits to chat with the sheriff about crime scene research for my books. The space was a little bigger than the Mayberry office of Andy Taylor that I knew from watching TV reruns as a kid, and this one was divided into small cubicles with a hallway leading back to a few enclosed rooms. Here, they had up-to-date, high-tech equipment and computers, and Sheriff Crawford had an actual office with a door. Laurelle, a dispatcher I'd met before, was at her desk wearing headphones and listening intently to the phone line. She waved to me, and I headed for the hall.

I glanced into Deputy Rosales's vacant space and looked into Sheriff Crawford's office as I passed. Also vacant. The voices had to be coming from the corner conference/interrogation room. The door stood open, allowing words to carry clearly down the hall. I slowed my pace, listening to the conversation.

"You were *right there*," a man said. "How could you not see anything? Are you blind?"

"It happened before I came in," a woman whined, "and you ought to treat me a little nicer. I could have been the one killed by those falling bricks, you know."

Pearl. Stretching the truth.

"I don't know much 'cause nobody's telling me the facts," the man said.

"Now, Mr. Devlin." Aunt Rowe's voice. "I think you're being a little too harsh with Pearl. Can't you see she isn't well? We need to get her home."

"The woman was found at the scene of my wife's death," he said. "Excuse me if I'm feeling a little *harsh* right now. If your friend's not talking, then there's somebody else I need to find. Maybe I can get some answers from *her*."

"Who's that?" Aunt Rowe said.

"Woman named Sabrina," he said. "I'm told she was right there at the scene with this one. You know her?"

I froze and thought about going back to my car. Something creaked off to my right, and Sheriff Crawford came around the corner from the copy machine alcove holding a sheaf of papers.

He smiled and raised his bushy eyebrows when he saw me. "Sounds like you're up, Sabrina."

11

"I'M NOT HERE to talk," I whispered. "I came to pick up Aunt Rowe and Pearl."

The sheriff moved closer to me and spoke in a low voice. "If you don't talk to Mr. Devlin now, he'll be askin' all over town about you. Is that what you want?"

"No, but there's nothing I can say that will help. I have no idea what happened to his wife."

"You can tell him what you do know," Sheriff Crawford said.

A chair scraped along the floor, and I heard Aunt Rowe. "Mr. Devlin, if you're not of a mind to help me with my friend, then could you at least get out of our way?"

I sighed. I wanted out of here as soon as possible even if it meant exchanging a few words with Lance Devlin first. I squared my shoulders and marched into the conference room.

Pearl had a grip on Aunt Rowe's shoulder as she tried to stand. I could hear her heavy breathing from across the room. Her hair looked like she'd walked through a windstorm, and her glasses sat askew. A man, Lance Devlin I assumed, stood between them and the door. He was dark-haired and tall, fiftyish, in jeans and a denim shirt. He held a felt cowboy hat in his right hand.

I walked up behind him. "Excuse me, Mr. Devlin."

He turned around, and I offered a hand. "I'm Sabrina Tate. I'm very sorry for your loss."

He switched his hat to his other hand and shook mine.

Aunt Rowe said, "Thank goodness you're here. Pearl is having trouble getting her breath."

"Should we call an ambulance?" I said.

"No," Pearl said, "I have some medicine at home, and I'm sure I'll be fine after I take that." She rapped her fist on the table. "Knock on wood."

There she goes again with that knock-on-wood business.

"Okay," I said. "I'm ready."

I looked at Devlin, who appeared to still be wrapping his mind around the fact that he'd uttered my name and conjured me up as if by magic.

"Hold on a second," he said in a deep Texas drawl. "You need to answer some questions."

"I already reported what I know, which isn't much, to the deputy at the scene. When I arrived, the bricks had already fallen. I don't know how it happened. There was nothing I could do to help your wife. I'm so sorry."

Devlin said, "Did you see anyone else in the area?"

I glanced at Pearl. Her complexion was flushed, and sweat beaded on her forehead.

"Pearl was there," I said. "She found Crystal. Before we could get help, the construction workers arrived and made the call. That's all I know."

"She had it in for my wife." Devlin gave Pearl a long once-over.

"Granted, they weren't best friends," Aunt Rowe said, "but Pearl wouldn't hurt an ant traipsing through her candy store."

The sheriff came into the room and handed the papers he held to Devlin. "I've made copies, so you can take these back home. I'll let you know if we find anything useful."

Devlin said, "Sheriff, a word in private?"

Sheriff Crawford nodded. "Let's go into my office. You ladies, see yourselves out. Pearl, stay close. We'll need to speak in more detail."

At least he didn't say "don't leave town," but I was pretty sure that's what he meant. I was surprised Pearl didn't have a comeback to that statement even though she didn't feel well.

Aunt Rowe took Pearl by her arm. I went around and supported Pearl's other side. She stood, breathing even harder, and let out a low moan.

I looked down at the woman. Her antics were making me suspicious about the whole illness thing.

"You should go straight to a doctor's office," I said on our way to the door.

"I'll be fine," Pearl said, sounding weak.

"Let's go to my house," Aunt Rowe said. "I can keep an eye on Pearl there, make sure things don't get worse."

"Okay," Pearl whispered.

The woman said she had medicine at home, but I'd rather get these two away from the sheriff's office than raise the issue.

"Where's your car, Aunt Rowe?" I said.

"In the shop," she said as we stepped outside. "I was there talking to the mechanic when I got the call from Pearl, so I walked straight over."

Pearl stopped short. "Good Lord, Sabrina," she said in a normal tone, "what's in your car?"

I glanced in that direction and saw Hitchcock sprawled on the dash above the steering wheel.

She leaned forward, squinting. "Oh my gosh, it's your cat."

"Hitchcock and I just came from a visit with his vet." I cast a glance at Cody and Mimi. The teenagers had moved down to the other end of the porch and were engrossed in conversation.

"You shouldn't bring him out in public like this," Pearl said.

She sounded stronger, as if the hot outdoor air had rejuvenated her.

"Get in the car, please." I opened the back door for the women and kept one eye on Hitchcock to make sure he didn't try to escape.

Pearl slid across the backseat. "I didn't say one word about the cat to the sheriff, I swear."

"Why *would* you mention the cat?" Aunt Rowe said.

I closed the back door after them, then got in and turned around to look at Aunt Rowe. "Pearl thought Hitchcock was in the building where Crystal died, but he wasn't and that's that. Let's drop the subject, please."

Aunt Rowe didn't comment. Pearl crossed her arms over her chest and looked out the window. I headed toward home, thankful that Pearl's breathing had seemed to ease and pretty much convinced she'd been faking the whole breathing problem. Hitchcock settled onto the passenger seat for the short drive. I wondered what the papers were that Sheriff Crawford had handed to Devlin. A copy of the police report, maybe, or something more?

We arrived at Aunt Rowe's house a few minutes later and Pearl climbed out of the car without assistance.

"I'm starving, but I need to make a call to the store," she announced and headed inside.

"Shouldn't she be resting?" I said to Aunt Rowe, wondering how long the two of them would keep up the charade.

"She will. C'mon in. You can join us for dinner."

I shook my head. "I need to take Hitchcock home. He's getting antsy in this harness the vet gave me."

"Bring him inside," Aunt Rowe said. "I have some of that smoked turkey he loves."

I thought Aunt Rowe didn't approve of feeding Hitchcock people food, but the cat's ears perked up at the word "turkey."

"Besides," she said, "you and I need to visit. It seems like I barely get to spend time with you."

"Okay, we'll stay for a little bit." I unfastened the harness, and Hitchcock couldn't slide out fast enough. We both followed Aunt Rowe into the kitchen.

"Have you eaten?" she said as she pulled a container of turkey from the refrigerator.

"Not since breakfast, and I'm having a serious chocolate craving."

"Glenda left a tortilla casserole for dinner." Aunt Rowe picked up a piece of paper where Glenda scribbled instructions as she often did. "All I have to do is heat it in the oven."

"How long will that take?" I said.

"Thirty minutes," she said.

"So long as you have the oven going, I'm going to mix up a batch of black bottom cupcakes." Luke Griffin's belated birthday treat.

Aunt Rowe turned on the oven to preheat, then chopped turkey into small pieces for Hitchcock. When she finished she placed a bowl of meat on the floor, and Hitchcock attacked it with gusto.

I got out the mixer and the cupcake ingredients. "Pearl seems to feel a lot better."

"Uh-huh." Aunt Rowe opened the refrigerator and took out the tea pitcher.

I made these cupcakes so often that I could practically mix them up with my eyes closed. I measured ingredients for the batter in one bowl and the cheesecake filling in another. Chocolate chips sprinkled on top added the perfect amount of sweetness.

"What did the sheriff say about Crystal?" I said.

"He wouldn't tell us much, but I heard him on the phone. He says she was dead before the bricks fell. Blow to the back of her head." Aunt Rowe filled tea glasses. "He's definitely looking for a murderer."

"It's awfully quick to know that for a fact. They'll have to do an autopsy, cross all their t's and dot the i's." I lined two cupcake tins with paper liners. "Any idea what those papers were that he handed back to Devlin?"

"Crystal's calendar, I think," she said.

"Huh." It made perfect sense for the sheriff to investigate the woman's recent activities and appointments. Hopefully, he wouldn't find derogatory notations about Pearl.

I looked at Aunt Rowe. "Things might not look great for Pearl, but I can't imagine he seriously suspects her."

"I hope you're right."

We worked in silence for a minute before Pearl walked into the kitchen and hopped up on a barstool at the island. She'd combed her hair and looked perky. "The store is running smoothly without me. Knock on wood." She tap-tapped the counter with a knuckle.

"Quit that," I said.

Pearl looked confused. "Quit what?"

"Saying the words 'knock on wood' changes nothing," I said.

"It makes me feel better." Pearl turned her attention to the stove. "What's for dinner?"

I rolled my eyes behind her back.

Aunt Rowe told Pearl about the casserole and handed her a glass of iced tea. I watched Pearl from the corner of my eye while I finished readying the cupcakes for baking and saw not one sign of trouble with her breathing.

Pearl took a sip of tea and sighed. "I hope this murder business gets cleared up before my little Julie gets here."

"When's she coming?" Aunt Rowe said.

"Supposed to fly into San Antonio day after tomorrow," Pearl said.

"Who's Julie?" I said.

"My granddaughter," Pearl said. "She's eight. Cutest little thing. Her parents are spending a day with her at SeaWorld before they head to Lavender. Then she'll be with me for two weeks."

"That'll be nice," Aunt Rowe said. "Reminds me of when Sabrina was a little girl. She came here to visit often, and I loved every minute."

Smiling at the memory, I slid the cupcake tins into the oven on the shelf below the casserole.

"Be a shame if I was locked up when Julie gets here," Pearl said.

"Don't be silly," I said. "They wouldn't lock you up unless they had evidence against you."

Pearl and Aunt Rowe exchanged a glance.

"*Do* they have evidence?" I said.

Pearl's face scrunched up. "I might have left a couple of, uh, not-so-nice voice messages for Crystal."

"You *might have*?" I said.

"She had me riled up about the real estate deal," Pearl said. "I blew off some steam on the phone. That's not what I'm most worried about, though."

I looked over at Aunt Rowe and shook my head.

"What worries you most?" Aunt Rowe said.

Hitchcock jumped up to the stool near Pearl and looked at her as if he was just as interested in hearing her next statement as the rest of us.

"What if the killer comes after me?" she said.

"The killer wasn't after you, Pearl," I said, "least not if what you told me was the truth."

"I'm not a liar," she said petulantly.

"You didn't see anyone," I said, "and chances are no one saw you in that building. No one knows you were there, except for me."

"A lot of loose lips in this town," Aunt Rowe said. "The killer might hear Pearl was there, think that she saw him, and come after her to shut her up."

"Good way to make your friend feel worse, Aunt Rowe," I said.

"It's a fact," Pearl said. "I already figured that out for myself."

I turned on the oven light and looked in the window to check the cupcakes. "What's with you two? I'm usually the one who comes up with all the weird plot ideas."

Aunt Rowe cleared her throat. "That's exactly why you should solve this case, Sabrina, before things get out of hand. You can think like a criminal, and you did a great job solving the last murder in Lavender."

"Oh, no you don't." I backed away from the oven, away from the women staring at me. "I'm not getting involved in a murder investigation."

"But you have to," Pearl whined. "How else will I get off the hook for good?"

I looked at her, my eyes narrowed. "How are you feeling, Pearl? You seem to be breathing with absolutely no problem."

She ducked her head and cut her eyes to Aunt Rowe. "She's onto us."

"Good grief, Aunt Rowe, you were in cahoots with her and the whole oh-I'm-so-sick-I-can't-breathe act?"

"I wasn't gonna stand by and let Devlin railroad Pearl straight into a jail cell." Aunt Rowe went to the pantry and stepped inside, possibly to avoid the conversation.

"I *did* feel bad," Pearl added. "Who feels fine when they're being questioned about a murder?"

I raised my hands. "I am not touching this case, it's not my job, I am no detective."

"You know all the tricks." Pearl set her glass down with a thump. "You write about them in your books all the time."

"That's different."

"It's not. I'm counting on you. Little Julie is counting on you, too. You wouldn't want her to see Grandma Pearl behind bars, would you?"

I shook my head. "There's nothing you can say to make me change my mind. Don't even try."

"Mrreow," Hitchcock said.

12

I STAYED AT AUNT Rowe's house long enough to grab a bite of dinner and finish making the cupcakes. Then I was out of there, without making any promises to investigate a murder. Not that I wished Pearl any ill will. My hope was she'd never be charged with anything. I mean, who indicts the candy-store lady for murder? I would mind my own business and hope for the best where Pearl was concerned. If all went well, my cat—or any cat for that matter—would never be mentioned in connection with this morning's events. The sheriff wouldn't even give the presence of a cat a second thought, would he?

No matter. Steer clear of the whole mess.

I carried a plate of slightly warm cupcakes into my cottage and found Hitchcock sitting by his empty food dish. He'd made it home ahead of me, and I didn't know if he'd stayed to hear the last of my conversation with Aunt Rowe and Pearl.

"I turned them down, Hitchcock," I told him as I doled out

his cat food. "We're not getting involved in any investigation. You're *not* already involved, right?"

He looked up from the bowl briefly before diving back into the food without responding.

Next on my agenda—how to go about getting these belated birthday cupcakes to Luke Griffin? I'd never been to his place, and it felt a little forward of me to assume he'd be okay with an impromptu visit. Invite him here? I'd rather not stay myself—not with Rita Colletti living practically next door. Her car was parked at the Paris cottage when I passed, and she was bound to hit me up again to do her typing.

First, see if Griffin's free tonight.

I picked up my phone and hit the button programmed to call the game warden.

Griffin answered on the second ring.

"Hey, remember those cupcakes we talked about?" I said.

"How could I forget?" he said with a smile in his voice.

I paused, thinking how to phrase this without sounding like I was asking him out. "They're ready, and I'm calling to see when and where you'd like to take delivery."

That sounded awkward—like I was calling from some cupcake shop.

"As soon as possible," he said. "I'm free after eight tonight. Heading out now to speak at a Boy Scout meeting."

"Really? About what?"

"Safety on the water, boating safety in particular. Scouts have a camping weekend coming up."

"Interesting," I said. "Is this part of your job?"

"Not exactly, but I'm a multifaceted kind of guy."

One of the things I liked about him.

"Where's the meeting?" I said.

"Eugenia Banks Middle School. You know it?"

"I do. Meeting ends about eight?"

"Right. You want to meet somewhere afterward?"

A thought came to mind, and I decided to go for it. "Is there by chance a place inside the school where I could sit and write while you're meeting?" I said. "This morning I knew exactly where the chapter I'm writing was headed, but things here right now aren't at all conducive to writing. I need to get the words down before they vanish."

"You want a hideout," he said.

"Exactly."

"There's cafeteria seating down the hall from the auditorium where we meet. Anyone sees you, they'll assume you're one of the moms waiting on the meeting to end."

"That sounds perfect, if you're sure it's not a problem," I said.

"I'll tell the security guy you're with me." He paused for a second. "I'll be glad to see you."

"For the cupcakes."

"Not only them," he said.

My cheeks felt warm as I disconnected the call, and I bustled around my kitchenette, gathering things to take along. Laptop, chapter notes, the cupcakes, something to drink. I started a pot of coffee and took out a thermos. While the coffee brewed I darted into the bedroom and changed into a fresh pair of khaki shorts and white eyelet top. By the time I ran a brush through my hair and put on some lipstick, Hitchcock was curled up and asleep in the center of my bed.

"I'm going out for a little while," I told him. "You stay inside and be a good boy, okay?"

He slitted his eyes at me for a moment before they drifted shut.

I smiled at the cat, then loaded up my things and took off for the school.

Eugenia Banks Middle School was located about five miles outside of town, halfway between Lavender and Emerald Springs. The school property was dotted with live oaks. A baseball diamond sat in the field next to the tan brick one-story building. A game was in progress when I pulled into the crowded parking lot, and the bleachers were filled with cheering spectators. I guessed the ballplayers weren't Boy

Scouts or, if they were, they'd chosen the game over the meeting tonight.

I left the cupcakes in a small ice chest in the car for fear I'd eat all of them before Griffin's meeting ended if I had them close at hand. A couple of boys in Scout uniforms, twelve or so years old, were dropped off near the building and headed inside. I looped my laptop case over my shoulder and followed them through a side door that took us straight to the auditorium.

I peered into the large room where other Scouts milled around, talking excitedly. Griffin stood near the stage, arranging handouts on a table. He wore his game warden uniform and looked very official next to a screen that showed a picture of a body of water with the heading "Boating Safety." As if he'd felt my presence, he looked up, met my eyes, and pointed—in the direction of the cafeteria, I surmised.

I gave him a thumbs-up, headed that way, and found the cafeteria without seeing any security guard. Maybe he was outside watching the ball game.

A sense of euphoria flooded me simply because I was alone in the relative quiet of a darkened building. A place to write. Alone at last. I booted up the laptop, which provided all the light I needed. I sat down and reviewed what I'd written first thing in the morning, before the interruption that had led me to Crystal's body.

Focus, Sabrina.

I forced thoughts of the morning's gruesome events aside. A few minutes later, I was writing at a steady pace. My FBI agent was sweating over the interrogation of a key witness— a young, frightened woman with no idea whom she could or could not trust.

My mind was completely wrapped up in the story, when I heard a murmur of female voices in the hallway about ten yards away. Maybe Scout mothers waiting for their sons' meeting to end. The top of a soft drink can snapped open. My laptop keys didn't make much noise, but I stopped typing and listened.

"I don't agree," a woman with a raspy voice said. "The husband's always guilty. You watch TV, right?"

"Happens a lot," said a second woman. "Saw on the news one time where this groom threw his wife off a cliff on their honeymoon."

"Yeah, I saw that. Hope he's sittin' in a jail somewhere."

"Me, too."

"The man must've had a cold, cold heart," the first woman said, "just like whoever committed this crime."

"I don't see Lance bein' that person, even if he did have a dozen reasons for wantin' her gone."

A sigh. "Could just as easily been one of her other men."

What other men? I took my hands away from the computer and leaned toward the voices.

"Ace McKinney's 'bout as cold as they come," raspy voice said.

"That's ancient history."

"To us, maybe not to him."

The women began walking, their footsteps on the tiled floor and their voices fading away from me.

Dang it. I had good intentions of ignoring this topic, but now my curiosity had kicked up. I stood to follow the women and keep up with their conversation, then stopped myself.

Write, Sabrina. Ignore the gossip.

I turned back to the computer, but couldn't quite grasp the rhythm of the story. My thoughts kept going back to what I'd heard. Did Lance Devlin have a dozen reasons for wanting his wife gone? Did Crystal have other men, as in lovers? What kind of ancient history did she have with Ace McKinney?

As I struggled to get more words on the page, eight o'clock came quickly. I had managed to write several pages and was glad for the draft to work on later. A buzz of people in the hallway alerted me to the end of Griffin's meeting. I packed up my laptop and returned to the auditorium, where I scanned Scouts and grown-ups who had either attended the meeting themselves or come to pick up the boys. Several women, but none were paired up. I had no way of knowing if they were the same women I'd overheard. I didn't recognize anyone.

As the last of the Scouts filed out the door, Griffin said his good-byes to a man I presumed was the Scout leader and headed my way.

"How'd it go?" I said.

"Pretty well until the kids veered off topic a bit, talking about safety in general and the lady who got killed. Whole town's gossiping, and the kids are no exception."

"Yeah, I heard some gossip, too."

"Let's go somewhere, and you can tell me all about it," he said.

Outside, Griffin retrieved his yellow Lab, Angie, from a friend who dog-sat for him while watching the baseball game. I'd seen Angie with Griffin many times, but had never met the dog up close and personal. Angie sniffed my hands and must have decided I was okay because she trotted by my side as we walked toward my car. I told Griffin I'd brought coffee and milk, in case he preferred one or the other.

"I know a perfect place for our cupcake break," he said. "A place we won't hear any more gossip, and it's one of Angie's favorite spots."

"Sounds great," I said.

We decided to take both vehicles, and I followed Griffin a few miles down the road to a turnoff I wouldn't have noticed just driving by. The dirt road led off the main highway to a pond next to a grove of trees. A rowboat tied to a small dock rocked slightly in the evening breeze. Griffin pointed out a picnic table shaded by the trees, and I brought out the cupcakes and drinks. Angie took off after a bird sitting by the pond.

"How do you know this spot?" I asked after we'd settled at the picnic table and I'd poured us each a cup of coffee.

He smiled. "Property's part of my late stepfather's ranch. Won't be able to enjoy it much longer, though. His kids decided to sell. Claim they love the place, but nobody's in a position to buy out the others."

"What a shame." I sat sideways on the picnic table bench and put my feet on the bench to hug my knees. "Sunset must be spectacular from here."

"You're about to see for yourself." Griffin peeled the paper off a cupcake. "These look great. You having one?"

"Probably, but trust me, I've already taste-tested my share."

He took a bite and made appreciative noises.

"So you'll have to move," I said. "Away from the ranch."

He wiped his mouth with a napkin and shrugged. "I knew that would happen, and Mom's ready to find a smaller place of her own. I'm hoping she'll stay close enough for me to keep an eye on her."

I grinned. "She probably says the same about you."

Angie must have realized there was food at the table and came back to sit by her master. I was about to apologize for not having a treat for the dog when Griffin produced a rawhide stick from a pocket.

"Grabbed it from my truck. 'Always be prepared' isn't only for the Boy Scouts." He finished the cupcake and took a swig of coffee. "Tell me about the gossip you heard back at the school. Were you outside at the ball game?"

"No, I stayed in the cafeteria writing." I told him what the women had said. "You hear any of this around town?"

He shrugged. "I try not to listen too hard. Crystal Devlin was out there in the public eye, of course people are gonna sling dirt. I hear she was a shrewd businesswoman. Probably wouldn't have won any popularity contests."

"Doesn't necessarily sound like the type who'd have the spare time to run around on her husband."

"Some women make the time," Griffin said, then hurriedly added, "but I know nothing about Crystal's private life."

"What about Ace McKinney? You know him?"

Griffin finished another bite of cupcake. "Unfortunately, yes. We had a showdown soon after I took over this territory. He and I didn't see eye to eye about the starting date of hunting season."

"You mean he's a poacher?"

"I don't know what he is today. That episode was over a year ago. Man was drinking, quite a lot judging from the smell of him. He definitely doesn't like other people telling him what to do."

"Or not do," I said.

Griffin nodded. "You get the picture. I backed down that day. Figured it was either let it go or risk being shot."

"He was that angry?"

"It was a bad scene. I wrote him a ticket. Made a report to my boss about the guy. Hate to come across as a coward, but there was no way I was gonna stop him from doin' whatever he felt like doin'."

"So you'd say Ace McKinney's the type of guy who could kill someone?"

Griffin turned his head toward the sun, still brilliant and surrounded by gorgeous shades of pink as it lowered toward the horizon. After a moment, he faced me. "I can imagine him killing. What I have trouble with is seeing a man like Ace climbing up on that scaffolding to patiently rig the bricks."

"What are you talking about?"

"Sorry. I forgot that's not common knowledge." Griffin wiped his hands on a napkin. "The bricks were rigged to fall. Set up so they'd go off quick and easy as soon as Crystal was in the right spot."

His statement contradicted what Aunt Rowe had said. "Who'd you hear this from?"

"Deputy Rosales."

"Who shouldn't be talking about such facts to anyone," I said, "no matter how much she craves your attention."

He gave me a palms up. "Let's not get sidetracked on that crazy woman."

"Okay, back to poor Crystal. I don't think Rosales had the latest information when she talked to you. Either that or she didn't tell you everything."

"What do you mean?"

"Aunt Rowe heard the sheriff say Crystal was killed by a blow to the head before the bricks hit her."

Griffin nodded. "Makes more sense than someone setting up bricks and hoping Crystal would show up and stand in the exact spot for the bricks to kill her."

"They could have been rigged," I said, "for the purpose of covering up the actual cause of death."

"Maybe," Griffin said, "but that still doesn't sound like Ace."

"Or Pearl. I can't see her climbing the scaffolding any sooner than I'd picture Ace McKinney up there."

"Good point."

"Bottom line is, somebody set Crystal up."

"That's what it looks like," he said. "We're talking premeditated murder."

13

FIRST THING IN the morning is typically my best time for writing, before everyday events crowd my brain. Sometimes I wake to find that problems and worries had spent the night and stayed for breakfast. Today seemed like one of those days, but I allowed myself a few moments to reflect on the peaceful time I'd spent with Griffin by the pond the night before. The joy of sharing cupcakes and watching the sunset, not the rest. Then, determined to write, I put my phone on "Mute" and opened my laptop. Before long, I was deep into the best type of conflict—the fictional kind.

Hitchcock sat nearby, watching me like a shift supervisor in a sewing factory to make sure I was actually turning out pages, not staring mindlessly at the screen for hours on end. After a while he apparently felt safe to leave me to my own devices and went outside to sit on the porch railing and annoy birds.

By early afternoon I'd finished a chapter and felt satisfied about meeting my most challenging goal of the day. I checked my phone, glad to see no one had tried to call. No unwelcome visits from Rita Colletti either. I didn't care where the lawyer was or what she was doing, so long as she wasn't bothering me. Next up—get those black cat event flyers printed and begin distributing them. I went outside, where the afternoon heat hit me like a slap in the face, and found my smart kitty dozing in the shade under the pink-flowering crepe myrtles.

"C'mon, Hitchcock," I said. "Want to go for a ride?"

His ears perked up, and he stood and stretched. Once we got into the car, he gave the harness a leery glance.

"If you wear this, we can walk on the street together," I told him as I looped the harness over his head. "Won't that be nice?"

"Mrrrreeooowww," he said, and I had a feeling that meant, *Are you out of your freaking mind?* in cat speak. Minutes later we were headed into town.

The only place in Lavender I knew of with a high-speed copier was, interestingly enough, Bunny's Beauty Shop. Aunt Rowe knew Bunny well because the shop owner colored Rowe's hair every six weeks. I knew *of* Bunny and the fact that she'd decided to make a little income on the side by renting a high-speed copier and charging by the page. Guess she'd heard enough people asking, "Hey, you know where I could get some copies made?" to figure she could profit by taking advantage of the demand.

I hoped Bunny wasn't one of those stylists who'd take one look at me and beg to have her way with my hair. I couldn't remember the last time I'd had someone lop a couple of inches off the bottom. Maybe it was time, but I wasn't in the mood to deal with hair issues today. Hitchcock watched without comment as I pulled my curly mop back and fastened it with a lime green elastic band. I checked the rearview.

There. Better.

As we approached the shop, I admired the lighted neon pink "Bunny's Beauty Shop" sign on the front window with a second smaller sign scrolled in purple beneath it—"Cuts 'n

Copies." Inside, the pink-and-purple theme carried on to the wallpaper, an upholstered bench along the wall, and the capes used to protect clientele's clothing. The pleasant scent of shampoo was barely recognizable, overpowered by hair-coloring chemicals.

A white-haired lady stood at a small checkout counter while a girl penciled her next appointment into a black date book. The salon had two styling chairs—one occupied by a woman in a pink cape. A middle-aged stylist with platinum blond hair—Bunny, I assumed, from things Aunt Rowe had said about her—was cutting hair and nodding while her client talked nonstop. A man, cape-free at the moment, waited in the second chair, presumably for the young lady at the checkout.

The white-haired client looked down and spied Hitchcock. "Oh my," she said, "he's a handsome fellow."

"Thank you," I said. "He's Hitchcock, the spokes-cat for the Love-a-Black-Cat adoption event coming up next month." I held up the flyer for her to read the details. "I've come to make copies."

The girl behind the counter stood on tiptoes and leaned over to get a look at Hitchcock, then hollered, "Hey, Bunny, copy job."

The older stylist waved and nodded. "Be with you in five," she said. "Have a seat."

The white-haired customer studied my flyer. "Sure is somethin' to see, a cat walkin' along with you like he's a dog."

"He's not exactly happy about it," I said, "but I like to keep him safe."

"Good for you," she said to me while giving Hitchcock's ears a scratch. "I'll tell all my friends about your adoption event."

After she left, I settled on the bench seat to wait and wished I could block out the strident tone of the woman having her hair cut. Hitchcock sniffed at a nearby carousel that held a variety of magazines. Through a glass door connecting the salon to a smaller second room I saw the copier, similar to those I had used plenty of times when I worked at the law firm. Left to my own devices, I could make a couple hundred copies and be out of here in a few minutes. I didn't blame Bunny, though, if she didn't want to risk having inexperienced customers jam up her machine.

The fortyish female customer kept up the nonstop chatter, which nearly drowned out the music coming through a wireless speaker mounted on the wall.

"I don't care what my soon-to-be-ex thinks he's gettin' outta the house," she said. "What he's *gettin'* is zilch. He's the one up and left, so the cash from the house goes to me. It was just about sold, too, till my agent went and got herself killed. I have like the worst luck in the world."

Really? Is she hoping to win a most-insensitive-person-on-the-planet award?

The man in the next chair glanced at her and exchanged a look with Bunny. The younger stylist came over and fastened a purple cape around the man's neck. She invited him to step over to the shampoo bowl, and they moved quickly as though eager to put distance between themselves and the other client.

Bunny said, "Crystal's death is a tragedy. If only she hadn't gone into that building."

Her customer said, "That's what she gets for her greed. Rushing off in hopes of a bigger commission, and now I'm left high and dry."

"What do you mean?" Bunny said.

"She was supposed to have an offer for me by today. I don't even have the buyer's name or I could call and finish the deal on my own."

"I'm sure she had records," Bunny said. "Her office will be able to help you."

The customer barked out a laugh. "You mean that little twit who wants the commission for herself now?"

I didn't know Crystal's assistant well, but she'd seemed very nice and down to earth.

"Jordan's a nice young lady," Bunny said, mirroring my thoughts, "and you're giving her a bum rap. Her family's fallen on hard times. I'm sure you can relate." Bunny turned the woman's chair and held a strand from each side of the woman's head, then stooped to compare the lengths.

"Hard times? That's what my husband's gonna feel. I got the perfect lawyer to file my divorce petition. She'll chew him up and spit him out."

During my years at the law office, I'd heard enough of that kind of talk to last a lifetime. I stood to move into the other room as Bunny swiveled her client's chair again, bringing the woman in line with me and Hitchcock.

"*What* is that animal doing in here?" she shrieked. "I'm allergic to cat hair. Get it out."

"Now, Claudia," Bunny said calmly, "if you sit still and keep your mouth closed, you'll be fine."

The woman's outburst had startled me, but now I had to stifle a laugh.

"I will *not* be fine. I'll start wheezing and break out in horrid red blotches."

Bunny continued, "The cat's been here for a few minutes already, and you didn't even notice. I'll be back in a moment." She motioned for me to join her in the other room, which I did gladly. We stood at a glass-topped counter adjacent to the copier.

"Sorry about her," Bunny said, keeping her voice low. "She's a . . ." She paused, searching for words.

"I got the picture," I said. "No need to explain."

"And she wonders why her husband left."

I smiled. "I'm sure she does."

"Now, let me see what you have." She pulled out an order pad.

"Nothing complicated." I showed her my flyer. "I need a couple hundred color copies."

Bunny looked at the page, then at me and Hitchcock. For a moment I thought she was going to comment about my hair. Then, thankfully, she said, "You must be Sabrina. Rowe talks about you and the cat all the time."

"I hope she has good things to say."

"Of course." Bunny stooped to run a hand down Hitchcock's back, and he purred in response. She quoted me a price, and after I agreed, she placed my flyer on the glass and pressed the "Start" button. "Claudia can wait for me to make your copies."

"I'm not sure I want to get on that woman's bad side," I said, "but I may never run into her again, so what the heck."

"Claudia plans to move away after she sells her house," Bunny said, "but I have a feeling you'll see plenty of her before that's said and done."

I frowned. "Why?"

"You live at Around-the-World Cottages with Rowe, don't you?"

"What does that have to do with *her*?" I tipped my head toward the salon. "Is she planning to rent a cottage from Aunt Rowe?"

"Your aunt says the lawyer, Rita Colletti, is staying out there," she said.

I nodded. "She's only there this week. Her office is in Houston."

"That may be," Bunny said, "but she's the lawyer Claudia hired to handle her divorce here in Lawton County."

My mouth went dry at the unwelcome news. As the machine spit out my copies, Bunny wrote up my order and collected my payment. She got a box ready for the copies, then excused herself to go back to the nasty client.

Why would Rita agree to handle a divorce all the way out here in the Hill Country? I supposed she might plan to negotiate a settlement with the husband's lawyer, but that could be done from her office in Houston. With e-mail and e-filing, it didn't matter that much where everyone was located. That is, so long as the parties didn't have to battle out every little issue in court. I looked over into the salon and saw Claudia jabbering away. She didn't strike me as the amicable-divorce type. If she had enough money to pay the fee, Rita would happily take her divorce case all the way to trial. I'd have to brace myself for the possibility of Rita coming back to Lavender if Claudia's case went to court.

I felt a tug, and the end of Hitchcock's leash slipped off my hand. He had jumped up on the counter and was trying to squish himself into the box Bunny readied for my copies.

"You silly cat." I chased him away from the box. He ran to the end of the counter and leapt from there to a desk in the corner. Boxes of completed copy jobs sat on the desk, aligned like cakes in a bakery case. Hitchcock pushed his nose against each box as if they had different scents and he was determined to find the most delectable one.

I grabbed at the end of his leash and missed a few times, until he paused at one box. I picked up the end and held it tight. Hitchcock rubbed the side of his face against the box, then straightened and looked at me.

"Mrreow."

I moved to pick him up before he could do any damage. Each of the boxes on the desk had a page taped to the top that identified the box's contents. The box Hitchcock stood by had a letter on Devlin Realty letterhead with a colorful house logo taped to the top. A letter signed by Jordan Meier, Realtor, that assured clients their contracts would receive the same care and attention from Jordan herself as they would have received before the tragic loss of the company's founder.

I said I wanted nothing to do with investigating Crystal Devlin's murder, but the mystery writer in me was admittedly nosy and had a wild imaginative streak that wouldn't quit. After hearing Crystal berate Jordan in their office the other day, I didn't imagine the girl was mourning the death of her boss. But Jordan's level of sorrow wasn't the issue here. The big question was, who gets the business?

I should have wondered about this from the start. Had Crystal's death left Jordan with the authority to control future real estate sales and to profit from them? If so, how far would the girl go to get that control?

14

HITCHCOCK AND I spent the next couple of hours visiting shops and businesses and asking for permission to post flyers about the black cat adoption event. Many people who loved cats, black or otherwise, were delighted to oblige and made donations to the event then and there. Unfortunately, we also ran into some anti-cat folks who set my teeth on edge. One man stated flat out he wanted no association with the event for fear that bad luck would come down on him like the plagues of Egypt. A lady at the dry cleaner's caught sight of Hitchcock and screamed before slamming the door in our faces and turning the lock.

Hitchcock was too bothered by the harness to pay much mind to whether people gushed over him or not. He rubbed the leather straps against every door frame we passed like a captured man trying to saw through a rope that bound him.

"I'm sorry, buddy." I picked him up and cuddled him against my chest, but he was too squirmy to relax. I'd have to come up with something a lot more enticing to gain forgiveness for the afternoon I'd put him through. "One more quick stop, and I promise you'll be quite welcome there."

He looked up at me with an expression I took to mean, *Yeah, right*.

We were on Saltgrass Road, two blocks from Wagon Wheel Antiques. Twila Baxter, the proprietress, would be happy to see Hitchcock. She'd already promised me a sizeable donation for the event.

"Keep in mind, this lady believes I'm a witch and you're my powerful sidekick," I told the cat before we went in. "Nothing I say will change her mind." I put him on the ground and ran a hand down his back. "If she gets to know you better, she might quit claiming you're the legendary bad luck cat that belonged to some lady named Hildegard Vesta way back when."

Hitchcock's ears twitched. "Mrreow."

"Oh, and she might go on about us having the power to restore her late husband's soul. Just ignore her." Hitchcock stood at attention with his nose pressed to the crack of the front door, eager to get inside. He didn't flinch when the door screeched horribly as I pushed it open.

When we stepped into the building the cat lifted his head and sniffed the air. He proceeded cautiously as if he expected a ghost to pop out of the woodwork. Twila's Halloween decorations were still in place. She claimed she'd last encountered her husband's spirit on Halloween years ago and thought it important that nothing change in anticipation of his return.

I heard Twila before I spotted her. "Sabrina, my dear, what a lovely surprise." She walked out from behind a walnut chifforobe, the hem of her midnight black dress trailing on the floor behind her. White curls surrounded her face like a puffy cloud. "What brings you and your trusty companion to my store?" She stooped to greet Hitchcock and made kissy noises at the cat.

I pulled a flyer from my tote. "Here's the announcement we talked about for your front window."

"Of course, my dear, I'm delighted to help the cause." She took the flyer and placed it on the counter, then handed me an envelope from the cash register drawer. "My donation. Now, come sit. We have grave matters to discuss."

I thanked her for the donation, then said, "What grave matters?"

"The murder, of course." She lowered herself to an antique love seat and patted the cushion beside her.

I decided to humor her and sat. Hitchcock jumped up on the back of the love seat and walked along behind our heads.

"You shouldn't concern yourself with murder," I said. "That's the sheriff's job. I'm sure he has the investigation under control."

Twila dipped her head. "As well he should, dear, but I'm very concerned. You should be, too. It's only a matter of time before the noose tightens around the necks of you and your bookstore friend."

"What?" I jumped up and Hitchcock jumped, too. He came back down on the love seat, the hair on his back bristling.

I carefully detached the cat's claws from the upholstery. "Tyanne and I have nothing to do with what happened to Crystal Devlin. Where on earth did you get such an idea?"

"People are talking about the two of you," Twila said. "You drove by the Devlins' house yesterday as if you were casing the joint. You were seen at Devlin's rodeo. Word is you were at the crime scene, and a customer spotted you with the husband earlier today."

Am I being tailed?

I glanced around the store and didn't see anyone else. "What people?"

"Several of the customers," Twila said. "I didn't take down their names."

"There's no one here," I said. "You're asking me to believe you had a crowd of customers in here discussing me and Tyanne? Where is this crazy talk coming from, Twila?"

She tsk-tsked and patted my arm. "You should keep a clear head, dear, so we can figure out what to do about this problem. Tell me, is it you who has an interest in the husband, or your friend?"

"We *don't* have any interest in Lance Devlin, neither of us. Did someone say that we do?"

"Not in so many words," Twila said.

I scooped Hitchcock up, smoothed the hair on his back, and attempted to slow my breathing. The cat's pupils were huge as he stared at the old woman, and I had a feeling mine looked pretty much the same. Was she making all this up in her wacky, fantasy-laden brain?

"If anyone dares bring up such ridiculous accusations again," I said, "you can tell them my friend is happily married, we were at the rodeo to discuss an event, and I certainly would have nothing to do with a married man."

"Who's now a widower," she said.

"I. Don't. Care." My head felt like steam was shooting out of my ears. "You can tell that to whoever is spreading these nasty lies. We're leaving."

I stormed toward the door, eager to get away.

"Don't forget to use your powers when you need them," Twila called after me.

Jeez. Powers. Like I'm a witch or something.

I blew through the front door, hanging on to my cat as if our lives depended on it.

"I know I told you we were making one stop," I said to him, "but we have to go see Tyanne."

He let out a yowl.

"I'm sorry, this is an emergency."

I hightailed it back to the car, then drove the short distance to Knead to Read. Hitchcock had visited the store with me before, and I usually took pains to introduce him slowly to Zelda and Willis so we didn't have a lot of hissing going on. Today, cat camaraderie wasn't high on the priority list.

I stomped into the bookstore, holding Hitchcock in my arms, and startled a group of youngsters seated on the floor in a corner. Ethan, dressed as a pirate, was apparently acting out a scene from a children's book. I strode across the store in search of Tyanne without stopping to apologize for the intrusion.

I found my friend in her office slicing the packing tape on cartons of new books. When I stopped in the doorway, she looked me up and down with a concerned expression.

"What's wrong?" She placed her razor knife on a table before coming over to me. "You look wild-eyed, both of you."

"So will you in a minute," I said. "Let's shut this door so no one hears."

"Okay." She took Hitchcock from me, and he wrapped his front paws around her neck like she was a long-lost friend. "What's the matter, baby? Your mama going all helter-skelter on you?"

I closed the door and pulled a folding chair out from the table. "Sit. You won't believe this."

"Might be the highlight of my day," she said, taking a seat. "I've been counting books for hours."

Hitchcock jumped to the floor and headed toward the corner where he'd find not only food and water bowls but also the cat box. Poor guy needed a break.

I took a deep breath before going on. "Have you heard any rumors about the murder?"

"A few things," she said. "Mostly from gossips who can't be believed."

"Yeah, me, too." I paced the room as I repeated what Twila Baxter told me.

Tyanne started laughing. "That's insane."

"Yes, but not one bit funny."

"No one will believe such a thing, knock on wood." She tapped her knuckles on a bookshelf.

"You, too?" I wondered if Ty had picked up the habit from Pearl. Or maybe she'd always knocked on wood and it never bothered me before.

"Me, too, what?" Ty said.

I shook my head. "Never mind. Twila believed the rumor, and she's encouraging me to use my *powers*"—I paused to add air quotes—"to deal with the problem."

Tyanne tried to keep a straight face, but she couldn't contain her laughter.

"No one around here will believe that I killed a woman to get my hands on her husband. Have you made a serious enemy I haven't heard about who would start such a rumor?"

"Now you're just ticking me off," I said. "This is bad, Ty. You don't want your reputation ruined because the town gossips say you're an accessory to a murder."

"Or that I'm interested in Lance Devlin." She struggled to maintain a serious expression. "Besides, he isn't the one who was fooling around during the marriage."

I frowned. "Do you know for a fact that Crystal was?"

"Rumor has it," Tyanne said.

"I'm fed up with rumors, especially the ones that could cause you and me harm."

"I agree," she said, "but I thought the sheriff's department was looking at Pearl Hogan as a likely suspect. Are *they* talking about us, too?"

"Not that I know of. At least not yet, and we can't let this rumor get that far."

"Did Twila tell you exactly who's throwing our names around?"

I shook my head. "She didn't name names, and I was too wound up to stick around and try to squeeze details out of her."

"I'd like to know who we're up against." Tyanne stood and went back to her boxes of books. "Whoever's accusing us might have something to hide themselves."

I stopped pacing and looked at her. "You may be right."

"Looks like we need to do some investigating."

"Exactly what I didn't want to do," I said. "Just this morning I resolved to keep my nose out of the investigation."

"Maybe the person spreading the rumors is doing it to force you to get involved."

My brain whirred. Would Pearl stoop to such a level to get me to do what she wanted me to do in the first place?

Nah.

A light knock sounded on the door, followed by a voice. "Mom? Can I come in?"

Tyanne went to the door and opened it for her daughter.

Abby, the eldest of three, was eight years old, a cutie with long curly blond hair and two missing front teeth. She smiled when she saw me.

"Hi, Miss Sabrina," she said. "Did I see Hitchcock come in here with you?"

I smiled. "You did. I think he's raiding the food bowl."

"Is the meeting over?" Tyanne said.

"Uh-huh," Abby closed the door behind her. "Better not let Zelda or Willis find out Hitchcock is after their food. They won't be happy."

"Those two are getting pudgy and can afford to share," Tyanne said. "Excuse me a minute. Ethan may need help at the checkout."

She left the room, and Abby looked around. She seemed a bit nervous.

"You can go on and pet Hitchcock if you want to," I said. "He likes little girls a lot."

"That's good," she said. "I'd like to bring a friend of mine to meet him when she comes to visit."

I nodded. "Let me know whenever you want to come, and I'll make sure we're home."

She walked over to me, twisting a strand of hair around an index finger. She looked up, her baby blues meeting my gaze straight on. "I need a favor."

I smiled. "What is it?"

"My friend is coming to visit her grandma in a couple days, only her grandma is kind of in trouble."

"And . . ." I waited.

"My friend doesn't live here, so I don't get to see her much," Abby said.

"What's the favor?" I already had an inkling of where she was going with this request.

The girl paused and regarded me earnestly. "Julie's Grandma Pearl might have to go to jail, unless you can figure out what really happened to that lady who died. So we need you to help, because we're planning to have a lot of fun while Julie's here—like you and Mom had when *you* were kids."

She knew where to aim the emotional dart.

"Your mom and I *did* have fun," I said. "Every summer when I came to visit. Whose idea was it for you to ask for my help?"

"Mine?" she said.

I gave her the eye and didn't say anything.

"And Julie's."

I kept waiting.

Abby did some more hair twisting. "Grandma Pearl told Julie to tell me to ask you, okay? Will you help?"

"I'll think about it," I said, "but do me a favor. Don't say anything to Julie or her grandma yet. Investigations work better if everybody doesn't know what everybody else is doing. Does that make sense?"

"Tell me when it's okay to talk." Abby made a zipper motion across her lips.

I'll be the first one talking, and Pearl's not gonna see me coming.

15

I DROVE STRAIGHT TO Sweet Stop and ignored Hitchcock's glare when I locked him in the car again with the air conditioner running. *This should be quick.*

I went inside to find Pearl and couldn't help but smile at a little girl standing stock-still, mesmerized by a six-foot-tall lollipop tree. There was no one waiting to check out at the moment, so I hurried over to the counter.

"Is Pearl here?" I asked the girl behind the counter.

"Nope." She smacked her wad of pink bubble gum. "She took off for some rehearsal."

"You don't happen to know where I can catch up with her, do you?"

The girl shrugged. "She'll be back in the morning."

Drat.

I bought a pound of nonpareils with multicolored sprinkles so this wouldn't be a completely wasted trip and downed a handful before I got back to my car.

"She's not here," I told Hitchcock as I slid into the driver's seat. "By the time I catch up with the woman, some of this aggravation will have worn off." I ate more chocolate. "Maybe that's a good thing."

"Mrreow." Hitchcock nosed at the candy bag.

"Sorry, boy." I put the sack on my lap. "No candy for you, but we'll go home for dinner now."

I headed for the cottages, thinking about Pearl. She undoubtedly planted the seed with her granddaughter to have me investigate, but was she behind the rumors Twila heard about me and Tyanne? That was a dirty, underhanded move, and while Pearl was sneaky, she wasn't normally mean. More likely whoever killed Crystal was busy throwing suspicion every which way to keep it off him or herself.

I hadn't committed to investigating anything, but I couldn't keep my brain from trying to fit the puzzle pieces together. No one needed to know what I was doing—unless I uncovered some earth-shattering clue, I could keep any crime-solving steps I might take to myself.

When we reached the Around-the-World cottages, I was relieved to see the empty parking slot at the Paris cottage. Rita Colletti wasn't around to bother me tonight. Maybe she was off meeting with her new client, the annoying lady from the beauty shop.

At my place, I freed Hitchcock of his harness and gave him a little food to supplement what he'd eaten at the bookstore. Before coming to his dish, the cat flopped down on a throw rug and rolled to and fro on his back. Celebrating his freedom. I had to grin at his exuberance.

While he ate, I made myself a ham-and-Swiss sandwich and took it with me to the bench on the deck. Laughter and voices of guests drifted up to me from the river as I nibbled on my dinner. The people sounded so carefree, and I felt anything but. My imagination swirled with questions.

Was Crystal having an affair for real?

What was her ancient history with Ace McKinney about?

Was her assistant Jordan profiting now that Crystal was gone?

Did the cliché about the husband always being guilty apply here?

I didn't know enough about the Devlins to get a feel for whether any family member had a motive to do away with Crystal. I could visit the ranch under the guise of expressing condolences and nose around a little, but I probably wouldn't be welcome out there after the run-in with Lance at the sheriff's office.

Maybe I could find another source for information about the family. I drummed my fingernails on the bench between bites of the sandwich, and finally the name of a promising lead sprang to mind.

Mrs. Morales—the woman who worked for Crystal. Of course, there could be hundreds of people named Morales in the county. How would I find the right one?

Maybe Aunt Rowe knew Paloma Morales.

I opened the door and stuck my head inside. "Hey, Hitchcock, I'm going up to the house." He paused over his chicken-and-salmon dinner as if logging in what I'd said, then continued eating.

I walked up to Aunt Rowe's and went in through the side garage door. Her car was gone. I texted Glenda: Know where I can find Aunt Rowe?

Her answer came quickly.

At the rodeo. Went to meet the goats.

Good grief.

TEN minutes later, after a change of clothes to jeans and tennis shoes, I was on my way to the rodeo grounds. The story Griffin had told about an angry and drunk Ace McKinney stuck with me, and I hated the thought of Aunt Rowe being anywhere near him. I had to see for myself that she was okay. I still hoped she and her friends would nix the whole senior rodeo idea. After the to-do with Lance, I didn't expect Rowe and Pearl to be welcome participants.

When I'd first heard about the senior rodeo, I thought the event sounded too dangerous for someone Aunt Rowe's age. Now I worried that people associated with the event were possible murder suspects. I wished Aunt Rowe would stay far away from the lot of them. Lord only knew what might be going on out there this very minute.

The faster I drove, the more my mind conjured up the worst possible scenarios. When I reached the Hill Country Rodeo sign I took the corner too quickly and skidded on the gravel.

Get a grip, Sabrina. This isn't the climax of a novel.

I forced myself to drive a reasonable speed until I reached the rodeo buildings and pulled into the closest parking spot. As I reminded myself to breathe, I saw Aunt Rowe's car parked amidst a dozen other vehicles.

Rehearsal night. Light crowd.

I went in through the front gate, relieved to find it unlocked. The area around the concession stands was deserted except for a couple of cats nosing around a trash barrel. I heard shouting in the distance and walked toward the voices. I circled the main arena and approached a smaller gated corral. The sound of women giggling reached me, and I took tentative steps toward the noise.

Aunt Rowe and Pearl stood inside the corral with their two friends. My aggravation with Pearl had eased a bit. Even if it hadn't, this wasn't the time to confront her. Each of the women held one end of a rope, the other end looped around a goat's neck. The goats were smaller than I would have expected, some white, some brown and white. Never in a hundred years would I have expected to see Aunt Rowe in this setting, and I almost laughed aloud.

"Okay, ladies," said a friendly-sounding man. "Take a

minute and get to know your goat. Don't worry. They're gentle."

Yeah, so why are you going to torture them in the rodeo?

The guy sounded familiar, but I couldn't place the voice and moved a few feet to my left to get a better look. Hayden Birch balanced on top of the fence and grinned as the women patted and talked to the animals. I wondered if this was part of his job description or if he'd volunteered to help the seniors with goat tying.

Whatever the case, there wasn't anything nefarious going on. My shoulders relaxed, and I let out the breath I'd been subconsciously holding. Ace McKinney was probably at home in his recliner guzzling a beer. My imagination had gone off on a tangent—a good thing in fiction writing, but too over-the-top for real life. I could leave before anyone spotted me, but why not check the place out while I had the chance.

I walked away from the goat meeting and rounded the building Hayden identified the other day as the horse barn. From this vantage point I could see the Devlin ranch house, maybe better described as a mansion, across the fields in the distance. I was so intent on surveying the property that I almost walked up on Mimi Trevino, her back against the side of the barn while she held her head in her hands.

The girl looked up at the same moment I noticed her, and swiped at her damp eyes. "What are you doing here?" she said.

I felt my face redden. Maybe she'd think the heat had gotten to me. "I came to check on my aunt. She's over—" I turned slightly to point back the way I'd come. "With the goats."

"Oh," she said.

"Sorry for the intrusion. I'm mindlessly wandering."

She nodded, but I got the feeling she didn't like it that I was here. Then again, why was *she* here?

"Are you okay?" I said.

She smiled, but it looked forced. "Better than Cody. He's messed up."

Now it was my turn to nod. "He'll be okay with time."

"Yeah, sure he will." Trying to convince herself.

"Is he here?"

She pointed toward the fields beyond the barn. "He's out there somewhere, riding."

"He didn't invite you?" Maybe that's why she'd been crying.

"I'm not that into animals," she said. "I don't mind waiting."

"The rodeo isn't your gig?"

"Hardly," she said. "Cody's either, but now he's suddenly into bonding with his mother's favorite horse. Like that's gonna change anything."

"He's hurting," I said. "Time will help."

"Yeah, you already said that."

"Sorry. Has the family made arrangements yet for a service?"

She shrugged. "I don't know."

I had a lot of questions I'd like to ask this girl about the Devlin family, but this was a bad time. She was being polite, but I could tell she wanted to be left alone.

"Well, take care." I walked back a couple of steps and paused.

Maybe one question.

"Hey, Mimi, do you know Mrs. Morales?"

"Sure."

"Could you tell me where she lives? I'd like to pay my respects."

"Over there." She cocked her head toward the ranch. "In the guest house out back."

I thanked her and walked away. When I was close enough to the corral to hear the excited voices of Aunt Rowe's gang, I made a detour. Seeing Mimi and thinking about Cody's loss had put me in a funk, and I didn't want to join in the fun and laughter. I didn't necessarily want Aunt Rowe to see me either, lest she think I was checking up on her.

Which I am, but that doesn't mean she has to know.

I made a turn, expecting to be on the parking lot side of

the arena. Instead, I stood facing four small wooden cabins lined up in a row. Could be the rodeo equivalent of trailers for the stars on a movie set. My internal GPS was apparently out of whack.

Before I could backtrack I heard a man's deep drawl. Ace McKinney.

Ugh.

I turned in a circle but didn't spot the man. I pulled out my phone and put it to my ear so I could pretend to be concentrating on an important call if McKinney saw me.

His voice, a low drone coming from somewhere nearby, didn't seem to move and grew more menacing in tone. Who was he talking to? I wondered if Lance Devlin was here, acting like this was any ordinary day in spite of his wife's murder. That would tell me something about the man.

I stepped tentatively toward the voice, listening for a second person.

"You tell 'im this is his last chance," McKinney said. "He doesn't come up with the payment by this time tomorrow, we start breaking fingers."

Dear Lord, was he serious? Was he drunk? Was he on the phone? I envisioned the man sending a pair of linebacker-sized thugs after somebody.

I needed to get away from the voice—and the rodeo—as fast as possible. Maybe Ace McKinney didn't literally mean fingers would get broken. Or maybe he meant exactly that. Whatever, that wasn't my business. I only wanted to get myself and Aunt Rowe away from here pronto.

Before I could move, though, McKinney walked out from between the cabins and looked straight at me. A chill crawled up my spine.

"You again," he said.

"H-hi." I attempted a smile.

"What're you doin' on that phone?"

I'd forgotten about the darn phone clenched in my fingers, and let my hand drop to my shoulder.

"Nothing, I mean, I was trying to find a spot with a good signal."

"Why are you here?"

Thinking fast, I said, "Actually, I'm a mystery writer, and I'm doing some research on rodeos."

He looked skeptical, and his scowl deepened.

"See, I'm writing this book." I lowered my arm and slipped my phone into my jeans pocket. "My agent thought it would be a nice touch to add some Texas flavor, and what better way to do that than a rodeo? Except I'm from the city, and don't know much about them, so I really need to spend some time—"

"Enough," he said, then called, "Remy, get out here."

A small man in cowboy garb approached from the same direction McKinney had come. Not one of my imagined thugs—this little guy wouldn't scare a fly.

"You wanna know the real deal about the rodeo, set something up with him." McKinney pointed a thumb over his shoulder at the other man. "I don't have time for this bull."

16

"**C**OULD BE A false threat," Glenda said the next morning after I shared Ace McKinney's statement about breaking fingers. In her pink gingham sundress, perfect for the predicted ninety-something-degree day, Glenda looked more cheery than she sounded. "What do you really know about this fella?"

"Not enough." I ran a damp cloth along Aunt Rowe's kitchen counter, sweeping up excess crumbs that had scattered during last night's insomnia-driven bake-a-thon. "Maybe he only acts like a jerk when I'm around, and he's a pillar of the community the rest of the time."

"I doubt that," Glenda said. "He didn't even know you were there when he made the threat."

"True. The point is, I don't like the idea of Aunt Rowe spending time near the man."

"I agree with you there." Glenda cracked eggs into a mixing bowl as butter melted in the skillet on the stove top beside her. "You want an omelet?"

"No thanks, I'll stick with fruit." Glenda rolled her eyes as I lifted the yellow plaid tea towel I'd used to cover a basket of fresh-baked goods and snagged a blueberry muffin.

"I'm going to have a serious talk with Aunt Rowe about the danger of hanging out over there at the rodeo."

Glenda watched as I took a seat on a barstool and peeled the paper from the muffin. "When she jumps into something like this goat thing, you know she's not gonna back out, right?"

I nodded, my mouth full of muffin.

"The harder you try to talk her out of it, the deeper she'll dig her heels in." Glenda took out a fork and started beating the eggs.

"I've known that since I was five years old," I said. "Don't worry, I know how to handle this."

"Whatever you say." Glenda poured the eggs into the sizzling butter.

"I'm curious about McKinney's little cowboy friend Remy, too. The fifteen minutes he spent showing me around the rodeo last night didn't tell me much of anything. I need to figure out whether the men are harmless, seriously scary, or something in between."

"Just how do you plan to learn the truth about these characters?"

I was contemplating my answer when Aunt Rowe walked into the kitchen in full makeup and dressed in a nice skirt and top, which usually meant she was going into town. I was glad to see she wasn't in her rodeo gear. Hitchcock trailed her into the room.

"Good morning," I said with forced cheer. "Hitchcock, were you Aunt Rowe's alarm clock this morning?" I hadn't even noticed when he left the kitchen in search of her.

"He came to my bedroom to tell me something," Aunt Rowe said. "Meowing all over the place until I headed this way. Don't know what was so all-fired important."

Hitchcock jumped up on the barstool next to me and perused the goodies I'd baked. Aunt Rowe looked down the length of the counter, taking in the muffin basket, a tray of assorted cookies, and a cake.

"So this is what he was trying to tell me," she said. "There must be a bake sale in town today that I didn't know about."

I smiled. "I made some of your favorites, Aunt Rowe. Applesauce cake, for one." I took the lid off the cake saver and waved it for her to get a whiff of apples and cinnamon.

"Tryin' to butter me up, I see," she said. "Let me get a cup of coffee goin' so I can be alert."

"Mrreow," Hitchcock said.

Aunt Rowe headed for the coffeepot. "Don't worry, boy, I'm onto her tricks."

Glenda and I exchanged a look.

Aunt Rowe filled the mug that Glenda had waiting by the coffeepot. "Sorry to interrupt your talk about characters," she said. "Discussing your book plot?"

I wadded up the paper from my muffin. "Uh, right. It's hard to keep those fictional people straight sometimes."

She turned toward me and took a tentative sip of the hot coffee. "Get a lot more done if you'd write when you can't sleep instead of baking. What do you hear from your agent?"

"Nothing yet." I couldn't remember the last time I'd checked my e-mail for word from Kree Vanderpool. "She's sending the book to one publisher at a time. It's a long process."

When it sells, you need to have the next one ready," Aunt Rowe said. "Tyanne tells me you're not very far along."

"When have you been talking with Tyanne?"

"Last night," she said. "After I heard the two of you are murder suspects."

Glenda turned away from the eggs, holding her spatula in midair. "Why on earth would Tyanne or Sabrina be suspected?"

"Don't have the answer to that one," Aunt Rowe said. "Asinine rumor going around."

"Who did you hear the rumor from?" I said. "One of your rodeo cronies?"

She frowned at the reference. "Helen's husband heard it at McKetta's. You can bet everyone and their brother who ate there last night heard the same thing."

I shook my head. I considered Daisy McKetta a friend, but I knew she was a world-class gossip.

Glenda slid an omelet onto a plate, added a piece of toast, and handed the plate to Aunt Rowe.

Aunt Rowe began to eat the eggs standing up and glanced at the clock.

"You have somewhere you need to be?" I snagged a peanut butter cookie and bit into it.

"I'm goin' to talk with Jeb," she said. "Find out who is and who is definitely *not* considered suspects by the sheriff's department. Hopefully get you, Tyanne, and Pearl off the hook."

She hadn't considered, as I had, that her friend Pearl just might be the person who started the rumor about me and Tyanne in order to convince me to investigate the case. I hadn't gotten the chance to confront Pearl. Maybe that was for the best since I didn't have any evidence.

"I appreciate that, Aunt Rowe, but I doubt the sheriff is ready to draw any conclusions. And he's probably not going to share his thoughts with you."

"Don't you worry. Rita can advise me on how to handle the situation."

"Rita?" Cookie crumbs caught in my throat, and I began coughing.

Glenda filled a glass with water and handed it to me. I gulped the water, trying to dislodge the crumbs stuck in my throat. The last thing I wanted was for Aunt Rowe to befriend the attorney. That woman needed to head back to Houston, the sooner the better.

"I don't think it's a good idea to involve *her* in anything," I said when my coughing subsided.

"Don't be silly." Aunt Rowe finished her eggs and placed

her plate in the sink. "Rita and I are going to town together. I'm not gonna lock her in the trunk while I talk to the sheriff."

"Why's she going with you?" I looked at Glenda, who was busying herself making a fresh pitcher of tea. I wouldn't be surprised if she was biting her tongue to keep from adding her own criticisms about the lawyer.

Aunt Rowe eyed the applesauce cake with a wistful expression, then said, "We're going to meet with Jordan at the real estate office."

I turned my palms up. "For what?"

"If you must know, to discuss Pearl's purchase of the property next to her store."

"I thought someone else was buying the place."

"Hasn't bought it yet," Aunt Rowe said. "Pearl put her money down in good faith and she signed a contract. She sure as heck doesn't want a cigar shop next to her candy store. Bunch of men standing around out front puffing on those nasty things could drive Pearl's customers away." She wrinkled her nose. "Rita's going with me to discuss the legal mumbo jumbo, see if we can salvage Pearl's deal."

"If Pearl presses the issue of buying that property, she reinforces her motive for wanting Crystal gone," I said. "This is a bad idea."

"So Pearl should just give up on her dream?" Aunt Rowe said. "I think not."

"You could send Rita to handle the problem," I said. "Steer clear so it won't look like you're in cahoots with Pearl."

"You don't think I can take care of myself?" Aunt Rowe said.

I cleared my throat. "Of course you can. I'm just pointing out that others may see things differently."

"That's nothing new."

My stomach knotted. "I worry about you, Aunt Rowe."

"No need," she said. "My friend needs help. The time to strike is now, before a sale goes through on the property. Somebody has to take action."

This line of conversation was wearing on my last nerve.

"That action should include steering clear of danger," I said, "not hanging out with shady characters, of which Rita is one, I might add."

Glenda tsk-tsked and muttered, "Dangerous ground."

"Go ahead and bad-mouth the rodeo," Aunt Rowe said. "I know you want to, so don't bother trying to hide it."

"Okay. I don't like the rodeo or anything it stands for. I'm particularly concerned about Ace McKinney. There's something shady about the man, and I'd feel a lot better if you'd stay far away from him."

"You done now?" Aunt Rowe said.

"Let's just say my writer's intuition is telling me he's a villain. What if he had something to do with Crystal's murder?"

"What if the man in the moon killed her?" Aunt Rowe said. "You're talking nonsense."

"I hope you're right. I'd rather you didn't take chances."

Hitchcock was looking from me to Aunt Rowe, following our conversation like a Ping-Pong match.

"Another thing," I said. "Rita is doing work for Lance Devlin, who I'm pretty sure is a member of the suspect list himself."

"And how do you know what your archenemy is doing?" she said.

"Rita asked me to work for her, an offer I wisely turned down."

"I don't care who else she's working for," Aunt Rowe said. "Today, I need her help. If I find out she's an accomplice in a murder plot, I'll turn her over to Jeb and be done with her."

"I wish you'd keep Rita out of it altogether," I said.

"You mind your business," Aunt Rowe said, "I'll mind mine." She stalked to the counter, where she kept her purse and car keys, picked them up, and left.

Hitchcock let out a low howling sound. I patted him on the head. "It'll be okay, boy. Settle down."

Glenda turned to look at me and raised her eyebrows. "That went well. I swear, if your characters get in half the trouble you do, your books will be bestsellers."

I N the aftermath of my conversation with Aunt Rowe, my stomach cramped something awful. Maybe it was the three muffins and half a dozen cookies I'd eaten. Clearly, Aunt Rowe wasn't going to take my advice. The only way to rid myself of all this worry was to figure out what really happened and make sure Aunt Rowe stayed far away from the villain.

A good first step would be to learn more about Crystal herself. Paloma Morales might shed some light on Crystal's life, enough to give me information I could use to unravel the facts surrounding her death.

It was midmorning when I pulled into the drive leading to the Devlin ranch house. I kept my eyes peeled for any sign of family members or, worse, Lance's pal Ace McKinney. I'd been told that Mrs. Morales lived in a smaller building behind the main house, which didn't mean she'd be there now. Crystal was no longer here to hand out assignments, so her personal assistant may have up and left.

I felt sad for the woman, but I had no way of knowing whether she and Crystal had a good working relationship or if it was more like the tense one Jordan had with Crystal at the real estate office. There was no sign of life at the main house. I followed the curving drive to the property in back.

The smaller structure was a one-story tan brick house with a Mexican tile roof shaded by huge oak trees. A row of flower planters hung from the roof over a covered veranda with a sitting area of white wicker furniture on a sisal rug. I pulled up in front, and noticed through the screen door that the inner door stood open.

Many people bring casseroles when making condolence calls, but I wasn't a main dish kind of person. I'd brought an assortment of my fresh-baked goods arranged in a basket over a floral napkin. I walked up to the entrance and knocked on the screen door.

Seconds later, a woman in a bright yellow Mexican Puebla dress embroidered with multicolored flowers approached the door. Her shoulder-length gray hair was held back on each side with clips. She spoke to me through the screen. "May I help you?"

I smiled at her. "Are you Paloma Morales?"

"Yes," she said.

"I came to pay my respects. I'm so sorry for your loss." I introduced myself, and Mrs. Morales stared at me hesitantly.

"I know you worked closely with Crystal. I can imagine how you feel because I once had a co-worker who died. It was so hard for me to believe she was gone." I lifted my basket. "A small token I brought for you."

The older woman pushed the screen door open and invited me in.

I stepped into the close air, moved slightly by three lazily spinning ceiling fans. I handed my basket to her.

"Gracias," she said.

"I hope there's something you like. When I start baking I can't seem to stop myself."

"I used to bake all the time," she said with a smile. "Crystal, though, she stayed on a strict diet. 'Stop the baking, Paloma,' she would say, 'or I will blow up.'" The woman chuckled, looked pensive for a moment, then turned to me. "Sit, please. May I bring you something to drink? I have a fresh pot of coffee."

"I'd love some, with cream, if you have it."

"Certainly."

I walked around the simply furnished living room while she was gone and came across a collection of framed photographs on a built-in shelf. There were several photos of Crystal Devlin, some of them with Paloma, some with Cody. None of Lance Devlin.

Mrs. Morales came back with a tray and placed it on the coffee table. She invited me to sit with her on the sofa. "Thank you for coming to see me," she said. "It is very quiet without Crystal. I feel like my ears, they quit working. The silence, it is not normal."

I leaned forward and added cream to my coffee. "You must have spent a lot of time together."

"Ah, yes, for more than fifteen years." She nodded slowly.

"Crystal was very vocal, I take it, and talked a lot?"

"Talking, shouting, criticizing," she said. "That was Miss Crystal's way."

"What did she criticize?" I said.

She eyed me warily. "Why do you ask that?"

"Just making conversation," I said. "I popped into the real estate office the other day. Crystal didn't seem very fond of that young woman who works for her. They had a bit of a situation and Crystal sounded, well, critical of Jordan." I sipped my coffee, an enjoyable mellow roast.

Mrs. Morales crossed her arms over her chest. "Crystal could be, what is the right word?" She thought a moment then said, "Impatient. Not always nice, but I should not say such things when I have not asked how you knew her."

"No worries," I said. "I met Crystal only once, the day before the, um, accident. She was very generous with a donation to a needy cause."

Mrs. Morales smiled. "Yes, Miss Crystal was always generous. Sharing the wealth, as she said." She picked up her coffee and relaxed against the sofa back.

"It's refreshing when the wealthy have that kind of sharing attitude." I looked out the window across the acres. "It's beautiful here. I guess Crystal and Lance own quite a bit of land."

"Yes," Mrs. Morales said. "Much came to Crystal from her family. She was a fortunate woman."

"Until recently," I said.

"You are right."

"Mrs. Morales, do you have any idea who might have wanted to hurt Crystal?"

The woman glanced at the wall where a clock hung. "How long can you stay?"

Her statement took me aback. Was she hoping for a lengthy visit, or did she mean what I thought she meant?

"You have a list?" I said.

"I could have, if I worked at it. Went through all of her sales records. These sales, they did not always go without a hitch."

"I imagine not," I said. "Has the sheriff come by to talk to you?"

"I spoke with a deputy," she said. "For only a few minutes. She did not put much stock in my words."

Detective Rosales at her finest.

"And did you tell the deputy about the people you suspect?"

"I told her some things," she said.

I drank more coffee. "Did Crystal and her husband get along well?"

She sipped from her cup. Her gaze darted about the room as she considered my question. "They kept up appearances."

"I hope you don't mind my asking about your employer."

"My employer is gone," she said. "I do not work for Mr. Devlin."

"That sounds like you don't like Mr. Devlin."

"He is not my favorite person," she said.

"Are you planning to leave?"

"No, I will stay, but only so long as Miss Crystal's son is home," she said. "I expect he will leave soon."

"For college?"

"Maybe," she said. "That was Miss Crystal's greatest wish."

I imagined that losing his mother might change Cody's immediate plans.

"Is Mr. Devlin on your list of suspicious people?" I said.

She paused, considering the question, then she shook her head. "I do not believe he would kill his wife."

"What about his pal Ace McKinney?"

She frowned. "He was old friend of Miss Crystal, not Mr. Devlin's."

"But he works at the rodeo, for Lance Devlin."

"Now, yes," she said. "He and Miss Crystal met in college. Maybe he was better then. Now, he is, how do you say?" She paused, thinking. After a moment, she said, "Self-destructive."

"In what way?"

"First it was the bull riding," she said. "He picked the most fierce till he got thrown off and hurt very bad. Then he turned to alcohol."

"Some might say that drinking goes with the rodeo cowboy way of life."

"No," she said. "This is much more."

"How did Crystal feel about his behavior?"

"She was very angry with him," Mrs. Morales said. "She would not tell me why. I do not think it was about the drinking."

"Were they romantically involved?"

She shook her head. "Oh, no, not like that."

"Did he come here to the house often?"

"No." A chiming noise sounded, and Mrs. Morales stood. She walked over to an antique chest and picked up her phone. Checked the screen. "I'm sorry, but I am needed at the main house," she said.

"No problem." I placed my cup on a side table and stood.

This woman probably had a lot more information to give, if only I knew the right questions to ask.

She showed me to the door. "Thank you for the basket. I am glad for visitors to talk with. I cannot live with all this silence."

*   *   *

WHEN I left Mrs. Morales, things still appeared quiet around the big house. I wondered whether Lance and Cody Devlin were home and requesting her presence or if she'd been summoned by the household help to lend a hand with some chore. I assumed the Devlins had live-in help to take care of the big house—there was surely enough room inside to house a full staff.

Looking at situations through a mystery writer's eyes, I couldn't stifle my tendency to investigate. Talking with Mrs. Morales had stirred up all sorts of questions. I wanted to talk with Jordan to see what she could tell me about troublesome relationships Crystal might have had with clients. Maybe I'd even continue my pretend research at the rodeo so I could learn what made Ace McKinney tick.

If I could find the time to work on all of this, I *would* solve Crystal Devlin's murder. If the resolution came quickly, I could get back to concentrating on my writing.

I climbed back in my car and was bombarded with blips, beeps, and vibrations coming from my phone, which I'd left in the cup holder while I was inside with Mrs. Morales.

Jeez Louise, what's the big deal? Has someone died?

I immediately regretted that thought and grabbed the phone. A row of text messages had come in—all from my agent.

My heart flew to my throat.

Before I could read the texts, the phone rang.

Kree Vanderpool's name showed on the screen.

With a shaky finger, I punched "Answer" and squeaked out a hello.

"Sabrina," Kree said. "Are you sitting down? Now don't get too excited, but I had to share this news right away. We have a nibble on your book from a very large house."

My heart pinged. "Oh my goodness," I managed. "Seriously?"

"Seriously," she said. "There's one little wrinkle."

I slumped in the car seat. "What is it?"

"The editor has pretty definite ideas."

"What kind of ideas?"

"He's asked for a few revisions," she said. "All you have to do is rework the subplot. If you have some time, I can go over the changes he wants you to make."

17

I DON'T KNOW HOW long I sat in my car with my mind racing after Kree and I ended our call. Long enough for Mrs. Morales to wonder what the heck I was doing and why I didn't leave. When I saw her peer out the front window at me, I started the car and drove away.

Kree and I planned a phone conference at one o'clock to go over the editor's suggested changes. My heart rate should be back to normal by then. I'd have time to look over the manuscript and refresh my memory about the story line before our call. I could sit at my desk and take notes.

Going back to edit that book would be a challenge. I had a hard enough time focusing on the story I was currently writing. Now I had to set aside the plot involving my FBI protagonist and immerse myself in the life of Scarlett Olson, my woman in jeopardy. The way I felt lately, with the recent murder and my conflict with Aunt Rowe, I should be able to relate to the character.

I had to leave the real-life murder investigating to the sheriff's department. Set aside my concerns about Aunt Rowe and the fact that she was running around town with Rita Colletti. Quit worrying about whose fingers Ace McKinney might want broken, so long as they weren't mine.

Or Aunt Rowe's.

Or Pearl's.

Or—

Stop. Go home. Get to work.

I considered going to the bookstore to share my news with Tyanne. She was my best friend, and she'd be as excited as I was. Her nagging me to spend more time on writing would start—it hadn't actually ended, just moved on to a different manuscript. She meant well. I might never have finished the book if it weren't for her. But what if little Abby was there at the store and asked me about investigating the murder again?

Stay on track.

I could call Tyanne after Kree revealed the editor's comments. At that point, I might be freaked out and overwhelmed. She would give me the logical advice I needed.

There *was* one friend I could share the news with right away.

I'm not sure how I made it to the Monte Carlo cottage, since my mind wasn't on my driving. I parked quickly and hurried inside, where I found Hitchcock sprawled on a living room chair. He gave me a quizzical look when I rushed over and fell to my knees in front of him.

"We did it." I placed a hand on either side of the cat's face. "An editor likes my book, the one I couldn't have written without you watching over me."

"Mrreow." He butted his head against my hands.

"That's right," I said. "This *is* big. You need to stay close to help me rev up the suspense in the rewrite."

Hitchcock's motor started running. I stroked his sleek black fur for a few minutes, then jumped up and turned my laptop on. As I waited for the computer, I thought about the prospect of holding my own published book in my hands. I'd have to get up to speed on the best marketing tactics. Set up book signings. Maybe hire a publicist, if I could afford one.

You're putting the cart before the horse, Sabrina.

I opened my book outline and reviewed the story line. Then I went to the manuscript and read my favorite scenes— the suspenseful passages I felt sure had captured the editor's attention. In one of them, Scarlett Olson was running from the one man who could help her, her biggest ally. Of course, she didn't realize that at the time.

The relationship between the two characters made me think about the friendship between Crystal and Ace. Mrs. Morales's statement that Ace was Crystal's friend, not Lance's, had surprised me. Ace looked at least ten years older than Crystal. Exposure to the hot Texas sun had prematurely aged his skin. I had a hard time imagining the two of them as pals. Recently, according to Mrs. Morales, Crystal had been angry with Ace. Why? I wondered if Ace knew Crystal was angry. Did he care? Was her anger a threat to him somehow?

I shook myself and regained my focus on the computer screen.

One o'clock came quickly, and Kree filled me in on what the editor had to say about my manuscript. He wanted the subplot to have a tighter connection to the rest of the story. To have more facets. He suggested I raise the stakes. Kree relayed his comments in addition to her thoughts on how I could accomplish these things. My hand cramped from taking fast and furious notes. Kree's voice kept rising in tone and speed until I worried she'd get so excited she'd trigger a stroke. Finally, she said she hoped to get the revised manuscript back from me soon.

As predicted, I felt overwhelmed by the end of the call. I fell back against the chair. The enormity of this project definitely called for a pep talk from Tyanne. I dialed her cell and got voice mail. I put in a call to the bookstore, and Ethan told me Tyanne and her kids were out to lunch with friends.

I sat and stared at the computer screen for a few more minutes. Reread my notes.

Jeez. Where to begin?

Hitchcock jumped up on the table. He sat next to the laptop and stared at me. Those green eyes of his sure were piercing.

"I can't just jump into this without a plan." I rolled my head, massaged my neck, then stood. "Let's go for a walk and loosen up."

I headed for the door. When I looked back, Hitchcock was still sitting by the computer.

"C'mon or I'm leaving without you."

"Mrreow." He leapt to the floor, trotted to me, and we left the cottage together.

A sweltering mid-July afternoon isn't the smartest time to take a walk. A swim, yes. I could hear people nearby, splashing in the river, but I needed to keep my focus on the project ahead. Best-case scenario, this walk along the shady riverbank would jog my brain and help me decide where to begin the revisions.

Rather than stick with me, Hitchcock opted to jump over fallen limbs and dive into dead leaves alongside the path. I loved to watch him run and play—a nice change from his usual, serious demeanor. Sweat trickled between my shoulder blades as I plodded along, doing my best to rearrange plot points in my head.

The next time I glanced along the path for Hitchcock he wasn't there. I stopped and turned around.

No cat.

I scanned my surroundings and caught sight of him heading back toward the cottages at a fast clip.

Was someone waving a can of tuna fish or what? I had to follow the cat and make sure he wasn't being lured by someone with less-than-friendly feelings toward black cats.

I cut through the trees to follow him and realized we were coming up closer than I'd like to the Paris cottage, where Rita Colletti was staying.

As I came through the tree line behind the cottage, I noticed a white pickup truck with a Devlin ranch logo on the driver's side door parked alongside Rita's BMW. Hitchcock darted across the lawn near the cottage and took a flying leap up to the back deck.

I opened my mouth to call the cat, then closed it again. I wanted to get Hitchcock home without the lawyer spotting us. I couldn't help wondering, though, who was visiting with Rita. Lance Devlin, maybe, or someone else who worked at the ranch or the rodeo?

Good grief, I hope it's not Ace McKinney.

I headed toward the cottage, praying Rita and her visitor weren't in a place where they could see this expanse of lawn. Hitchcock jumped up on a windowsill. I pictured the inside of the Paris cottage and realized he was outside the bedroom window. Was she in *there* with someone?

"Psst, Hitchcock." I made kitty-calling noises in hopes he'd come my way, but he didn't acknowledge my presence. He'd suddenly gone deaf. Selectively.

Darn cat.

I walked closer and kept up the noises in hopes he'd pay attention and obey. When I got within a few yards of the cottage, I heard a repetitive thumping sound. I paused for a few seconds before realizing someone was knocking on the cottage's door.

I walked to the corner and peered around the edge to look at the front porch.

Cody Devlin stood by the door, looking gangly and out of place. He tried again—*thump, thump, thump*—but no one answered. Rita and Aunt Rowe might still be in town.

I took a few steps toward Cody. "Hi there. Help you with something?"

He jerked and spun toward me, then tried to cover his embarrassment at being taken by surprise. "No, ah, I need to talk to the lawyer."

I smiled. "Ms. Colletti went out with a friend earlier."

"Her car's here," he said.

I shrugged. "They probably took the friend's car. I guess they're not back yet. I can leave a message for her if you like."

He shook his head. "No. This is private."

"Most things that bring someone to a lawyer are confidential. I worked for Ms. Colletti for many years." Insinuating I could be trusted to give a private message to the attorney for him.

"Who are you?" he said.

I told him my name and pointed out the Monte Carlo cottage where I lived.

"I saw you somewhere," he said. "The other day."

I nodded. "Yes, I saw you in town. Twice, in fact."

He pointed at me. "You were with that woman. The one who killed my mom."

I shook my head vigorously. "No, that's wrong."

"Yeah, you were with her. The candy-store lady."

"She didn't do anything to your mother," I said. "The phrase 'innocent until proven guilty' was invented for circumstances like this."

The kid was beginning to look like he wanted to put a fist through the door. "That's bull," he said. "She sent my mom a text to meet her at that building, then she waited there and—"

"Hold it, hold it." I put up a hand. "What text?"

He stopped talking, and his brows drew together. After a moment he said, "Never mind."

"Are you saying Pearl Hogan sent your mother a text the morning of the incident?"

He nodded slightly.

"Huh. I didn't hear anything about a text message."

"Why would you?" he said.

My mind raced. Pearl said she happened to look out the window that morning and saw Crystal entering the building, then rushed out on the spur of the moment to confront her. Was she lying all along? Had she sent a text message to Crystal?

"The sheriff knows about the text message, right?" I said.

More foot shuffling. The kid wouldn't look at me. I waited him out, and finally Cody looked up at me. He didn't speak.

"Where's your mom's phone now?" I said.

"At the house."

"What's on the phone that you don't want anyone to see?" I said, voicing a suspicion.

"We fought." His voice cracked, and he cleared his throat. "A lot. In texts."

"Kids and moms fight. That's a fact of life."

"Not like us."

He didn't know me and my mother.

"You don't want anybody to know about the fighting," I said.

I watched him. After a few seconds, the kid shook his head. Funny, he was quick to accuse Pearl, yet he held back evidence that might help to convict her.

"You didn't threaten to kill your mom or anything like that in the texts, did you?"

"No."

"Okay, good."

I didn't think the boy was guilty of anything except wanting to keep his less-than-ideal relationship with his dead mother a secret.

He ought to turn over the phone. If he did, what would happen to Pearl? Had the woman committed premeditated murder? Lured the victim to the scene of her death by sending a text message?

I didn't think so.

"What does your dad have to say about all this?"

"I didn't tell him," Cody said.

I cocked my head and inspected the kid's face. He was hurting. According to Ethan, this boy's parents didn't give him the attention he needed. Now one of them was gone forever.

"Why do you need to see the lawyer?" I asked.

"Personal business. I'll come back." He turned to leave, then jumped. "What was that?"

I caught a streak of black out of the corner of my eye. "Oh, that's my cat. Hitchcock."

The cat had gone through the porch railing into the ligustrum bushes. Cody leaned over the railing to look in the shrubbery. "Is he pure black?"

I nodded. "Why? Are you superstitious about black cats?"

"No." He shook his head. "They're cool."

"Yes, they are. Hitchcock is my good luck charm."

He snorted. "I could use some of that."

My feelings about the kid softened a bit. "Things will be tough for a while, but you'll come out okay on the other side."

He rolled his eyes and dipped his head.

I leaned over to look for the cat and noticed a white car heading down the drive, coming from the main entrance.

A sheriff's department car.

Cody lifted his head, saw the car, and seemed to stiffen.

"I won't say anything about your mom's phone or the text message if you don't," I said.

The sheriff needed to have this information, but I didn't necessarily want to be the person to turn over the evidence. I wanted to talk with Pearl and see what she had to say for herself.

"Deal," he said.

As the car grew closer, I closed my eyes and made a wish that Sheriff Crawford would be inside and not one of his unlikeable deputies. When the crawl of tires over gravel grew closer, I opened my eyes.

Luck wasn't with me. Deputy Rosales climbed out of the car and came straight toward me. She had a piece of paper in her hand and held it out.

"I have a warrant here," she said.

My heart rate sped up. "A warrant for what?"

"I need to collect a hair sample to match hair found at the

murder scene." Her eyes glittered as she clearly enjoyed delivering this news.

They found my hair at the scene? Rosales was looking straight at me, but maybe she was talking about collecting hair from Cody. Except she wouldn't have known to come here looking for the kid.

"Hair from me or from him?" I pointed at Cody.

"Neither," Rosales said. "I need the hair of the cat."

18

I RELUCTANTLY TOOK THE piece of paper from Deputy Rosales and looked at it. "Seriously? You're testing my cat's DNA?"

"That's right." Rosales twisted to scan the area, and her heavily starched uniform rustled. "Where is it?"

"He," I said. "A cat is not an *it*. Rather, a cat is a *he* or a *she*."

"Okay then, where is *he*?" The lines around her mouth deepened, giving her even more of a don't-mess-with-me expression than usual.

I'd always heard that waiting for DNA test results took weeks. Surely they wouldn't hold off on a murder investigation while they waited for results from testing cat hair. I suspected Rosales had dreamt up this ridiculous idea about testing cat hair on her own.

"If you came here to harass me, fine," I said, "but don't threaten my cat."

Rosales shook her head. "This isn't about you. I'm here to see the cat. You want to complain, talk to the sheriff."

Cody said, "Does this have something to do with my mother's death?"

"Yes," Rosales said.

"Oh, please," I said. "You can't charge a cat with murder." *She couldn't, could she? I'd rather retrieve Crystal Devlin's phone and throw Pearl under the bus than let that happen.*

"Fetch the cat and quit wasting my time," Rosales said.

The woman was delusional if she thought I'd hold Hitchcock so she could pluck hair from his body. I did want her to leave, though, and she probably wouldn't until she got what she'd come for.

"He roams," I said. "I'll have to track him down."

I couldn't see Hitchcock from where I stood, but the bushes he'd darted into were moving. There was no wind. Cody, to his credit, didn't point in the cat's direction.

"What'll the cat hair prove?" he said.

"You'll have to ask Sheriff Crawford." Rosales frowned as she looked at him. "What are *you* doing here anyway?"

Cody fidgeted under the deputy's attention. "Um, nuthin'. I'm leaving."

"Hold on." Rosales put a hand on the boy's arm. "Odd place to come for no reason. What's going on?"

"He came to see the lawyer." I didn't see the harm in answering this question truthfully. "She's not here at the moment."

Rosales kept her eyes on Cody. "What's your business with the lawyer? She prepare your mom's will?"

The question struck me as overly nosy, but I found myself curious about the answer.

"No, ma'am," Cody said. "I mean, I don't know."

"You have legal questions, ask your father," she said. "You're a minor, so—"

"I'm eighteen next month," Cody blurted. "Old enough to talk to a lawyer by myself."

Rosales's eyes narrowed.

"I have to go," Cody muttered.

The deputy nodded. "Go on then. We'll talk later."

The boy hurried to his truck. I watched him drive away and wished I were going with him instead of standing next to Rosales.

"What's he want with the lawyer?" she said.

"He didn't tell me."

"Has he been here before?"

"Not that I know of," I said.

"How about Crystal Devlin? She come here?"

"I never saw her here."

"Did Colletti draw up the mother's will?"

I shrugged. "I wouldn't know."

"You worked for her."

The fact that Rosales knew my employment history creeped me out.

"Even if I knew the name of every client Rita Colletti ever had, I couldn't share confidential information."

"Fine," Rosales said. "Get the cat. Now."

I sighed. "I don't understand why you're singling out my cat in this investigation. Any type of animal might have been drawn in by the garbage strewn about and left hair at that scene."

"We have hair in a car, hair on a person, and hair at the scene," Rosales said. "We connect the perp and the cat, along with the right witness statements, and we make our case."

"But—"

"If you don't cooperate," Rosales interrupted, "I'll find the cat myself and take him with me."

She knew how to get my attention.

THIRTY minutes after Rosales collected the hair, I parked in front of Sweet Stop. Hitchcock, who appeared unaffected by the ordeal, sat on the passenger seat. I'd outfitted him with the harness and leash, determined to keep a tighter handle on the cat so I wouldn't have to worry about things like him being snatched by someone out to cause bad luck for an enemy, or a certain deputy out to connect him to a murder.

I was hot under the collar, thinking about Pearl taking off with Hitchcock and then lying to me about it. Not to mention the alleged premeditated text message. The candy-store lady didn't know what was about to hit her.

I turned off the car and picked up Hitchcock's leash. "C'mon, boy, let's go get some answers."

"Mrreow." Hitchcock jumped out of the car behind me, and we headed into the candy store. The store wasn't an animal-friendly environment, but in my current frame of mind I didn't much care. Besides, I wasn't staying long.

Inside, I saw only one couple. This was the late-afternoon lull, when tourists were more likely to search out their dinner than buy candy. A perfect time to interrogate Pearl. I spotted her behind the counter, filling little rectangular cartons with chunks of fudge.

"Hi there, Sabrina," she said when she noticed me, and her gaze traveled to the floor beside me. "And Hitchcock."

She scanned the store, saw the customers, then glanced at her employee behind the cash register. "I don't think it's such a good idea for you to be in here with"—she dropped her voice to a whisper—"the black cat."

"That's right," I said harshly. "You believe my cat is bad luck."

"No, no." She closed the top of a fudge box and wiped her hands on her red-checked apron.

"Let's go outside," I said. "You don't want anyone over-hearing this conversation."

Pearl came around the counter and followed me to the back door. "What's wrong, Sabrina? You look upset."

We stepped outside, and Pearl closed the door behind us.

"Upset is too mild a description," I said. "My poor cat is being subjected to a DNA test."

"Why on earth?" Pearl said.

"Because *you* took Hitchcock from Aunt Rowe's house."

"I already told you I didn't do anything with your cat."

"The sheriff's department is collecting evidence, Pearl, and they have cat hair that ties things together."

She waved a hand. "Not to your cat it doesn't."

I blew out a breath. "Explain."

"I had *a* black cat, not *your* black cat."

"I told you not to take Hitchcock, so you found a substitute black cat?"

"Exactly," Pearl said.

"Why would you do that?"

"I wanted Crystal to think the bad luck cat crossed her path."

I remembered the upheaval at Crystal's office the day before she died. "Did you take your random black cat to Crystal's office?"

"Yup," Pearl said. "I don't feel so proud about that trick anymore, now that the woman's dead."

I shook my head. Was it some sort of law that postmenopausal women lost their marbles? And what did it say about me that I could follow Pearl's logic in the whole mess?

"What about the text message?" I said.

Pearl's lips pursed. "What text? I don't text."

"I know about the text, Pearl. Go ahead and fess up. I might be one of your best friends right now."

"You don't sound like a friend." Pearl's lower lip quivered.

"I'm trying to help you, for the sake of your granddaughter and her friend Abby, if no one else. You sent Crystal a text message the morning she died."

"No, I didn't," Pearl said.

"Let me see your phone." I looked at Pearl's large apron pockets. No telltale bulge.

Hitchcock walked over to Pearl and stood with his paws propped on one of her knees. He sniffed at her apron.

Pearl patted the cat's head. "I don't have a phone on me, honest, Hitchcock, Sabrina. I have the darnedest time keeping up with that gizmo."

"Is it in the store?"

"I'm not sure. I keep losing the slippery thing."

Was she being truthful or trying to keep me from inspecting her phone?

"When's the last time you saw it?"

"I can't remember. I don't need my phone to keep the town stocked up on Tootsie Rolls, Sky Bars, Mallo Cups—"

"Good grief, Pearl, think. This is important."

"We can look inside, but I'm telling you I didn't send any text message."

"I hope not, 'cause plenty of people know you and Crystal were at odds."

"I wouldn't kill a person," she said. "What good would hurting Crystal do me anyway?"

Pearl had a point, and that brought me back to the question of who stood to gain with Crystal out of the way.

"Did you spread the rumor about me and Tyanne?"

"What rumor?"

Pearl looked sincere, and this time I believed her. If she wasn't behind any of these things, who was?

"Let's go find your phone. And don't you say one word about Hitchcock coming into the store with us."

Pearl made a zipper across her lips with a forefinger, and we went inside. I followed her behind the counter, and she reached onto the shelf under the register.

"I try to keep the phone here." She stooped slightly to get a better reach onto the deep shelf. "Found it. Somebody pushed it to the back."

She handed the phone to me. "I don't remember how to send a text. I'd rather just call a person if I have something to say."

I nodded to acknowledge her statement as I checked her phone's screen.

The couple shopping, now with a basket full of candy to purchase, approached the counter. I stayed where I was, keeping Hitchcock out of the customers' sight. Pearl greeted them since her employee was across the store stocking shelves.

Hitchcock wormed his way around my legs, wrapping me with his leash. I found the text message icon on Pearl's phone and punched a button.

A screen popped up with only one text showing. The message Cody had described.

I'm ready to make an offer for asking price on the restaurant property. Meet me there. Eight a.m. sharp Tuesday or lose the sale.

My heart sank. How could Pearl have expected to keep this message a secret? A few yards from me, she chatted gaily with her customers while ringing up their candy purchases. She claimed she didn't send text messages. Maybe she was telling the truth.

I placed her phone on the counter, wishing I'd never touched it and wondering who else's fingerprints might be on the device. Because if Pearl didn't send this text message to Crystal Devlin, that meant someone else had. Someone who was setting Pearl up and doing a darn good job.

19

WANTED TO DROP Pearl's phone into one of those little white fudge boxes and pretend the text message didn't exist. I believed her—she had not sent the message. Someone else had. Pearl wanted to buy the property next door. Killing the real estate agent wouldn't help her accomplish her goal. To the best of my knowledge, Pearl had nothing to gain by hurting Crystal.

So who did?

A person who knew this particular message would cause Crystal to rush over to the property. A villain who wanted to frame Aunt Rowe's friend. But who had motive and opportunity? An employee of the candy store? A customer? Or someone who saw Pearl outside of work? Oh, jeez, she'd been spending time lately at the rodeo grounds with Aunt Rowe—a place where many people were well acquainted with Crystal Devlin.

I walked over to the counter and slipped on disposable

gloves used to handle the candy. I picked up the phone and slid it into a white candy sack.

Pearl finished with her customers and came my way. "What are you doing with my phone?"

"Preserving evidence."

She frowned. "What evidence?"

"There's a text message from your phone to Crystal's."

"There can't be."

"I'm afraid there is."

I explained my theory that someone could have easily grabbed Pearl's phone when she wasn't looking and sent the message to Crystal's number, which Pearl had stored in her phone.

"Who would do such a thing?" Pearl said.

"I don't know, but we need to turn this over to Sheriff Crawford right away."

"Who we?" Pearl spread her arms. "I can't leave now. I'm working."

"What's more important?" I said. "Helping to solve a murder or working? The store's about to close anyway."

"That doesn't mean I'm finished for the day. Far from it." She looked frightened, and I didn't blame her.

"You have no choice, Pearl."

"Maybe tomorrow," she said. "I have to practice with the lasso tonight. I don't have much time to get my skills up to speed before the big rodeo."

I propped my hands on my hips. "Please don't put the importance of that darn rodeo above tracking down a killer."

Pearl's face contorted as she thought up her next excuse. "Okay, never mind the rodeo, but I have a lot to do before Julie gets here day after tomorrow. Why don't *you* take the phone to the sheriff?"

"Pearl, Pearl, Pearl. Unless you want to be behind bars when your granddaughter arrives, you're coming with me."

* * *

S OLVING a crime in a book is easy. I can revise what I've written until all the clues, facts, and character actions fit perfectly together and lead my protagonist to the solution. If only things were so easy in real life. I had no idea who had killed Crystal or why they had chosen to frame Pearl, if indeed that's what happened. As I waited for her to close the candy store, I realized the dead woman might have a dozen enemies I'd never heard of.

I needed to be home writing, but I couldn't seem to disengage myself from the drama unfolding around me. Besides my natural inclination to nose into things, I couldn't forget that Tyanne's daughter was counting on me. Abby might call any second to ask if I'd solved the crime and saved her highly anticipated summer vacation with Pearl's granddaughter from being ruined.

The authorities had involved my cat, for goodness' sake, and I wanted the case solved before anyone brought his name up again in connection with this murder investigation.

I called ahead and arranged for us to meet Sheriff Crawford at his office at half past six. Ideally, I would have dropped Hitchcock at home before taking Pearl to the meeting, but I didn't trust Pearl to show up on her own. I had to keep the woman in line for her own good, so I offered to drive her to the sheriff's department and back home after the meeting. When we walked in, the dispatcher left her desk and joined us.

Laurelle knelt on the floor next to Hitchcock, whom she adored, and brought her nose to his. "You are such a big, handsome fella," she said, rubbing the sides of his face. "What a good boy you are, comin' to see me."

She didn't mention the testing of his hair, and I wondered if the whole DNA thing was only a charade on Rosales's part to aggravate me. After listening to a minute of Laurelle's cat-baby-talk, I cleared my throat.

"The sheriff is expecting us," I said.

Laurelle looked up. "Right. He told me. He's finishing a

meeting." She sat back on her heels. After a final pat on the cat's head, she stood on creaking knees. "Make yourselves comfortable. He should be out in a minute."

Laurelle went back to her desk, and we walked over to a row of hard-backed chairs lined up against the wall. I sat down and Hitchcock promptly jumped on my lap.

"Who can be comfortable *here*?" Pearl muttered, eyeing the chairs before she sat. "I could've lived happily my whole life without ever seein' the inside of this place."

"Let's just hope for a quick in-and-out meeting," I said. "Settle down." Those last words applied to Pearl and Hitchcock. The cat stood with his front paws on my shoulder, and I felt his body tense as he prepared to jump. I held on to him for a moment and looked back at the windowsill behind me then decided *why not?* and let him go. Hitchcock leapt up and paced the wide sill with his leash trailing. I knew Laurelle wouldn't complain, and thank goodness neither of the deputies were in at the moment.

Pearl crossed her legs and checked her watch. "Can't stay long."

"Don't start." She'd complained the whole way over, and I'd heard enough.

After a few minutes, a door opened and I heard voices in the hallway. Sheriff Crawford's deep tone and a second slightly familiar man's voice. The clomping of footsteps sounded on the hard floor. A door closed. After a moment, the sheriff poked his head around the corner. He was alone.

"Pearl, come on back," he said.

Pearl shot me a you-started-this-mess glance, and I stood to join her. I picked up Hitchcock, then turned and saw the sheriff holding up his hand. "Sabrina, I'll see you after Pearl and I are through."

The two of them disappeared.

I'll see you? About what? Does he think I want to see him, or does he want to see me?

I'd come to make sure Pearl told the sheriff everything she

knew. I was counting on the fact that he'd track down Crystal's phone on his own and match up the message at both ends. This would lead to the discovery of the texts between Cody and his mother that the boy didn't want anyone to see. I was sorry about that, but at least I wasn't directly telling the sheriff what Cody had shared with me in confidence.

Of course, I'd love to ask the sheriff some of the questions running through my head. Like how many suspects did he have on his list? Had he thoroughly investigated the husband? Did he seriously think testing a cat's DNA would lead to information to solve the freaking case? I was pretty sure Sheriff Crawford wouldn't answer any of those things even if I asked.

Hitchcock, up on the windowsill again, rubbed against the back of my head as if he was trying to transfer his thoughts into my brain.

A sudden paranoia hit me. What if Sheriff Crawford wanted to ask me questions about Hitchcock? Or worse, take the cat? I'd feel a lot better if I got Hitchcock out of here. Maybe that's what Hitchcock was trying to tell me.

Let's get the heck out of Dodge.

I stood abruptly and hand signaled to Laurelle that we'd be outside. I was dialing Tyanne before the door closed behind us.

After a half ring, she answered with a jolly tone. "Well, it's about darn time you called me, star writer Sabrina Tate. Where have you been? Busy editing, I suppose. Well, I can't blame you for getting a head start before I put in my two cents. Kree e-mailed me the fab news. Are you on cloud nine or what?"

My brain took a second to switch gears.

"Uh, yeah, of course. Listen, I need a big favor. Are you still at the store?"

"Yes." She hesitated. "Why? Where are you?"

"Sheriff's department," I said. "Again. There's been a development."

"How are you involved?"

"Pearl's turning over an important piece of evidence."

"And you are—?"

"I drove her here. I'm waiting with Hitchcock, but that's the problem. The sheriff sent Detective Rosales earlier to collect some of his hair and they're doing a DNA test."

"Hitchcock's hair? Seriously?"

"Yes, and it's crazy. Now we're here—Hitchcock was in town with me—and the sheriff wants to talk to me. All of a sudden I'm scared to death he's going to do something to Hitchcock, and I'm hoping you can cat-sit for a little while."

Tyanne's sigh came over the line. "You come up with some doozy ways to avoid writing," she said, "but you've reached new heights. I'll be right there."

I picked Hitchcock up and walked around to the back of the building. I crossed a wide lawn to a stand of trees where we could wait in the shade without being spotted from an office window.

I scratched Hitchcock's head. "This is probably silly, but I'll feel better if you go with Ty for a bit."

About fifty yards from where we stood, the back door of the sheriff's department opened. I moved behind the trunk of a tree and peered at the door. A man in a ball cap and sunglasses stuck his head out and looked around before emerging from the building. He turned up his shirt collar and walked with furtive steps toward the nearest side street.

Was he a delivery person of some kind? Or had he been the person meeting with Sheriff Crawford when we arrived? In either case, why would he use the back door? Why would he turn up his collar on such a hot day? The guy was acting like an escaped felon, or was that my imagination running wild like it was prone to do?

As I continued to watch, the man pulled something from his pocket. A phone. He touched the phone and put it to his ear, presumably talking to someone, though I couldn't see his face from my vantage point. He kept moving down the sidewalk and had walked quite a distance from me when a red pickup pulled to the curb ahead of him. About that time, I saw Tyanne's SUV heading my way from the other direction. She passed the man and the pickup. When she pulled into the parking lot, I carried Hitchcock over to the driver's side door. Ty had already powered the window down. Abby sat in the passenger seat.

"Sorry I don't have a cat carrier with me," I said. "I sure appreciate you coming over."

Abby held out her arms. "I can hold the kitty."

Tyanne didn't say a word. She was focused on her rearview mirror. I turned to watch as the red pickup's passenger side door was flung open, presumably by the driver. The man left the sidewalk and ran around the back of the truck to jump in. He pulled the door shut behind him.

I realized who he was at the same moment Tyanne said, "What the heck is Hayden Birch doing over there, and who's that woman who just picked him up?"

"Mrreow," Hitchcock said as he squirmed in my arms.

I turned to look at the truck again. As though determined to find out the answers to Ty's questions himself, the cat sprang away from me and raced toward the truck as it started to pull away from the curb.

"No, Hitchcock," I shouted. "Stop."

I couldn't believe my eyes when the cat made a long graceful arc through the air, the leash flying behind him like a skinny Superman cape. I prayed that the end of the leash wouldn't get caught on the trailer hitch, and let out a whoosh of breath when the cat and leash disappeared into the pickup bed.

"Dear Lord," Tyanne said, her gaze still glued to the rearview. "Did you see that?"

I had, and I was already in her backseat.

"Hurry, Ty," I said. "Follow that truck."

20

TYANNE TURNED IN her seat. "Follow that truck? Are you kidding me?"

"Please." I kept my eyes on the pickup as the truck moved down the road. "They have Hitchcock."

"Your cat hitches rides with people all the time. You picked the perfect name for him. I don't know—"

"Mama, go," cried Abby. "They're getting away."

Tyanne sighed and shifted into drive. "I'm not starting a high-speed chase."

"They're not exactly racing from the scene," I said, though I wouldn't be surprised if the truck went tearing down the road after the way Hayden had acted.

After about a mile, the pickup took a left on Oleander Lane and we followed.

Tyanne said, "I thought you told me the sheriff wanted to talk to you."

"Oh, yeah." I grimaced. "I'll call Laurelle and explain why I had to leave."

I made the call to the dispatcher and told her what had happened.

"That Hitchcock is very resourceful," she said. "Maybe he's sending you a message."

Sounded like something Twila might say.

"Right," I said, "I'll let you know if I figure out what the cat's trying to tell me. Meanwhile, could you make sure Pearl gets a ride home?"

"Will do," Laurelle said, and we disconnected.

"Why did Hitchcock jump in that truck?" Abby said after I ended my call.

"Maybe he thought it would be fun. He didn't understand we'd worry about him."

"I *am* worried." Abby turned to her mother. In profile, I saw her little brows knitted together.

"Cats are very talented. He'll be fine." Ty's eyes met mine in the mirror and she nodded, trying to reassure me, too.

I hoped she was right. My heart raced as I worried about Hitchcock. What if this truck was headed to Dallas? What if they got on a freeway and he tried to jump out when they were speeding? What if he burned his paws on the metal truck bed?

Stop it, Sabrina. You're getting hysterical.

I took a deep breath. It was late in the day, and the sun had started to set. Hitchcock's paws would be fine. If they weren't, he'd have jumped out by now. Still, I hoped there was something in that truck he could hang on to.

We were headed in the general direction of the rodeo, and I was convinced that's where Hayden and the woman were going. The truck took a sudden turn, however, and Tyanne did, too. She kept her distance as the truck drove up a narrow street and approached a one-story house with flaking white paint.

The vehicle ahead had barely rolled to a stop in front of the house when Hayden jumped out and slammed the door behind him. A plume of dust kicked back as the red truck motored on and Hayden walked toward the house.

"Now what?" Tyanne said.

"Keep following the lady, Mom," Abby said.

"Right," I said. "Hitchcock is still in there. We'd have seen him if he'd jumped out."

"I could get closer and start honking the horn for her to stop," Ty said.

"That would probably make her drive faster, and who knows what Hitchcock would do then. Let's stay with her."

"I think your cat's a lot more resilient than you give him credit for," Ty said.

She was probably right. For all I knew, Hitchcock took pickup rides like this twice a week and was no worse for the wear. Didn't mean I had to approve of his daredevil nature.

We negotiated several turns before I concluded that the woman driving the pickup was, in fact, headed to the rodeo. We turned into the lane at the Hill Country Rodeo sign and followed in her cloud of dust. I was feeling optimistic about getting my hands on Hitchcock until the dust cleared and I saw Ace McKinney standing in the parking lot. As the red truck took a left and headed away from us, Ace motioned for us to stop. I was disappointed when Tyanne obeyed.

She powered her window down when Ace approached the car.

"Barrel racing tryouts tonight, ma'am," he said. "We're closed to the public."

Ty said, "But—"

"Next public show is end of the month," McKinney said.

My last interaction with the man had been unpleasant. As my brain raced for a way to get us in without mentioning a cat, Abby cleared her throat.

"Mo-o-om." Abby drew the word out to three syllables. "Come on. I'm gonna be late for tryouts."

Ace bent from the waist to peer in the window at the girl. I averted my gaze and hoped he wouldn't recognize me.

"Ain't you a mite young for barrel racing?" he said.

"I'm short for my age," Abby said assertively.

Either she convinced him, or he got distracted, because

McKinney waved Tyanne through. Her window powered up and the car moved forward. Only then did I turn my head to see McKinney's attention had already moved to cars coming in behind us.

"That was quick thinking, Abby," I said.

"I'm not sure I like your talent for conning people," Tyanne said.

Abby ignored her mother. "I bet that man doesn't like cats. He looks mean."

Girl has good instincts.

I unhooked my seat belt. "Stop here. I'll go after the truck on foot."

"Are you sure?" Tyanne said.

"Me, too," Abby was so fast that she was out of the car before me.

I called over my shoulder. "I'll keep her with me, Ty. Promise."

Tyanne was forced to move along when an SUV came up behind her. The horn sounded. I grabbed Abby's hand, and we ran down a row of parked vehicles, behind Ace McKinney's back, until we came to the red truck.

Abby grabbed the top edge of the truck bed and jumped to peek inside. I was tall enough to see without jumping. Hitchcock wasn't there.

"Where'd he go?" Abby whined. "Did he hop out?"

"I would've seen him. He's here somewhere, and we'll find him." Sounding more optimistic than I felt.

I stood on the truck's running board and scanned the area, then stooped down to peer under the vehicles.

"There she is," Abby cried.

I jumped up to find Abby had climbed into the truck bed where she had a better vantage point, and she was pointing toward the horse corral.

"There who is?" I said.

"The lady who was driving this truck."

"Is Hitchcock with her?"

Abby looked in every direction, then frowned. "No."

"Get down, and we'll go find him."

Abby was out of the truck in two seconds. We rushed to the entrance and slipped through with three teenagers outfitted in jeans and boots—obvious barrel racers. Abby and I looked completely out of place in shorts and sandals. We made it through the gate, though, and I pulled the girl off the path the others were taking.

"Think like a cat," I said. "Would he go with the crowd of people or off by himself?"

"Depends on why he came," she said.

"Why who came?"

The man's voice startled me, and I spun around to see the wiry little man named Remy approaching us. He was covered in a layer of dust, from his Stetson down to his worn boots and including the shotgun he held in his left hand.

My gaze flew to the weapon, and I put an arm around Abby and pulled her close. "What's that for?"

"Never know when my Remington will come in handy," he said.

Good grief. Was the guy named after the danged weapon?

"Wait for me," Tyanne called, and I could see her rushing toward us from the corner of my eye.

She stopped short when she saw Remy, then walked quickly to her daughter's side.

"Sir, would you mind keeping your weapon out of sight?" Ty said. "I don't appreciate my daughter seeing such things."

"Then you shouldn't be here," Remy said. "I hope you broads aren't after Mr. D, and I gotta say it won't help you brought the cute kid along for the ride. He ain't interested."

"Is Mr. D a cat?" Abby said.

Remy snorted.

"He's talking about Lance Devlin," I said, "the owner of this property." I looked at Remy. "Am I right?"

"Give the lady a star," he said, "but you're not gettin' in to see him."

"We're not interested in seeing the man," I said. "We're here looking for my cat."

"The cat came here with a lady in a red truck," Abby said.

I was surprised this man with the shotgun didn't seem to faze the girl, 'cause he gave me the heebie-jeebies.

Remy's dusty brown eyebrows drew together. "This rodeo ain't a cat-friendly spot."

I'd seen cats here before, but the way the guy sounded made my gut churn. "Why not?"

"Ace doesn't like varmints hanging around."

"Fine," Tyanne said. "We'll find the cat and take him with us. Just please put that weapon away, and let us go on."

"I'm not holdin' nobody hostage," Remy said. "Go ahead and look for the animal, makes me no difference."

I didn't believe that for a second. This guy wasn't giving us the run of the place without keeping a close eye on what we were doing.

"We'll split up," Tyanne said. "Abby and I will stay together. We're familiar with the area nearest the barrel racing."

"Fine. I'll go the opposite direction. Whoever finds Hitchcock, call the other."

We went our separate ways, but I could feel Remy's eyes boring into my back as I walked away. I forced thoughts about the weird little man to the back of my mind. I was soon immersed in the search, calling Hitchcock's name every two feet.

My voice was beginning to have a desperate edge by the time I reached the cabins where I'd run into Ace and Remy on my last visit. I rounded the corner of the first cabin and stopped when I heard a grating voice I knew far too well.

Rita Colletti. What the heck are you doing here?

I walked casually by the window of that cabin and peeked inside to see the lawyer sitting at a table with Lance Devlin. Documents sat on the table between them.

I forged on and kept up with the kitty-calling noises, but I couldn't help wondering why Lance Devlin needed legal counsel. Was the sheriff investigating him in connection with his wife's death? Rita wasn't a criminal attorney, but that wouldn't stop her from getting involved if he paid her a fee. After all, she'd gone with Aunt Rowe to the real estate office earlier in the day even though she wasn't a real estate lawyer either.

Did Hitchcock lead me to this place to see these two together?

If so, then why couldn't I find him?

My hair would turn gray before its time if the cat kept scaring me like this. As I griped to myself about the cat chase, my phone pinged with a text message.

The text was from Ty.

Doc Jensen found Hitchcock. We're with her. In the barn.

Relief flooded through me, and I responded with shaky fingers.

Be right there.

Hayden Birch had shown me the barn the other day when he took me on a tour, and I practically ran the whole way there.

I found Hitchcock sitting on top of a bale of straw next to Tyanne and Abby. The three of them watched as Magnolia Jensen tended to a horse.

Hitchcock looked up at me, calm as can be. "Mrreow."

"You little dickens." I rushed over to the cat and gave him a kiss on the head.

"This is Doc Jensen's horse, Sweetie-Pie," Abby said. "Isn't she pretty? Mama, can we get a horse?"

Tyanne said, "That's a question for your dad."

Passing the buck, and I didn't blame her. Watching Maggie

brush her horse with long smooth strokes, I wondered how far Abby would get with her request.

After a minute, the vet looked up at me. "You know, Sabrina, when I gave you that harness I didn't mean for you to leave it on the cat twenty-four seven. You should always detach the leash before the cat is left to his own devices."

"I know, but he took me completely by surprise when he got away."

"I understand," she said. "But this is the most dangerous place he could have come. You have to watch out for that little creep with the shotgun. He's been known to do away with things he considers a nuisance."

I didn't want to think about that. I fell to my knees next to the straw bale and gathered Hitchcock into my arms.

21

B Y THE TIME I got Hitchcock home I felt like I'd run a
marathon and barely lived to tell the tale. Due to our
unplanned rodeo escapade, Abby was running late for
a piano lesson so Tyanne took me straight home without going back into town for my car. I told her not to worry. I didn't
have any plans tonight, and I was sure Thomas wouldn't mind
driving me to town in the morning.

The open laptop on the table reminded me I should have
stayed home and worked on my book all day. I didn't know
if I had it in me to be creative tonight, but I'd try. First, I
wanted to share my news about the call from my agent with
Aunt Rowe. We'd parted ways that morning on bad terms,
and I was eager to clear the air between us.

Hitchcock finished his dinner and was curled up fast asleep
against the pillows on my bed when I left the Monte Carlo
cottage. I walked up to Aunt Rowe's house and found her in
the guest room. The bed, usually centered on a wall, was
pushed to one side, squished up against the dresser and a

chair. A weight rack, complete with a row of various-sized barbells, sat against the opposite wall. Aunt Rowe lay on a black bench, wearing fuchsia leggings with an oversized T-shirt and sneakers. Her arms were out to her sides. She held a small barbell in each hand and muttered to herself. Counting, maybe. Or cussing.

I walked into the room. "Aunt Rowe, what on earth are you doing?"

She turned her head to scowl at me and kept up the exercise.

"Polishing my nails. What's it look like?"

Her mood obviously hadn't improved. I eyed the weight set and tried a different approach.

"When did you get the new equipment?"

"It's not new," she huffed. "Picked it up at a garage sale."

"Huh. You never mentioned that you wanted to take up weight lifting." I crossed the room and sat on the bed.

Aunt Rowe placed the weights on the floor. "I need to advertise every move I make now? You have a problem with this?"

"Me? No, I think it's a fine idea."

"Okay then." She picked the weights back up and stood to place them on the rack.

"So long as your doctor approves," I said.

She turned to look at me. "Hooey. I'm not asking permission. Doctors always harp about how everybody needs exercise."

"But, Aunt Rowe—"

"Stop right there," she said. "Maybe you don't think I can handle it. You'll change your tune after I get on a program with my personal trainer."

Was she serious?

"We're starting next week, and wait'll you see him. He's easy on the eyes."

I wondered if something in particular had brought on her new plan. Maybe something as simple as a magazine article touting the benefits of building muscle through weight lifting? This didn't seem like a good time to ask a bunch of questions.

"Can't wait," I said.

Aunt Rowe pointed an index finger at me. "And I don't need you, or Glenda, or anybody else with an opinion I didn't ask for to give me a hard time about activities I choose."

I guessed she was referring to the rodeo.

"You're taking good care of yourself, and I admire that, Aunt Rowe. Truly I do."

"Damn straight," Aunt Rowe said.

I wondered what had gotten her so riled up. Then I remembered she'd spent part of her day with Rita Colletti.

"How'd your meeting go this morning?" I held my breath, hoping the question wouldn't send her off on another rant.

"Fine," Aunt Rowe said.

"Rita behaved?"

"She acted the way I expected after all the things you've told me about her."

"Annoying, huh?" I said.

"In control," Aunt Rowe said. "Aggressive. She took charge of the situation just the way I wanted her to."

I frowned. Aunt Rowe liked Rita, and I couldn't for the life of me figure out how that had happened.

"Did Rita say anything about her plans for this evening?" I said.

"No. Why?"

"I saw her in a meeting with Lance Devlin about an hour ago."

"At the Paris cottage?"

"No. In a cabin at the rodeo."

"She didn't say anything to me about any meeting with the man. What were they doing?"

"I didn't stop to ask."

Aunt Rowe frowned. "Were you over there checking up on me?"

"No, I was not."

"You sure you're not trying to talk those men into booting me out of the rodeo lineup?"

"If I thought that would work, I might try," I said truthfully, "but I'd rather stay on your good side."

"Always knew you were a smart cookie," Aunt Rowe said with a hint of a smile.

"I went to the rodeo looking for Hitchcock. He rode over there in the back of a pickup."

Aunt Rowe snorted. "Well, if that doesn't beat all. I take it you found the little fella."

"He's back home now, safe and sound." I curled my legs under me on the bed and leaned back against the pillows. "Tell me more about what happened at the real estate office. Maybe something that led Rita to meet with Lance Devlin tonight?"

"I wouldn't know," Aunt Rowe said. "Rita made it clear to Jordan Meier that Pearl is reviving her offer to buy the property next to her store for the listed price."

"Does Jordan have any say-so in the property sale?"

"Somebody has to sell it now that Crystal's gone," Aunt Rowe said. "The brokerage company owns the listing, and Jordan's a licensed agent."

"I didn't know that. Crystal treated her like a menial servant the day I saw them together."

"That was Crystal," Aunt Rowe said, "but there's nothing to keep Jordan from selling that property to Pearl."

So long as Pearl isn't in jail.

"What about the developer who was supposed to buy the place?" I said.

"Nobody seems to have a fully signed contract."

"Then why wouldn't Crystal sell to Pearl?"

Aunt Rowe shrugged. "We may never know the answer to that one."

"Jordan might become the new queen of Hill Country real estate."

"Maybe off in the future. Girl is barely keeping her head

above water now. Mother's in that expensive assisted living place, though, so this turn of events could be a blessing in disguise."

"What do you mean?"

"I'm sure Jordan could use commissions flowing her way. She's making sure her mom gets the best care available in spite of the price."

"I'd do the same for you," I said.

"Bite your tongue," Aunt Rowe said. "You won't have to deal with any nursing home. I'm living to a hundred, then I'll die peacefully in my sleep."

"You'll be one of the lucky ones. Let's change the subject. I have good news to share."

I told her my book news, and Aunt Rowe clapped her hands.

"That's cause for a celebratory drink," she said, "and I hear my pitcher of Texas Tea calling our names. One quick drink, though, because you need to skedaddle back to your place and get those fingers busy. I don't know what you're thinking, standing around gossiping when you should be writing."

I FELT a little tipsy as I headed back to the Monte Carlo cottage after only one glass of Aunt Rowe's Texas Tea. My mind was stuck on the topic of real estate commissions going to Jordan Meier, who needed the cash influx to pay for her mother's care. Commissions that Crystal Devlin might have kept for herself had she lived. I wondered if she'd shared *any* of the commissions with Jordan. Crystal's condescending attitude the day I saw them together had annoyed the heck out of me. Getting rid of the snotty boss and gaining an income stream in one fell swoop was more than enough motive for murder.

Quit that. You barely know the girl.

I got back home, grabbed a bottle of water, and went

straight to my laptop, intent on writing for the next couple of hours. Hitchcock wound around my legs, and I bent to run my hand down his back as I reread the chapter I'd worked on earlier. I was pleasantly surprised with the edits made and sat with my fingers poised over the keyboard as I mulled over changes needed in the next section.

My phone rang, and I stared at the device sitting more than an arm's length away on the kitchen counter. After three rings, I sighed and pushed my chair back.

Another danged interruption.

I grabbed the phone on the fourth ring and answered.

"Good evening, Sabrina," Sheriff Crawford said.

My heart fell to the pit of my stomach as I remembered the sheriff's request to speak with me.

"Sheriff Crawford, I forgot. I mean, I'm sorry. I didn't avoid you on purpose. Tyanne brought me home, and it never occurred to me that—"

"Sabrina, calm down," he said. "You're fine. I didn't call about that."

I opened my mouth to speak, then closed it. Maybe I didn't want to know why he called.

After a few seconds of silence, he said, "I need to ask you for a favor."

"O-kay," I said slowly. "What is it?"

"Can you please talk some sense into your aunt? Get her to drop out of that rodeo?"

"Why?" I said innocently.

"She's gonna break her neck," he said vehemently, then quieted. "I don't want her to hurt herself."

"Is there some reason you haven't had this conversation with her yourself?"

"Oh, I have," he said. "More than once. She's dug her heels in even harder."

And this surprises him?

I had no intention of doing what he asked, but I could take advantage of having him on the phone.

"I may be able to help you out," I said, "if you answer some questions."

"Are you trying to blackmail me?" he said.

"I wouldn't do such a thing, but I find myself personally involved in the Devlin murder investigation. I can't concentrate worth a darn on writing my book with all the information about the case constantly running through my head."

"You have no personal involvement," he said.

"I've been told that Tyanne and I are considered suspects. I'm hoping that's just the village gossip, and you don't have me on a list somewhere."

"You're not on my list," he said. "Neither of you."

"Whew." I blew out a breath. "That's good to know. I guess the perpetrator is spreading the rumors to throw the heat off of him or herself."

"That sounds like one of your stories," he said.

"I'm sure that plot's in plenty of books, but I have a personal interest in figuring this out. To clear our names."

"Far as I'm concerned, your names *are* clear," he said.

"Tyanne's daughter Abby has a personal interest in the case being solved, too."

He sighed and it came out more of a groan. "Why?"

I explained the upcoming visit of Pearl's granddaughter, Abby's best friend.

"Pearl was released for tonight," Sheriff Crawford said. "Abby can rest easy."

The "for tonight" part of his comment didn't escape me.

"We can *all* relax after the killer is behind bars," I said, "which brings me to another question. Who do you think has the most to gain from Crystal's death? I imagine it's her husband."

"I can't discuss the case," he said.

"Why did Hayden Birch come to see you today?"

"I said I can't discuss the case."

"Are you checking out the men associated with the rodeo?"

Silence.

"Don't tell me. You can't discuss it."

"Right," he said.

"Any one of them could have had access to Pearl's phone and sent that text message to Crystal."

"Same answer."

"Why are you testing my cat's hair?" I said.

More silence, then, "Why am I *what*?"

"Testing Hitchcock's hair. His DNA."

"Why in tarnation would *anybody* care about your cat's DNA?" he said.

"Deputy Rosales came by my cottage earlier today," I said. "She collected hair from Hitchcock to compare to cat hair found at the scene of the murder."

"I see," he said.

I could practically feel my blood pressure rising. "You didn't know about that?"

"I counted on you being as worried about Rowe as I am," he said, avoiding my question. "Guess I shouldn't have called."

"Did Rosales cook up the cat hair DNA thing to get me riled up?" I said, "Because if she did, it's working."

"Uh-huh."

"But don't tell her it's working, because I'm going to sit back and act like it's not really a big deal. Even though it's a *huge* deal."

"Time to calm down."

"Don't tell me to calm down," I said. "Your deputy is harassing me for no good reason."

He cleared his throat. "I'm sure she has a fine explanation. I'll find out her angle in the morning."

"Maybe I should be there," I said, "to make sure everybody knows what everybody else is doing."

"No, Sabrina, that's not appropriate."

"And Deputy Rosales's behavior is?"

"Now, let's not—"

"I'll see you in the morning, assuming it's okay for me to keep my car parked at your office until then. I'll have someone bring me by to pick it up."

"Fine."

"You won't give me a ticket for parking there overnight, will you?"

He cleared his throat again. "I won't," he said, "but I can't speak for Deputy Pat."

22

I WOKE THE NEXT morning feeling irritable and in the mood to confront Deputy Rosales.

You have a problem with me? Then face me like an adult, don't involve my cat.

My logical mind told me confronting the woman could backfire. She had a serious chip on her shoulder.

And a vindictive personality.

And a badge.

I rolled over to check the clock. Way past the time I'd intended to get up and start writing. Next to the clock sat a plate of crumbs—what was left of the Texas Cowboy Cookies I'd baked during the night when I couldn't fall asleep. I'd eaten a dozen of them around three and now felt slightly queasy.

I sat up and scanned the room. I didn't see Hitchcock, and it was odd that he hadn't come around to bite at my hair or tap my face with his paw.

"Hey, buddy," I called out. "Where are you? Ready for breakfast?"

No answering meow.

I hoped he was simply enjoying the morning sunshine and not off on one of his journeys. I threw on shorts and a T-shirt and went outside to walk around my cottage. I didn't see Hitchcock hanging out in any of his favorite spots. I strolled around the grounds to look for him.

Rita Colletti's car sat outside the Paris cottage along with another car I didn't recognize. The lawyer sure had been a busy bee lately, and I wondered what she was up to. I wished she would hurry up and head back to her office in Houston.

I kept walking, scanning the grounds and peering under bushes. As I neared Aunt Rowe's house I noticed her driveway filled with vehicles. I looked at the cars for a moment and realized that her rodeo gal pals were here again. A timeworn green pickup I didn't recognize sat amongst the cars. I heard laughter and followed it around the house to Aunt Rowe's backyard. There was Hitchcock, sitting on the split rail fence under the shade of an oak tree, watching the action like an umpire following a ball game.

Aunt Rowe and two of her friends stood in the yard around a wooden four-legged figure that I supposed was meant to represent a goat. Hayden Birch, holding a rope, stood with them.

He held up the rope and said, "Adele, come on over and give this a try."

Adele, dressed in a red T-shirt and denim capris, stepped reluctantly toward him. "Could you demonstrate for us one more time?" she said.

"I think someone's stalling," Hayden said with a smile. "How about this? I'll stand behind you and guide the motion."

Adele giggled as she turned toward her friends. I caught a glimpse of her waggling her eyebrows. Hayden put his arms around her from behind to demonstrate how she should hold the rope. I walked to the fence, and Hitchcock looked up at me.

"Mrreow."

"I agree. No poor goat should be so mistreated." I scratched the cat's head, and he began to purr.

The back door of the house opened and Pearl emerged, but she didn't join the others. Instead, she sat in a chair on the deck and moped. She watched her friends, but there was no joy in her expression. Guess I couldn't blame her after the events of the past few days.

I watched as Hayden finished showing Adele the steps to taking hold of a goat and flipping it over. I cringed, even though they weren't using a live animal. Normally, I liked to be supportive of Aunt Rowe in all her endeavors. Not this time. Now that I could rest easy about Hitchcock's whereabouts, I'd head back to start my writing day.

Pearl looked up when I began to walk away, and I gave her a little wave. She returned a wan smile. Feeling sorry for the woman, I walked over to the deck.

"Good morning, Pearl."

"Only if you're close to solving the mystery," she said. "Otherwise, my son isn't bringing Julie for her visit."

Uh-oh.

"He got wind that I'm being investigated by the sheriff," she went on. "I don't know who told him. Sure wasn't me."

Pearl's son had grown up in the area. No doubt he had friends who still lived here.

"I'm so sorry, Pearl. That's disappointing news."

"Julie and Abby are out of their minds about this," Pearl said. "They were *so* looking forward to their week."

"I know."

Pearl looked over the deck railing at me. "Are you getting anywhere? *Somebody* killed the woman, for crying out loud, and it wasn't me."

Even though I *was* hoping to figure out what happened to Crystal, I didn't appreciate Pearl's tone or the fact that she assumed I could solve everything and tie it all up in a great big bow. I didn't want to get into it with her right here and now.

"I'm doing the best I can, Pearl, and I'm headed back to work."

Work that wasn't what Pearl had in mind, but if I stopped for every little thing, I'd never make progress with the book. I walked back to where Hitchcock was still fence sitting.

"I'm headed home, writing buddy. Wanna come?" I had turned toward the Monte Carlo cabin and taken a few steps in that direction with Hitchcock on my heels, when I heard a voice behind me.

"Sabrina, wait up."

It was Hayden. I didn't want to hear one word about the goat tying, and heaven forbid the man suggest that I give it a try myself. That wasn't going to happen.

I stopped walking and picked up Hitchcock. Hayden approached me with a silly grin on his face. What was that about? Seemed to me this good-looking clown was enjoying the fact that the senior ladies were making complete fools of themselves.

"You get your kicks from making fun of elderly women?" I said when he joined me in Aunt Rowe's side yard.

His grin vanished. "I'm not making fun, I'm coaching them."

I nodded. "Sure."

"What got your goat?" he said. "Pardon the pun."

"I don't like rodeos."

"I can tell. Last I checked, no one needed your permission. The Lavender rodeo's older than you." He lifted his cowboy hat and ran a hand through his dishwater blond hair before replacing the hat. "It's a legend, kind of like your cat here."

He reached a hand toward the cat, and Hitchcock allowed the man to pet him.

"Hitchcock is *not* a legend. Any legend that has anything to do with a cat around here is about some cat who lived decades ago."

Hayden grinned. "Whatever you say, Miss Sabrina. Didn't mean to set you off."

I flipped my hand in a no-big-deal gesture. "I don't like my aunt being involved in dangerous activities. That's what gets my goat. Best thing I can do right now is walk away and put this whole rodeo performance out of my mind."

"How 'bout you and I go out for dinner sometime soon, and I'll wipe the rodeo and everything else right out of your memory." His hand drifted forward, and his fingers trailed down my arm.

Knock it off, mister. I barely know you.

I took a half step backward and ducked my head to hide the shock that must show on my face. "This isn't a good time. I have a tight book deadline to meet."

"Cool," he said. "We'll go out and celebrate when you're done."

I didn't want to be rude, but I didn't want to go out with the man either. He seemed like the type with a lot more on his mind than dinner. This was a good time for a change of subject.

I snapped my fingers. "Hey, what were you doing skulking around the sheriff's department yesterday?"

Hayden frowned. "I was at home yesterday."

"You were acting a little weird, then you got into that truck."

He shook his head. "You must have me mixed up with somebody else."

"Tyanne and I both saw you."

"Wasn't me," he said.

Why was the man lying? "We saw the red truck drop you off at a house."

His eyes narrowed. "You were tailing me?"

"We followed the truck," I said. "Hitchcock was in the back."

He looked from me to the cat. "Why?"

I shrugged. "Don't know, 'cause he got a wild hair to jump in? We weren't gonna let him take off in the truck by himself, so we followed."

Hayden scuffed a toe in the dirt and glanced around nervously. "Glad you got him back," he said. "Cats pull some crazy stunts, huh?"

He was trying to change the subject.

"Anyway," I said, "Sheriff Crawford wouldn't tell me what you and he were talking about."

Hayden looked up. "You talked to Crawford about me?"

"I didn't intend to, but he called me last night—"

"For what?" Hayden said.

"He's a friend of my aunt's."

I noticed a white pickup coming down the drive. Pearl was involved in the goat tying practice now, completely uncoordinated as she tried to pick up the pretend goat. I looked at Hayden, who was watching the approaching pickup—Luke Griffin's truck, I realized, when I saw the yellow Lab riding shotgun.

Hitchcock jumped to the ground. He'd seen the truck, too, and he looked excited to see his friend Luke Griffin again. I could relate.

"Tell me what you and the sheriff said about me." Hayden turned his attention back to me.

"He wouldn't talk about the case," I said.

"I got nothin' to do with any case," Hayden said.

"If you say so. Sheriff didn't tell me a thing. I saw you at his office. We followed the truck to a house where you got out. The truck went to the rodeo, so that's where we went to get the cat. End of story."

Luke Griffin climbed out of his truck and headed our way. I was glad to see him, but I wondered why he was here.

"You were at the rodeo last night?" Hayden said.

"Yes, that's what I just told you."

"Did you talk to anyone there?"

"Ace, Remy, Doc Jensen. Why?"

Hayden lowered his head and rubbed his forehead. "I seem to recall you owe me a favor, so don't talk to anyone about me, especially not about seeing me in town." He looked up, his eyes hard and dead serious. "Promise me."

"Or what?"

"Let's just say I can't afford to lose my job and leave it at that. We never had this conversation."

His statement insinuated that someone with the power to fire him wouldn't like him talking to the sheriff. Had he passed on incriminating information about Lance or Ace?

Before I could ask another question, Griffin walked up to us. "How do." He tipped his head to me and Hayden before checking out the women practicing their roping skills.

"I see you got one of those goat dummies," Griffin said. "That helping?"

"Not much, doesn't look like," Hayden said. "Ladies have no experience, so it's gonna take a while. Something I can do for you, Warden?"

"Nope." Griffin shook his head. "I came to see Sabrina."

"Oh?" Hayden looked at me. "Are we clear?"

"Perfectly," I said.

Hayden strode toward Aunt Rowe and friends.

"Mrreow." Hitchcock jumped up on a decorative fence by Aunt Rowe's rosebushes and perched on the end post where he could rub against Griffin's elbow.

"Sorry, didn't mean to ignore you." Griffin rubbed the cat's head, then looked at me and lowered his voice. "What was that smarmy son of a gun cozying up to you about?"

"I'm not sure. Wants me to keep quiet about something, so I will. For the time being."

"I don't like the sound of that," Griffin said.

"It's not a big deal, but I do have news that's a very big deal."

"What's that?"

"Let's walk," I said and motioned for Griffin to follow me around to the other side of the house, where we wouldn't be overheard. Hitchcock jumped down from the fence and followed us. I led Griffin to the front porch bench, and we sat. Griffin put his arm on the bench behind me and crossed one ankle over a knee.

"Your *friend*, Detective Rosales, took a sample of Hitchcock's hair to test his DNA," I said.

Griffin faced me. "For real?"

"She claimed the hair was needed for the murder investigation, but Sheriff Crawford seemed pretty darn surprised when I mentioned it to him."

"Why'd she do it?"

"To annoy me, I'm afraid."

"Why?"

"Because she doesn't like me."

"She doesn't like a lot of people."

"But me especially," I said.

Griffin's eyes met mine. "She's a very poor judge of character."

"Except for the fact that she likes *you*, because you're very likeable."

He grinned. "I'm glad you think so."

"We have a mutual admiration society going on here, don't we?"

"Mrreow," Hitchcock said.

We looked down at him, sitting on the porch in front of us, and burst out laughing.

When our chuckles subsided, I said, "Did you have a special reason for coming over this morning, Warden Griffin?"

"I came to check on you," he said. "Saw your car parked at the sheriff's department last night. When I noticed it's still sitting there this morning I started to worry Rosales had arrested you and threw away the key."

"Did you go inside to see?"

He shook his head. "Rosales's car was there, too, and I didn't want to get into anything with her. Besides, it's not such a long drive out here to check on you in person."

"You could have called."

"Then I wouldn't have gotten to see you."

I felt the heat of a blush creeping up my cheeks.

"I have a question for you, Luke."

"What is it?" he said.

"Have you ever come out and told Rosales to back off?"

"Sort of," he said. "Guess I wasn't clear enough."

"Have you ever told her how you feel about me?"

As I turned to look at him, he put his arm around me and pulled me closer. "Not yet. I figured it'd be best if I told you first."

23

LUKE HAD TO get back to work, but not until after he'd convinced me with a kiss that he wanted us to spend more time together.

A lot more time.

We planned to meet for a late dinner to delve into the relationship discussion a little further. I couldn't quit grinning as I walked back to my cottage. The thought of a future with Luke appealed to me, but I was letting my imagination jump way ahead. Maybe that was normal for a woman closing in on forty. The same advice applied, though, no matter what a person's age. Follow the path, slow and easy, and see where it leads.

Hitchcock had somehow returned to the Monte Carlo cottage ahead of me. I'd been so distracted thinking about Luke that the cat could have ridden home on my shoulder and I probably wouldn't have noticed. He was sitting on the porch and meowed when he saw me.

"Bet you're ready for your breakfast, aren't you?" I said.

He darted in through the kitty door, and I took that as a yes.

I hit the "Power" button on my laptop on the way to filling Hitchcock's food dish. Time to turn my brain dial to fiction, if I could manage that with this warm fluttery feeling I had going on.

Fifteen minutes later we'd finished breakfast, and Hitchcock lay on the desk next to the laptop as I tried to concentrate on writing. My thoughts kept drifting back to Luke Griffin. As often happens after a divorce, I went through a period of swearing off men. Until I'd met Luke a few months ago, that hadn't been a problem. Now that he'd made the first move, I couldn't help daydreaming about what his second move would be like.

And the third.

My cheeks warmed as my thoughts turned racy. I shook my head to bring myself back to the present.

You're a professional writer, Sabrina. Act the part.

The book. The publisher. The revisions.

"This is what I've looked forward to my whole life," I told Hitchcock. "Being an author, I mean."

He lifted his head. "Mrreow."

Bolstered by the cat's support, I moved to the part of the manuscript where I'd left off the day before. After a few minutes, I knew the good luck Hitchcock brought to my writing was working big-time today. I checked off numerous items on the requested revision list, then planned out a critical scene the editor had suggested adding.

Scarlett Olson, my protagonist, had managed to outrun the killer thus far. At this point in the book, Scarlett didn't know the killer's identity, but she had suspicions about three people. A reader would have the benefit of knowing Scarlett's point of view, which provided valuable clues in figuring out the villain's identity.

I stopped typing and looked out the window. Too bad no one could know what was in Crystal Devlin's head before she was killed. Would knowledge of her thoughts—if we could read her point of view on a page—solve the crime?

I tipped my head to one side, thinking that through.

So what was the next best thing to knowing what Crystal thought?

Asking someone she confided in. Either that or someone who spent a lot of time with her. I'd already talked with Paloma Morales, but hadn't gotten enough useful information from the woman.

You don't need to solve the crime. That's the sheriff's job.

Sooner or later, the killer would be caught. Pearl would be back to working in her candy store with nothing bigger to worry about than how many cartons of Reese's to order. Pearl sure had known where to stick the knife, though, by mentioning Julie and Abby. I had such fond memories of summers spent visiting Tyanne, back in our girlhood. If Crystal's murder was solved—soon—the girls' fun summer vacation might be salvaged.

I have to do something—for the girls' sake.

What was the harm in asking a few questions of the appropriate people?

I clicked "Save" on the laptop and closed my document. Then I said bye to Hitchcock and headed into town. Jordan Meier had spent a lot of time—more than she wanted to, I'd bet—with Crystal Devlin. She *had* to know things about the dead woman that no one else knew.

A BELL tinkled over the door when I walked into the real estate office. A fresh bouquet of flowers sat on the reception desk. Easy-listening music played in the background. The phone trilled a soothing ringtone, and the young lady behind the desk answered "Good afternoon, Devlin Realty" in a melodious voice.

She wasn't Jordan, and I looked twice when I realized it

was Cody Devlin's girlfriend, Mimi. Wearing a simple black dress with her blond hair tied back in a ribbon, she looked more mature than she had when I saw her before.

"Ms. Meier is with clients," she said into the phone. "May I take a message?"

I glanced toward the office Crystal Devlin had entered the other day. Through half-open blinds on the glass office wall I saw Jordan seated behind the desk, across from a man and woman. The man looked none too happy, almost like he was shaking a fist at Jordan as he talked. The office door was closed, so I couldn't hear their discussion.

"Closing is set for next Wednesday." Mimi ran a finger across a spreadsheet on the desk in front of her. "You'll get a call from us the day before."

I was surprised at the business-as-usual routine, but people had contracts to deal with and deadlines to meet.

Mimi ended her call and turned toward me. "Welcome to Devlin Realty. How may—" She stopped short when she focused on my face. "Oh, hi."

I smiled. "Hi yourself."

I felt awkward, having come here to nose around for information about Crystal, her boyfriend's mother. I glanced at the real estate papers lining the desk in front of her. Turning around and leaving would be more awkward, and I hated making a wasted trip.

"You work here now?" I said, "Or maybe you've always worked here and I didn't know."

She shook her head. "I came to help Jordan. She's kinda overwhelmed."

"I was curious what would happen," I said. "Who's handling the properties?"

"Jordan is," Mimi said.

"I thought she was an assistant, but then I heard she's a licensed agent."

"Right. She is."

"Good for her." The fact made me more curious about the way Crystal had treated Jordan. "This will be a rough patch for a lot of folks. Nice of you to help out."

Mimi shrugged. "I'd gag if I had this job full-time, but I can answer phones for a little while. The other day when we were in here, it was ringin' off the hook, Jordan was meeting with like three customers at once. Looked like she was gonna lose it."

"I guess Mr. Devlin isn't involved in the business," I said.

Mimi wrinkled her nose. "He'd rather spend all his time on that smelly old ranch."

I laughed. "You're a city girl, like me."

"You call this a city?"

I didn't consider Lavender the city, but before I could respond the phone trilled again. Mimi rolled her eyes and held up a finger while she answered.

I strolled to a wall that held assorted pictures of people in front of houses, standing next to Sold signs with big smiles on their faces. Crystal Devlin was in many of the photos with the new homeowners.

A door opened behind me, and I turned to see Jordan emerge from the office with the couple.

"Don't you worry," Jordan said. "We'll have the inspection report by tomorrow, and we'll close in time. Trust me."

"We'd better," the man said.

Jordan walked them to the door and said good-bye, then let out a loud sigh when she closed the door behind them. She glanced my way and smiled. Like Mimi, she looked like a different person today, dressed in a navy skirt with a white blouse and heels.

"Good to see you." She came over to me and offered her hand. "What can I do for you today?"

We shook, and I glanced at Mimi. The girl's chair was turned toward the wall, and she was hunched over with the desk phone tight to her ear. A personal call, I guessed.

I looked at Jordan. "Could I ask you a few questions about Crystal? If you have a moment."

Jordan's smile vanished. "What kind of questions?"

"Just a few things about her acquaintances." I lowered my voice a notch. "Better done in private."

"Sure. Come on in to my office." She headed that way. "Crystal's office, I mean. This is very awkward, but there's so much to do and someone has to get these deals put to bed."

We entered the office, and I settled in a chair across the desk from her.

"I understand my Aunt Rowe and that lawyer paid a visit. Hope they weren't too much bother."

Jordan waved a hand. "No, no. They were fine. Well, the lawyer was aggressive as all get-out."

"Don't I know it. I used to work for her in Houston."

"Poor you." Jordan made a face. "I know how it feels to work for someone less than nice, but no worries about that property Pearl Hogan wants to buy. I think I can make it happen for her."

"I didn't realize until Aunt Rowe told me you're licensed. The other day you were—"

"I know, mopping the floor," she said, "acting more like the janitor."

I nodded. "Right."

"Crystal liked to pretend I wasn't official," she said. "I hired on as a company employee, partly so I could get the company benefits even if I had to do all the clerical stuff."

"I see. You did the behind-the-scenes work and Crystal took all the credit."

Jordan smiled grimly and nodded. "And the money."

"None of the listings were yours," I said.

"Nope. Crystal made the commissions. I'm paid a salary, plus I get the health insurance."

"You could have purchased health insurance elsewhere," I said.

"Sure I *could*," Jordan said, "but I wanted the real estate experience. There isn't a better place in town, and I had to stay in Lavender because of my mom." Jordan glanced fondly at a picture of an elderly couple perched on the edge of the desk.

"I guess things have changed for the better, now that Crystal isn't in charge anymore."

"What do you mean?" Jordan said.

"You're the licensed agent in charge," I said, "so you can make the commission."

Jordan frowned. "I hope that's what will happen, but I'm not bothering Mr. Devlin with questions right now." She straightened some files that sat on the desk, then looked up at me. "You wanted to ask me about Crystal's acquaintances, and here we are talking about me."

The girl had to realize I was suspicious, but she didn't call me on it.

"You're right," I said. "Since you began working with Crystal—how long ago was that?"

"Four years and ten months," Jordan said without consulting a calendar.

"In all that time, did you notice if Crystal made any enemies?"

"You mean someone who'd want her dead?" Jordan said, straight-faced.

"Exactly."

The desk phone bleeped, and Jordan glanced down. "Excuse me."

She punched an intercom button. "Yes, Mimi."

"That woman is on the phone again," the girl said.

Jordan's complexion seemed to pale. "Tell her I'm in a meeting."

"I tried that. She's acting, um, kind of nasty—"

Jordan's hand hovered over the phone. "Sabrina, would you mind if we do this later?"

I stood. "Not a problem. I know you're busy."

"Thank you." Jordan smiled. I took note that she didn't pick up the phone until I was out the door and closing it behind me.

Mimi appeared to be sorting the papers on her desk and looked up at me. "Have a good day."

"I guess this can be a nasty business sometimes," I said. "I hate to see clients treating Jordan badly when she's clearly trying to help."

"That woman on the phone's beyond nasty," Mimi said. "She's from some place called Manor House, not a client. Something about a bill that needs to be paid or else."

24

TEN MINUTES AFTER leaving the real estate office, I walked into Hot Stuff. I recognized the song coming through the speakers—"Shake Your Groove Thing." My dad, an avid seventies disco fan, used to quiz me about song titles and artists. *Peaches and Herb*, I thought. *Wonder what became of them?*

Jordan Meier didn't give me the answers I wanted. Now I had new questions. Maybe I could learn something here at the coffee shop. If nothing else, at least I'd get a much-needed caffeine buzz. Though it was steamy outside, the shop's air-conditioning was set to light-freeze and I was up for my usual hot drink rather than the iced versions they sold. I walked to the bar, and Max Dieter greeted me with a big grin.

"Hey, Sabrina," he said. "Where have you been? That corner table's missin' you and your laptop."

I glanced toward the spot where I liked to sit and write and noted it was, in fact, empty.

"I've been writing at home, Max."

I ordered my usual. When he placed a steaming mug on the bar in front of me, I said, "What do you know about a place called Manor House?" Neither of us were natives of Lavender, but Max heard a lot more than I did through the grapevine.

"Assisted living home on the highway," he said. "Few miles out of town."

"Any idea how much they charge?"

"I hope you're not thinking of sending Rowe over there." Max laughed, enjoying his joke for a moment, then sobered. "She's okay, isn't she?"

"Aunt Rowe is fine, and no, I wouldn't send her there. I don't even want to think about that."

"Don't blame you." Max wiped his hands on a towel he had stuck in his belt. "She's nowhere close to needing a home. I understand she's gonna be in that senior rodeo."

I rolled my eyes. "I don't want to talk about the rodeo either."

"Okay," Max said. "About Manor House, then, I'm sure they charge a pretty penny. All those places do. Couple or three hundred a day is what I hear."

I did a quick mental calculation. "That's a chunk of change."

"Lucky I never had to know more," Max said. "Been to visit some folks over there, though. Why're you askin'?"

I sipped my coffee. "Guess I'm worrying for Jordan Meier's sake. I just came from seeing her at the real estate office."

Max nodded. "Her mother's at Manor House. Has been for a couple of years."

"The bill must be eating them alive," I said.

The next disco hit, "Le Freak," started playing. Max whipped the towel from his belt and wiped the counter in time with the song. I got the impression he had something to say and was considering whether or not to spit it out. After a few

seconds, he bent to look across the counter. Apparently satisfied with his wipe-down, he came back to me and leaned on
the bar.

"I think Jordan's okay now," he said. "While back, I heard
she might lose the family homestead. Jordan's living there by
herself."

"Does she have any brothers or sisters to help out?" I said.

"Don't think so."

"I'm glad things are better for her." Not all that good if
Manor House was making nasty collection calls.

Max went to take care of other customers, and I was left
tapping my foot against the bar rail. Max thought Jordan was
"okay now." Crystal hadn't been gone long enough to assume
her death had caused the improvement in Jordan's financial
condition.

I finished my coffee and headed out, but I barely cleared
the door when one of Max's employees, Lacy Colter, came
out behind me.

"Bless your heart, Sabrina," she said, "Did you really work
for that woman? The lawyer?"

"Rita Colletti?" I squinted against the sun. "Unfortunately, yes."

The young woman blew out a breath. "I swear I don't know
how you did it. I see her for a few minutes every morning,
and that's more than enough."

"I hear you."

"I guess the coffee y'all use over at Around the World
Cottages doesn't meet her standards."

I shook my head. "Doesn't surprise me."

The girl leaned closer. "Is she after Mr. Devlin?"

"After?" I said.

"You know, interested, like romantically."

I studied Lacy's expression. Her face was wrinkled up like
she found the thought disgusting, and I couldn't disagree.

"I have no idea," I said. "Rita never discussed her personal
life with me, and I'm fine with that. Honestly, I can't picture

her caring about anyone except herself. I am curious, though, where you got that idea."

Lacy shrugged. "My boyfriend does some work at the Devlin ranch. Told me the lawyer was here in Lavender before, three weeks or so ago. Now she's back, the wife is murdered, and they're together a lot. It's eerie."

I felt like my eyebrows had raised clear up to my hairline. How the heck had I missed Rita being here weeks ago? I made a conscious attempt to relax my face. Even though I had seen Rita with Lance Devlin, I never considered there was something romantic going on. Could there be?

"Rita handles all kinds of legal work," I told Lacy. "I'm sure Mr. Devlin's involved in a lot of business transactions where he needs the help of a lawyer."

"I suppose you're right," Lacy said.

"Has your boyfriend seen anything specific that made him think they were romantic?"

She shook her head. "I don't think so."

"Mr. Devlin just lost his wife," I said, "and he sure doesn't need to take up with that lady piranha."

Lacy giggled. "I hope she leaves town soon, so I don't have to deal with her."

"I second that."

THE what-if section of my brain jumped into overdrive on the way home. What if the connection between Rita and Lance *was* about something more than legal work? What if they were longtime friends who came together in a plot to rid Lance of a wife he had tired of? What if there *was* a romantic relationship between the rancher and the lawyer?

Yeesh. I'd rather not envision that.

I couldn't help but wonder what the heck the two were meeting about. If Rita was in Lavender weeks ago, though, she was probably handling a matter totally unconnected to Crystal's death.

Or was it?

I took note as I drove toward my place that Rita's car was still parked at the Paris cottage. The woman never took a vacation in the years I worked for her, yet here she was in Lavender, a fun Hill Country vacation spot. For the second time.

But not vacationing.

I went on to my place and parked. Hitchcock came out through the pet door and sat on the deck. I sat on the top step next to him.

"You didn't know me when I worked for Rita Colletti," I told the cat. "Took every ounce of patience down to my toenails."

He looked up at me and blinked.

"Okay, toenails don't have patience. If they did, dealing with Rita used up a hundred percent."

A germ of an idea formed as I stroked the cat's back. I checked my watch. Luke wouldn't get off work for another two hours.

"I could start getting gussied up for my dinner with Luke," I said aloud, "or go start a simple conversation with Rita. Find out what's going on with her and Lance Devlin." I stood and looked down at Hitchcock. "I'm feeling daring. Want to join me?"

My common sense screamed at me as I walked toward the Paris cottage with Hitchcock on my heels. I went up to the door and knocked.

"Mrreow," Hitchcock said as we waited.

"It'll be okay," I said.

I knocked a second time, and a few seconds later I heard Rita's loud voice approaching the door from the other side. She was talking to someone. The door wrenched open and there she was, dressed in her standard black slacks with white shirt. Not vacation garb. She wore pointy-toed, high-heeled shoes that were out of place in Lavender. Her head was bent at a painful-looking angle as she held a cell phone pressed between her ear and shoulder.

"Hang on a sec," she said into the phone, then stared down at my hands. "You bring the ice?"

I frowned and shook my head. Behind Rita, the living room looked like a paper blizzard had blown through. It annoyed me to see she'd moved Aunt Rowe's Paris mementoes from the coffee table—her Eiffel Tower replica and a lovely white-glazed crock from a Rue Saint-Honoré boutique—and placed them on the floor in a corner.

"I'm out of ice, and I need more," Rita said. "When's it coming?"

"I don't know." I gave her a palms up. "Your ice maker not working?"

Rita held up an index finger. "Bad idea," she said into the phone as she walked back into the living room. "Keep your mouth shut for the time being. We want to take him by surprise, right?" A pause. "Why not? Tell me what you're thinking."

I looked down at Hitchcock, knowing I ought to turn around and go back the way I'd come. Instead, I said, "Wait here" to the cat and went inside.

I walked into Rita's kitchen and opened the freezer to take a look at the ice maker. I pulled out the ice container and sure enough, found it empty. Before I got the container pushed back into place, ice fell and hit the shelf where the container would have been had I left well enough alone.

Just my luck.

I turned to look at Rita, who was still on the phone but busy shoving papers from the sofa into her briefcase.

"Hang tight," she said, "and I'll call you first thing in the morning for a status update."

I grabbed a big spoon from a drawer, shoveled the scattered ice into the container, and closed the freezer door.

I turned to face Rita, who was gathering piles she'd arranged on the floor into one messy heap. Not the first time I'd seen her sorry attempts at getting organized.

"You now have ice," I said.

Rita set her phone on the small kitchen table she'd dragged over beside the sofa.

"Won't last long," she said. "I asked for a full bag."

"You didn't ask me."

"No, it wasn't you," she said in a snippy tone. "It was the maid."

"You mean Glenda," I said.

"Whatever. I need ice."

I'd heard this complaint maybe a thousand times back in the office, and each time I'd obediently taken her superhuge water cup and traipsed down the hall to the kitchen to fill the cup with ice. A co-worker always joked that the habit of eating ice was caused by lack of a sex life. Rita was apparently still eating a big quota of ice, so maybe there was nothing to this rumor about her and Lance Devlin.

"I'll see about the ice in just a minute," I said. "You sure look busy."

"I am."

Rita continued shoving papers around, turning them face-down as if concealing some deep, dark secret from me.

Maybe she was.

"How's your friend Lance Devlin?"

Rita straightened and looked at me. "He's hanging in there," she said. "Tough blow."

"Have you known him long?"

"Not very," she said. "Why do you ask?"

"I'm making conversation. Aunt Rowe's usually the one who gets to know the guests. She's always telling me I should do the same."

"You already know me," Rita said.

Boy, do I ever.

I forced a smile. "Yes, I do, but it's been a while."

"Your aunt's a gem," Rita said. "Has nothing but good things to say about this town and her friends. And you."

Was it my imagination, or had her tone changed with the word "you"?

"I'm sorry I couldn't help you the other day." Watching the way Rita turned over the papers was making me curious as all get-out. "If you still need a hand, I could—"

"Fetch that ice," Rita said. "And you could check on dinner while you're at it."

I paused a second, dumbfounded. "Dinner from where?"

"Up at the house," she said. "Rowe told me there's chicken-fried chicken tonight. Best in the county, according to her."

Glenda *did* make fabulous chicken-fried chicken, but I couldn't imagine she'd agreed to cook for Rita. I might faint if I saw Glenda carrying the food down here for this particular guest. Wasn't going to happen.

"Did Aunt Rowe invite you to join her for dinner again tonight?" I said.

Rita sat on the sofa and pulled some papers into her lap. "Nope. She's out at the rodeo doing a practice run. Isn't she a hoot and a half, playing cowgirl in that rodeo at her age?"

"She sure is."

"Told me dinner would be brought down when it's ready," Rita said.

"Oh, she *did*?"

When hell freezes over was on the tip of my tongue, when someone knocked on the door.

No way.

"Could you get that?" Rita said.

Shaking my head, I went to the door and pulled it open. My jaw dropped.

Thomas stood there, holding a room-service-type tray in one hand and carrying a bag of ice in the other. I wondered if he used his head to knock on the door.

Hitchcock leapt to the bench beside the door, and Thomas jumped. "Could you keep that cat away from me?"

"He's not hurting anything," I said. "You're delivering dinners now?"

"Flipped for it with Glenda," he said in a low voice, "and I lost."

That made me grin.

"Let me take the tray," I said.

"Thanks."

"Here's your dinner, Rita. Have you met Thomas?"

Rita barely glanced up from her documents. "Who? Oh, yeah."

Thomas threw the ice bag into the freezer. "Enjoy the meal. I have to run."

"What's the rush?" I said.

"Girls' night out for the wife," he said. "I get to stay with the kids."

That might be easier than my self-imposed task of getting information out of Rita. I told him good-bye and turned back to her. "So, what kind of work are you doing for Lance Devlin?"

"This and that." She'd already uncovered the food and was cutting the chicken into bite-sized pieces.

"Anything I can do to help?"

Rita popped a piece of chicken into her mouth and nodded. "Mm-hmm, yes there is. Wait."

She pushed her plate aside, paged through papers sitting by her computer, and pulled out some documents paper-clipped together.

She finished chewing and swallowed. "These things need to be e-filed. You can use my log-on."

This was more than I'd bargained for. "I don't know, Rita. It's been too long—"

My cell phone sounded off.

"Hold on, let me get this." I pulled the phone from my pocket and answered without checking caller ID.

"Sabrina, it's Helen," Aunt Rowe's friend said. "I don't want to alarm you, but we need you to come out here to the rodeo right away."

My heart rate kicked up. "Why? What happened?"

"This goat got the better of your aunt and knocked her down. I'm sure she'll be okay, but she needs attention."

Adrenaline flooded my body. "Did you call for an ambulance? I'm coming, but they're faster. Don't wait on me."

"We called, but she's arguing."

"Of course she's arguing." I headed for the door. "That's what Aunt Rowe does. If she needs a hospital, make sure she goes. And let me know. I'll be there shortly."

"You should have Thomas drive you over," Helen said. "That way you can take Rowe's car home."

"Thomas is busy," I said. "We can figure out the car situation later."

I was halfway out when Rita grabbed my arm. "Sounds like Rowe needs help," she said. "I'll take you."

25

As WE SPED down the lane in Rita's car, I thought that perhaps I'd judged the woman a little too harshly. She might not care about all of the people all of the time, but she cared about Aunt Rowe. That meant a lot in my book, especially under these circumstances.

"What happened over there?" Rita said.

"Sounds like Aunt Rowe was knocked over by a goat. I thought they used baby goats for this roping, or tying, or whatever the heck they call it. They're mistreating the poor things, that's all I know."

"Probably doesn't hurt the goats," Rita said. "They're pretty hardy."

"That doesn't make me feel any better. I just hope Aunt Rowe's okay."

"She's hardy, too," Rita said.

We reached the main highway, and Rita surprised me by hanging a right on a road I wasn't familiar with.

"Wait. The rodeo's that way." I pointed in the direction I would have turned.

"This is a shortcut," Rita said. "Trust me. I've been over there often enough."

"If you're sure." I grasped the door handle as she made a sharp left and headed up a hill. Her car negotiated the incline and switchbacks easily. Below us, the Glidden River sparkled in the early evening sun. If I didn't feel so overwhelmed with concern for Aunt Rowe, I'd appreciate the scenery from this height. As we came down the other side of the hill, I caught a glimpse of the rodeo buildings through a clearing in the trees.

"There it is," I said.

"What?" Rita said. "You didn't believe me?" She allowed the car to pick up speed as we went down. When we reached a dip in the road, she worked the gas in a way that made my stomach fall in a roller-coaster sensation.

"How'd you like that?" she said.

I wasn't sure if she was trying to annoy me or amuse me. Or maybe she wanted to take my mind off of Aunt Rowe.

When the road leveled off, Rita nudged the accelerator harder and we sped along beside the river. I thought briefly about Hitchcock and the way he managed to slip into vehicles without anyone noticing. I checked the backseat and was relieved to find it empty.

When we arrived at the rodeo grounds, Rita didn't even slow down at the parking lot. She drove around the perimeter of the arena building to an open gate and went straight on through.

"They're practicing in the big arena tonight," she said. "Looks like that's where the action is."

I didn't bother asking how she knew the practice details. Beyond the fence surrounding the arena, ambulance lights flashed. Several people I couldn't recognize from this distance sat in the stands. Others congregated near the ambulance's open back doors.

"Thanks, Rita." I jumped out of the car, then clambered

over the fence and ran headlong across the dirt floor toward a stretcher that appeared to bear an occupant. A white sheet was pulled up to the person's chin.

"Aunt Rowe," I called, approaching the stretcher at a dead run.

One of the EMS guys moved aside as I flew up beside him.

"Aunt Rowe." Tears came to my eyes as I looked at my aunt's still form. I looked at the guy. "Is she gonna be okay?"

Aunt Rowe raised her head and opened her eyes. She had dirt smudged across her cheek, and her hair was matted with what looked like mud. "I'm right as rain. You don't think I'm gonna let a dang goat get me down, do you?"

I blinked back tears and reached for her hand. "I was worried, Aunt Rowe. See, this is why I don't like you involved—"

"Hush," she said. "Jason here says I need to rest and lay low on taking criticism."

I looked at the paramedic, who grinned, then back at Aunt Rowe. "No, he did not. Where are you hurt? What exactly happened?"

From the corner of my eye, I noticed Remy approaching the ambulance. Since I wasn't leaving Aunt Rowe's side, I didn't see a good way to dodge him.

"That goat head-butted her," he said. "She went down like a box of rocks. Not a big deal."

"Maybe not to you," I said, my confidence bolstered by the fact that he wasn't carrying a weapon today. At least not one that I could see. I noticed Aunt Rowe's goat-tying posse crossing the dirt from the stands, coming our way.

Jason said, "We're monitoring your aunt's vitals. Blood pressure's up, and we'd like to take her in for a thorough check. She doesn't agree."

Aunt Rowe propped herself up on her elbows. "I'm fine, and I'm going home."

Adele, Helen, and Pearl were close enough now to hear the conversation. "You should listen to the paramedic, Rowe," Adele said. "We're not spring chickens anymore, you know."

"Even if we can do a pretty good imitation." Helen held her arms like wings and began walking with the gait of a chicken.

Pearl wore a calm and serious expression. "You scared me, Rowe. I've already seen one dead body too many this week."

"Load 'er up, Jason," Remy said, "Mr. Devlin requires injured participants to go to the hospital."

Aunt Rowe swung her legs around and sat up. "Mr. *Devlin* doesn't require me to do jack."

"Wrong," Remy said. "You signed some papers."

"Papers schmapers," Aunt Rowe said.

"I'll go speak with Ace about this," Remy said.

Exactly what we don't need. Ace McKinney's two cents.

Remy moved off toward the stands. I squinted at the people sitting there and picked out Lance Devlin speaking with Rita. I scanned the other onlookers and spotted Cody Devlin standing at arena level. A shorter person in jeans and hat was facing the boy, and they appeared to be in the middle of a heated discussion. I didn't see Ace.

Behind me, Aunt Rowe said, "I don't blame the goat one bit for getting annoyed, do you, girls?"

Her friends chorused their agreement.

Pearl said, "Sabrina, did you know they tie those poor things to a stake in the ground so we can ride up and throw 'em down to tie 'em up? Where's the fairness in that?"

"The whole event ought to be outlawed," I said, "but at the moment I'm more concerned about getting my aunt out of here. Jason, may I take her to the doctor myself?"

"I have a car," Aunt Rowe said, "and I can take myself out of here."

Jason held up his arms, palms out. "Don't get me in the middle of this. If she won't agree to ride to the hospital, I can't force her. I'll just need a signature."

"Show me where to sign," Aunt Rowe said.

"Give me a sec." Jason walked around to the front of the ambulance.

"I'll drive you in your car," I said, "no ifs, ands, or buts. Rita brought me over here."

Aunt Rowe's brows rose. "Bet that was an interesting ride."

"She was okay," I said, "because *you* needed help. She really likes you."

Aunt Rowe smirked. "Doesn't everybody?"

"Darn tootin'." Helen walked over to the gurney. "Here, take my arm."

Aunt Rowe cooperated, holding on to me on one side and Helen on the other, and stood beside the gurney.

"You feel okay?" I said.

She took a couple of steps and rolled her shoulders a few times. "I might feel about eighty in the morning, but for now I'm good to go."

The sun was setting fast by the time Aunt Rowe signed Jason's papers and listened to his advice about icing any aches and pains resulting from her fall. Remy came back and reported that Ace cleared Aunt Rowe to leave. Like we'd have waited without his clearance.

As we walked toward the exit, I noticed Rita was still in the stands with Lance Devlin. I wondered what the devil they were up to, but I'd have to think about that later. Right now, Aunt Rowe needed to get home and settle in with some ibuprofen and an ice pack. The way she was chattering with her friends, I believed she truly felt fine—for the moment.

I waved to get Rita's attention and called to her that I was taking Aunt Rowe home. Lance Devlin had a cell phone to his ear. Cody and his friend were gone. The arena lights flicked off, one by one, and other onlookers drifted toward the gate.

Pearl agreed to drive the other ladies so I could head home with Aunt Rowe. I decided to take the new route I'd just learned today. It wasn't a straight shot, but it was definitely a shortcut. Aunt Rowe didn't comment as I headed north and up the hill.

"Should have seen the show Hayden Birch put on tonight," she said.

"His clown performance?" I said.

"Not exactly, but he did act like a fool."

"What'd he do?"

"Had a fight with one of the barrel racing gals," Aunt Rowe said. "Right out there in the arena, big as you please."

"What'd they fight about?"

"Sounds like he just broke things off with her. Guy his age shouldn't be dating a girl barely out of her teens anyhow, and is she ever ticked off. Threatened to tell all about his fling with Crystal."

"So it's true they had an affair?"

"Apparently so."

"Who heard all this?"

"Me and the girls were in the ring, waiting on the goats to be brought out, when the fight started. Didn't see anyone else, but that hollering was bound to attract attention."

"Interesting." I steered carefully along one of the switch-backs, thinking about this new development. "I guess Hayden didn't deny what the girl said."

"Nope. He was tryin' to shut her up, though. I'm guessing Lance knows nothing about whatever his wife had going with Birch."

"Huh."

I wondered if Crystal and Hayden were still an item when she died. Or had he broken things off with her, too?

A set of bright headlights shot up the hill behind me. When we reached a straightaway, the vehicle passed me and I recognized Rita's black car.

"Wonder why she's in such an all-fired hurry," Aunt Rowe said.

I'd put my cell phone in the cup holder and it began ringing.

"I'll get it." Aunt Rowe had the phone to her ear in a flash.

"Well, hello, Luke Griffin," she said. "What a pleasant surprise."

My shoulders fell. Oh, jeez. How could I have forgotten meeting Luke for dinner? I glanced at the dash clock and saw that I wasn't too terribly late, but I felt awful just the same.

"Dinner with Sabrina, you say?" Aunt Rowe said with a grin in her tone.

With the treacherous switchbacks I couldn't take my eyes off the road or my hands off the wheel to snatch the phone from her. There wasn't even a shoulder for me to pull over.

"She's right here with me," Aunt Rowe said. "Driving me home, and I'm truly sorry I took her away from seeing you, but—"

A pickup truck roared up behind us, seeming to come out of nowhere, and flew around me to speed ahead.

"Jeez Louise," I said.

"We're coming over Vaquero Pass," Aunt Rowe said into the phone. "You know how steep that hill is. Not a place suited to speeding. Looks like we have a maniac out here."

We reached the top and came over the ridge to spot the truck on the downhill side, a quarter mile ahead of us. Another vehicle was on the road in front of the truck, and I assumed the larger vehicle was closing in on Rita's car.

Darn tailgater.

"Good God," Aunt Rowe said. "What's he doing?"

I watched in horror as the pickup truck sped up and rammed into the back of Rita's car.

"No, stop!" I yelled.

"That truck's trying to run her off the road," Aunt Rowe shrieked into the phone. "No, not us. Rita Colletti."

I glanced in my rearview, saw empty road behind me, and tapped my brake pedal. There was nothing either one of us could do to keep the truck from crashing into Rita's vehicle again. This time the force sent her car off the road. My heart seemed to stop as I watched the truck race away. Rita's car tumbled down the hillside toward the river.

26

"SEND HELP," AUNT Rowe yelled into the phone. "Car went off the road. South of the ridge. Near the old Rockwell place."

She paused to listen, then, "No. Can't see the car from here."

There was barely a smidgen of daylight left, and we couldn't see much of anything. Maybe the trees on the hillside had kept Rita's car from going too far off the road, or at least kept the car from hurtling into the river.

"Okey-doke." Aunt Rowe disconnected the call. She turned to me. "Luke says stay right where we are. Help's on the way."

I looked at her in the dim light of the car. "Do *you* think we should stay right here?"

"Hell no," Aunt Rowe said. "We need to help Rita."

I shifted into drive and started down the hill.

"That Rita's a tough cookie," Aunt Rowe said. "She'll make it."

"Bet you're right."

I drove to the spot where the car had plowed through grass and weeds beside the road.

"Park it." Aunt Rowe opened the glove box and rifled through the contents, pulling out a small flashlight. "Here. Take this. I have a bigger one in the trunk."

I edged off the road as far as I could, threw the car into park, and turned on the hazard lights. Aunt Rowe's door was lodged too close to the bank for her to open it. I wished she would stay inside, but didn't waste my breath telling her so. She crawled over the console without hesitation to follow me out my side.

"Take it easy, Aunt Rowe."

"No time for that." She grabbed the car key from me and punched the button to open the trunk. "Got a first aid kit and a blanket. First we find her. Ah, here's the big light."

She flicked the switch on the long silver flashlight, and the beam illuminated the area around us. We ran to the place where Rita's car left the road. Aunt Rowe shined the beam back and forth across the foliage on the hillside.

"Let's go on down a little farther," she said.

"You could wait here," I said.

"We'll both go." She was already off into the weeds and grabbing at tree trunks to catch her balance every few steps.

We caught a glimpse of the car bumper about twenty yards down the hillside. The vehicle had landed with its left side crushed against a rocky ridge. Thank goodness it hadn't tumbled all the way into the river. It had rolled, though, judging from the dents in the roof. A dim glow told me the headlights were on, but the nose of the car was buried in thick foliage that nearly blocked all the light.

"Good Lord," Aunt Rowe said.

I shined my light at her face. She didn't look good.

"Sit down *now*," I said, surprised when my aunt listened and lowered herself to sit on a flat rock.

We looked at the car for a few seconds, and I knew we

were both thinking the same thing. To get out of that car, Rita would have to climb up to the passenger side door and hoist herself out.

If she could open the door.

If she could move.

If she was alive.

My heart threatened to slam right out of my chest. I didn't hear any hissing or ticking noises coming from the car. Nor did I hear any cries for help.

I reached my hand out toward Aunt Rowe. "Give me the light."

For once, she didn't put up a fuss and handed over the heavy-duty flashlight.

I negotiated the rocky hillside as best I could in my sandals. Thorns jabbed my calves and pricked my feet. When I got within a few yards of the car I called out.

"Rita, can you hear me?"

No reply.

Sirens sounded in the distance.

Please hurry.

I shouted Rita's name several more times with no response. I looked at Aunt Rowe, still seated and watching me with an eagle eye. Then I turned my attention back to the car. Sweat ran down my back as I climbed up on the ridge beside the car. I stretched, but the door handle was a good two feet above my fingertips. No way could I miraculously jump up, grasp the handle, and open that door.

Even if I could—

Aunt Rowe called to me. "Sabrina, let's go flag down help. You can't get in there."

Reluctantly, I jumped down from the rock and started to climb. When I reached Aunt Rowe, I helped her up and we headed for the road. We were almost there when I heard a door slam, followed by Luke's voice.

"Sabrina? Where are you?"

"Here," I called.

His flashlight beam shined through the trees. When he barreled through the brush ahead of us, relief swept over me.

"The car's down there." I turned and pointed the way we'd come. "It's on its side, and we couldn't get to Rita. I didn't see how—"

"You're okay." He wrapped his arms around me in a quick hug before backing away and looking at Aunt Rowe. "You're both okay. What a relief. First responders are right behind me."

The words were barely out of his mouth when I heard a vehicle screech to a stop up on the road. Doors slammed and voices came our way.

Deputy Ainsley was the first person I saw, followed by firefighters and EMS techs.

"Safer if you wait by the car," Luke said. "You need a hand getting there?"

"We're good," Aunt Rowe said. "Stay and help get Rita."

Luke nodded. I took Aunt Rowe's arm and we hung on to each other to negotiate the slope back to the road. The strobe of blue-and-red police car and ambulance lights cast an eerie glow on our surroundings. The emergency vehicles had parked haphazardly around our car.

"We're blocked in," I said. "Guess we're not going anywhere anytime soon."

"That's okay," Aunt Rowe said. "I'd like to wait and see about Rita."

I studied her face. "You sure you're okay?"

"We got medical people nearby if need be," she said.

"But how do you feel?"

"I could use some cool air."

We got into the car, and I started the ignition to run the air-conditioning.

I wiped my damp forehead with the sleeve of my T-shirt. "Wish we had some water."

"We'll survive," Aunt Rowe said, "and Rita will, too."

She looked out the window for a few moments, and I could almost hear her brain cells clicking when she turned back to me. "Now tell me, who do you think's out to get Rita?"

I shrugged. "No idea, not that it's hard to imagine someone wanting to do her in."

"Watch out they don't try to pin it on you."

"They can take one look at this car and tell it's not the one that rammed into Rita's."

"You must have something by now that would help figure out who was driving that truck."

"What do you mean I must have something?"

"From your investigation," she said. "A clue."

I rolled my eyes and looked away. "I'm not investigating. I told you that from the beginning."

I could feel her glaring. "You think I don't know you better than that? There was a murder. You couldn't keep your nose out of it to save your life."

I sighed, reluctant to tell her the bits and pieces I had picked up. Good thing I *wasn't* the investigator on the case, 'cause I was doing a poor job.

"I may have learned a few things, but nothing that would tell me how or if Rita's involved in the murder."

"Go on."

"Okay." I twisted in my seat to face Aunt Rowe. Maybe it would help to voice the thoughts running around in my head. "Rita is doing some work for Lance Devlin. Whatever that's about, she's keeping it close to the vest. Devlin's son, Cody, came to see her at the cottage. I don't know why, and he wouldn't tell me. Did she say anything to you about the Devlins?"

"Not a word," Aunt Rowe said. "I saw her with Lance tonight. If she's working for him, he wouldn't run her off the road."

"Makes sense, but we know this incident is connected to Crystal's murder."

"How so?"

"Devlin's wife is murdered and now, mere days later, someone tries to kill his lawyer? That's too weird a coincidence to be unconnected."

Aunt Rowe drummed her fingernails on the center console. "The kid was out there at the rodeo. Hate to think of a boy killing his mother, but it happens."

"True, but Cody Devlin doesn't strike me as that kind of kid."

A flashlight came bobbing up the hill. An EMS tech hurried to the ambulance. He reached inside, took out a gray box, then ran back the way he'd come.

We sat in silence for a little while. I tried to think positive thoughts for Rita and the people helping her.

Aunt Rowe cleared her throat. "You know that crotchety old cuss, Ace McKinney?"

"We've met," I said. "I don't really know him, and for that I'm grateful."

"Likes people to think he's mean as a grizzly bear."

"Yeah, I've witnessed his behavior."

"I hear he makes some money on the side on rodeo nights."

"How?"

"Taking bets."

"What does that have to do with anything?"

"I'm not sure," Aunt Rowe said. "Also heard he and Crystal were pals way back when."

I perked up. "I heard that, too. From Crystal's personal assistant. And?"

"Lately, Ace had nothing but criticism for Crystal. Couldn't stand the sight of her is what I heard."

"Because?"

"Don't look at me," Aunt Rowe said. "You're the investigator."

"No, I'm—" I stopped in midsentence when I saw Luke climb over the ridge.

He headed our way, and I got out to meet him.

"Is she—" I said before he reached me.

"She's alive," he said. "They're getting her out of the car, but it's slow."

Aunt Rowe joined us. "Did she say anything?"

He shook his head. "She's unconscious."

"Oh, jeez." I looked at the ground, taking in the new information.

Luke put a finger under my chin and tipped my head up. "Keep the faith."

I attempted a smile.

Then he looked down and stooped in front of me. "You're bleeding."

"No big deal," I said, then cringed when he touched a deep scratch where thorns had caught my leg.

"That needs cleaning up," he said. "I'll be right back."

Aunt Rowe nudged my arm with an elbow. "Hunky game warden wants to touch my leg, I'm not gonna argue."

I gave her a light punch in the arm, then Luke was back with a first aid kit. I sobered my expression.

"Why don't you get her to sit on your tailgate?" Aunt Rowe said. "Give you a better view of your subject."

I shot her a glare. "It's dark out here, Aunt Rowe. This can wait, really."

Luke said, "Sit in the car. I have antiseptic. You don't want an infection."

I could clean the scratches myself, but I sat obediently on the back car seat with my legs stuck out in front of me where the dome light could shine on them. Luke knelt beside the car and opened the first aid kit on the floorboard. Behind him, Aunt Rowe grinned at me, and I looked down to avoid meeting her eyes.

"This will sting," Luke said as he moistened a cotton square with liquid from a brown bottle.

He was right, but I managed not to cringe as he thoroughly cleaned off the dirt and blood. My legs resembled a road map of scratches and cuts. When he finished the cleansing process, he pulled out a tube and began to cover the wounds with antibiotic ointment.

"Well, isn't this special?" said a voice coming from behind Aunt Rowe.

We all looked up to see Detective Rosales approaching us. I must have been all tuned in to Luke touching my legs since I didn't even hear a car approach. Of course, she had to park behind at least three other vehicles with flashing lights, so maybe it was no wonder none of us had heard her arrival.

Luke held my left calf in his hand, finishing the ointment treatment, and he kept right on going. "Evening, Deputy," he said.

"Luke," she said.

"Accident's over the ridge," he told her. "I'd say they'll have the victim up here to the ambulance shortly, but you may need to assist."

"I came to start the interview process," she said, eyeing me.

I glanced at the notebook and pen she held, then said, "I'm surprised you have time for this."

Rosales frowned. "Why is that?"

"Because you haven't solved Crystal Devlin's murder yet. But then you've wasted some time there, I guess, doing odd things like testing cat hair that doesn't need to be tested."

Luke raised his gaze and met my eyes. He shook his head ever so slightly, but I wasn't finished.

"Maybe if you had arrested the murderer by now this accident wouldn't have happened."

In the strobe of the emergency lights, with her hair pulled back into the tight bun she favored, her harsh gaze reminded me of Snow White's wicked stepmother.

"Ms. Tate," she said tightly. "We are not talking about that case. I'm told you witnessed a truck ramming a car off the road up here."

"That's right," I said.

"Me, too," Aunt Rowe chimed in.

Rosales flipped her notebook open and clicked her pen. "Why were you out here at this time of night?" She'd directed her question to Aunt Rowe. "Don't you have a business to run?"

Even in the dim light, I could see my aunt's temper flare.

"Her business has no connection to tonight's accident," I said.

"I'll judge what's connected and what's not," the deputy said.

Luke finished his ministrations, put the ointment back in the first aid kit, and latched the lid. He stood and looked down at the deputy. "Lighten up on the ladies, Pat. They've had a bad night."

He looked at Aunt Rowe. "I have some water in the truck if you'd like some. I'm sure the deputy wants to talk to you separately. That's the usual MO."

Aunt Rowe nodded and followed as Luke walked away. Rosales watched them for a moment before returning her unfriendly gaze to me.

"Need I repeat my question?" she said.

She'd directed her prior question to Aunt Rowe, not me. I didn't point out the error and proceeded to explain that Aunt Rowe had been at the rodeo and about the call I received.

"This isn't your car." She tipped her head toward the vehicle I was still seated in.

For a moment I wondered if she knew what kind of vehicle everyone in Lavender drove or if she had specifically kept dibs on me and my car. I suspected the latter.

"This is Aunt Rowe's." I explained that I'd gone to the rodeo in Rita's car and was driving Aunt Rowe's back because of her high blood pressure issue.

"Tell me what you saw."

I went through the whole story up to and including the arrival of the emergency folks.

"Can you identify the truck that rammed into the lawyer's car?"

"It was a light color," I said. "Other than that, no."

"Could you ID the driver?"

"No way." I shook my head. "The truck went flying past us, much too fast for me to get a look, even if I'd tried. And we were a good distance away when the ramming started."

Rosales paused for a moment, then said, "So you originally were in the car that went over the ridge."

"That's correct."

"And the truck purposely rammed the car."

"Yes. More than once."

"Do you believe the truck's driver intended to cause physical harm to Rita Colletti?"

"Yes," I said. "If you'd been here, you'd have no doubt. That driver tried to kill Rita Colletti."

Rosales frowned. "I'm curious about one thing."

Her tone sent a tingle of dread up my spine. I waited for her to accuse me.

After a few seconds, she went on. "You were in that car this evening."

"Uh-huh."

"Then how do you know the driver wasn't after you?"

27

Deputy Rosales's words stuck with me during the drive home. No way would I repeat them to Aunt Rowe, who had reclined the passenger seat and closed her eyes. The last thing I needed was her worrying that some nut-job killer might be out to get *me*. Much easier to have her assume the pickup driver was after Rita, which was likely the truth. Still, the possibility nagged at me.

And gave me another reason for solving the whole mess.

From the start, I wanted to believe Pearl Hogan innocent of murder. Going with the assumption that Crystal's killer drove that pickup tonight, Pearl was in the clear. No way could I see her doing that daredevil driving. If I could prove her innocence, two little girls might enjoy their summer vacation together after all. If I pinpointed the villain, I might be saving my own hide as well.

I already knew I couldn't depend on Deputy Rosales to look out for my best interests. For her, jealousy seemed to overshadow good sense. Maybe others in the sheriff's department had better focus when it came to gathering essential clues to solve a case, but would they figure things out anytime soon?

In my mind, everyone who had anything to do with the real estate agent was suspect.

Her assistant.

Her husband.

Her son.

The rodeo guys—Ace, Remy, Hayden.

Maybe an unhappy client or two.

The suspect pool could be huge. Which of them also had a connection to Rita or, if I was the intended target, had a bone to pick with me? Why would they? Maybe someone who thought I asked too many questions. I blew out a breath.

Aunt Rowe said, "Lots of pieces to fit together, huh?"

There she goes, reading my mind again.

"About as many as those huge puzzles you and I used to put together."

"Fun times," she said. "We should get one of those."

"Okay," I said, but until the mysteries were solved and my book edits finished, I wouldn't be able to concentrate on much else.

I was yawning hard by the time I reached the turnoff to Aunt Rowe's a little after ten. Crime scene officials had kept us from moving the car for a good while after the ambulance took off for the hospital with Rita. When word came from the authorities that she was conscious and her condition had stabilized, we all heaved a sigh of relief. Rita was still being watched carefully in the intensive care unit. I was betting she'd be back to her aggressive self in no time.

After delivering Aunt Rowe home and using her monitor to make sure her blood pressure was okay, I headed to my place. What should have been a pleasant evening with Luke had turned into a disaster. He would leave for a game warden conference in Austin in the morning, and we'd make up our missed dinner when he came back. No official date yet, so the memory of him as he applied ointment to my legs would have to hold me for a while. As unromantic a moment as that might be, the gesture made me feel closer to him.

A sliver of moon barely illuminated the Monte Carlo cottage as I dragged myself from the car and up to the porch. I stood still for a moment, listening to the gurgling rush of the river. Then I noticed the outside light had burned out already. Odd. I'd just changed the bulb last week.

An alarm sounded in my head, and I took a step backward. What if the killer was lying here in wait for me after realizing I wasn't in that car when it went off the road?

"Mrreow," came out of the darkness.

Hitchcock. He didn't sound troubled. He meowed a second time, and I found him sitting on the porch railing. His rumbling purr worked its soothing magic on the tension in my shoulders.

"You're a good boy." I stroked his sleek fur. "I'm so glad to see you're here at home where you belong."

"He's glad to see you, too."

I jumped at the voice coming out of the darkness and spun to look at the bench. Twila, from the antiques store, sat there, almost invisible in her jet-black dress. I picked her out by the eerie glow of her snowy white hair.

"What are you doing here?" I said.

"That hardly matters at this point," she said, waving a hand.

I pulled out the little flashlight Aunt Rowe gave me earlier and flicked it on. "Tell me why you're here."

And how you got here, while you're at it.

There was no car, and I was pretty sure the lady didn't fly in on a broomstick.

Twila laughed. "Oh, my dear, there's no need to be frightened. You're home now, and all is well."

I smiled slightly but didn't respond.

"My son Ernie has friends staying in your Barcelona cottage," Twila said. "He was heading over for a visit, and I asked to come along. To check on you and Hitchcock."

I had met the guests in Barcelona—Lawrence and Patti Logan, a middle-aged couple from Lubbock. I was pretty sure they didn't start entertaining this late in the evening.

"So you've been here for hours?"

"No. I visited with them and walked over here a little bit ago. Needed a rest before I walk back, but here you are."

"I hope you didn't come to report more lies about me and Tyanne," I said, remembering our last conversation.

"Heavens no." Twila shook her head. "I was worried about you when I heard about the accident. I knew Hitchcock would be, too, and that he'd need consoling."

I frowned. "What are you talking about? Who told you I was in an accident?"

"Ernie has one of those police thingies. The news blasts out of that little box. Gives me heartburn."

"You didn't hear my name, did you?"

"No, but I made a few calls and learned who was up there in the hills."

"As you can see, I'm fine and so is Aunt Rowe. In fact, I just dropped her off at home and she's probably already asleep."

Hinting about the late hour.

"Oh, dear," Twila said. "I don't mean to keep you up. Ernie will be here shortly."

As if on cue, I saw headlights coming down the lane from the direction of the Barcelona cottage.

Twila stood with a few creaks of her joints, and I guided her toward the tan Suburban that pulled up out front. Hitchcock followed us and plopped into the monkey grass bordering the flower bed. Ernie Baxter got out of the car, leaving the engine running, and came around to help his mother. I thought of Ernie as the good son as opposed to his twin brother, who hung out at the local honky-tonk.

We exchanged greetings, and I said, "How was your visit?"

He smiled. "Good, good."

"The Logans seem like nice people," I said.

He gave Twila a hand as she stepped up on the running board and settled in the passenger seat. "They are. They're planning to buy a place here in Lavender. Matter of fact, they're shopping for property on this trip."

Twila said, "I hope they don't work with that flighty girl."

Ernie said, "I already recommended they use an agent from Emerald Springs instead of her."

"Her who?" I said.

"Jordan Meier." His brow wrinkled. "I hope she's not a friend."

"No worries," I said, "but now I'm curious about why you're recommending the Logans go elsewhere."

"Meier has issues," Ernie said.

"She seemed like a very nice young lady when I met her," I said. "What's the problem?"

"She came to us a few months ago, sold us all of her family's antiques," he said.

I waited.

"Thought at first she wanted us to take them on consignment, but she insisted we buy them outright, so we did. Good-quality stuff. A week, ten days later, she comes in with cash in hand to buy them back. Fell apart when I told her we couldn't do that."

"Why not?" I said.

"We'd already sold them. You know how tourists flock into town lookin' for a deal."

I nodded.

"The Meier antiques were snapped up in the first few days after we bought them from her."

"Jordan's having a stressful time," I said. "With her mother's situation."

"I know," Twila said. "That's why it shocked me to see her with all that cash."

I perked up. "How much cash?"

Twila looked at Ernie, and he shrugged. "Five thou, maybe."

A considerable amount of cash for anyone to carry around. "Maybe she worried her mother would be upset if she found out the antiques were gone. Felt like she had to get them back no matter what it took."

"I thought that," Twila said, "until she showed up a few days ago with more to sell."

I tipped my head. "Really?"

Twila folded her arms over her chest. "She brought in a valuable set of antique china and some silver serving dishes."

"Don't forget the Martha Washington sewing stand," Ernie added, "and that treadle sewing machine."

"You bought those things from her, too?"

Ernie nodded. "Tried to turn her away, but the woman insisted she *had* to sell. The sooner the better. She used those words. Promised she wouldn't come back like she did before."

"How long ago did this happen?"

"Day after her boss died," he said. "She was so wrapped up about selling her stuff. Seemed odd her mind would be on anything besides the murder."

"Odd indeed," I said.

"Anyhow," Ernie said. "I doubt she'll be back."

"Poor dear probably doesn't have much left in the home," Twila said.

"Speaking of which," Ernie said. "I need to get you home, Mom. It's late."

Twila waved a hand. "It does an old body good to get out every once in a while. And it was wonderful to see my friends, Sabrina and Hitchcock."

Hitchcock meowed at my feet and rubbed against my legs.

"Be careful driving home," I said.

"Will do." Ernie nodded and closed the passenger side door. He was walking around the vehicle when Twila opened her window a few inches.

"Good luck with the investigation, Sabrina," she said. "Stay close to Hitchcock. He'll keep you safe."

Like the cat has special powers.

I watched them drive away, then looked down at my furry friend. "People are putting some pretty big expectations on our shoulders," I said. "Think we can handle it?"

"Mrreow." He turned and ran back to the flower bed where he'd been sitting earlier.

I squinted and walked over to him. He batted at the monkey grass with a paw.

"What is it?" I knelt and made out something white in the grass. A balled-up piece of paper. Hitchcock's favorite cat toy.

"Are you littering again?" I smiled at the cat as I picked up the scrap paper. "C'mon. Let's go inside."

He followed on my heels, meowing all the way to the cottage door. Inside, I flicked on the lights and tossed the ball of paper into a trash can.

"Mrreeooooowww!" Hitchcock darted over to the can.

I looked down at him. "What's wrong?"

He stood on his back legs and put a paw on the top of the can to tip it over. An empty water bottle, a used paper plate, and the ball of paper slid out.

Hitchcock sat by the paper. "Mrreow."

"Okay, okay," I said. "I won't throw your toy away."

I righted the can and put the other things back. Threw the balled-up paper toward Hitchcock.

He ran to the makeshift toy and picked it up with his teeth. Trotted to me and dropped the ball in front of me.

"It's late, buddy," I said, yawning wide. "I need to get some sleep. We can play more tomorrow."

He batted the paper toward me, and it landed at my feet. I knelt and beckoned for Hitchcock to come closer.

"Are you trying to tell me something?"

He walked over and sat in front of my knees. His piercing green eyes stared into mine.

"Mrreow."

I picked up the paper and unfolded what turned out to be a portion of a page with a jagged edge as though someone had ripped it in half. I smoothed the paper against my leg to iron out the crinkles and began reading typewritten words on the page. Unless I missed my guess, Rita Colletti had written this. It read like a cover-her-butt letter that I'd seen plenty of times. The kind that outlines her legal conclusion about a given situation, states her advice, and points out why the client should absolutely not do whatever it was he wanted to do, and that it wouldn't be her fault if he went ahead and did whatever he pleased against her advice.

Adrenaline shot through my veins, and every trace of fatigue vanished when I realized she'd written this letter to Lance Devlin.

28

WILD HORSES COULDN'T drag me away . . .

I hummed the tune as I walked at a fast clip toward the Paris cottage with Hitchcock trotting beside me. I needed to read the entire letter Rita wrote to Lance Devlin. I wished Hitchcock could tell me where he'd come up with the scrap in the first place—it wasn't like Rita to throw confidential client documents in the trash. Usually, she insisted on shredding every tidbit.

"I shouldn't go in there," I said to the cat. "The cottage isn't hers, though, it's Aunt Rowe's, and I go in the cottages all the time."

"Mrreow," said Hitchcock.

"Yes, I know that's a technicality. I could call Sheriff Crawford and ask him to come straight over, tell him why this letter could be the clue that breaks Crystal Devlin's murder case."

I considered and quickly discarded the idea. He'd probably send a deputy, and I wasn't going to risk that.

"The sheriff wouldn't let *me* go into the cottage, though,"

I said, continuing my one-sided dialogue with the cat. "The cottage may be considered part of a crime scene given the accident. Don't worry, I won't mess up any fingerprints." I patted a pocket that held disposable gloves I'd plucked from the cleaning supplies under my kitchen sink.

I wasn't too worried about my prints being found in the Paris cottage. After all, I was with Rita earlier in the evening. If anyone asked, I'd tell them how Rita asked me to do work for her.

I swear that's the truth, the whole truth, and nothing but the truth. Kind of.

We arrived at the cottage, and I pulled on the gloves. Used my master key to open the door. I looked down at Hitchcock.

"Okay, let's go in. Try not to shed."

He trilled a response, and we went inside.

I flipped on the lights. Nothing had changed in the last several hours. Haphazard piles of papers sat on the table, sofa, and floor. I went to the table and picked up the paper-clipped documents Rita had wanted me to e-file. A final order in a Houston case and an original petition to file in Lawton County for a woman named Claudia. The chatty lady from Bunny's Beauty Shop.

I laid those papers aside and sat on the sofa to pick up the nearest pile of documents. I leafed through bank statements, tax returns, pay stubs, phone records—in various names of various clients. Nothing useful. I slowed down when I got to real estate documents with the Devlin name on them. Some property was in both Devlin names, some in Lance's, some in Crystal's. Dates ranged all over the place.

I heard scratching and looked down at Hitchcock. He was across the room on the floor, pawing at Rita's briefcase, where it rested against the side of a living room chair.

"Good idea, boy." I left the other papers and went to sit cross-legged on the floor by the cat. I pulled the briefcase toward me and paused.

"Feels like I'm crossing a line," I said, "but this is important."

"Mrreow," he said, clearly agreeing with me.

I unlatched the briefcase and rifled through the contents—another assortment of documents from various people and a bunch of office supplies. Tablets, manila folders, mailing envelopes. My pulse quickened when I spotted a document titled "The 1992 Morrison Family Trust, Crystal Eloise Morrison Devlin, Trustee." I slid that document out of the briefcase and leaned against the chair to read. The legalese was somewhat over my head, but I concluded that Crystal's parents had set up a trust and put her in charge. They named their grandson, Cody, as sole beneficiary of the trust. He'd receive the entire lump sum sitting in the trust when he turned eighteen. The document didn't say how much money was involved. I remembered the boy saying he'd turn eighteen soon.

Why did Rita even have this document? Did Cody know she had it? Had Lance given it to her for some reason? After a moment of mulling over possibilities, I set the trust document aside. It had no connection to the letter I was looking for, so I got up and moved to the laptop. I touched the mouse with a gloved finger, and the computer sprang to life. Lucky for me, Rita hadn't changed her password. When I entered the name of her childhood Chihauhau—Bullet—the lawyer's electronic calendar filled the screen. I read through her appointments over the past few weeks, noting that she'd had a phone conference with Lance Devlin back in June. No explanation for how or why Devlin hooked up with a Houston attorney. A notation for two days ago interested me even more. Apparently Rita had met with Jordan Meier and Lance Devlin at the Devlin Realty office.

I mulled that over for a minute and wondered if the meeting had thrown Jordan into a tizzy. Or maybe she'd called the meeting herself. Offered to manage the business for him.

I closed the calendar and went into the electronic client

files. Luckily, Rita's digital files were more orderly than the paper she had strewn about the cottage.

"Oh my," I said aloud when I found the Devlin file. Rita had two subfiles under Devlin—"Divorce" and "Trust."

Hitchcock came over and jumped onto my lap, partially blocking my view of the screen.

"He doesn't need a divorce anymore, now does he?"

I found the letter I was interested in and noted the date—two weeks ago. I quickly scanned what Rita had written.

"Holy cow, Hitchcock," I said. "Crystal Devlin had the money in the family."

Hitchcock looked up at me and blinked. My thoughts raced as I ran a hand down the cat's back. If Lance had divorced Crystal, she'd have a fortune in separate property. Lance might still own plenty of land, but he'd be cash poor.

Which gave the rancher a powerful motive for avoiding the divorce route.

A FTER a fitful night spent tossing and turning, morning came way too quickly. Sunshine streamed through the crack in the bedroom curtains and hit me in the eye. Hitchcock must have felt the late night, too, because he was still curled up on top of the covers.

I thought about Luke and wondered what he was doing this morning at the game warden conference. Hoped he'd hurry back so we could make up our missed dinner date. I'd never forget how he rushed to help me and Aunt Rowe the night before or his relieved expression when he saw that we were okay. That I was okay.

Details of the accident—that wasn't an accident at all, but a purposeful crime—flitted through my head like frames of a movie played back in slow motion. Rita passing us on the road, fine one minute, then forced off the road the next. The memory gave me chills.

I rolled over carefully onto my back, and the cat kept right on snoozing. I stared at the ceiling and remembered what I'd found in the Paris cottage.

Lance Devlin had a definite motive for wanting his wife gone. I couldn't know what Crystal's will said, but most wives left their estate to the husband. She might have specified that her separate property went to someone other than Lance. If so, the beneficiary of her substantial separate property estate could be Cody—who was also coming into a pot of money from his grandparents' trust.

I swung my legs over the side of the bed and sat up. Hitchcock squirmed, then resettled. I padded out to the kitchen and the coffeepot. My stomach rumbled, and I wished I'd have used my sleepless hours to bake something for breakfast as I often did. Instead I settled for a breakfast bar from my pantry, peeled back the wrapper, and took a bite. I looked at my laptop and the manuscript pages sitting on the table. With everything that happened and all the unanswered questions, the circuits in my brain were fully loaded. Today wouldn't be a good day for writing even if I tried.

I wanted the crimes solved in the worst way for many reasons.

Keep Aunt Rowe safe.

Clear Pearl's name, not to mention my own.

Get back to my book writing.

None of those things would come true until the killer was identified and put away so no one else would get hurt. I reviewed the facts I knew and the documents I'd read the night before. It looked like Lance and Cody Devlin both profited in a very big way from Crystal's death. The sheriff needed to know the information I'd uncovered. Realistically, though, none of it proved wrongdoing.

Rita could shed some light on the subject.

Assuming she was recovering well in the hospital.

Snippets of story plots flashed through my head—those where a person recovering in the hospital is attacked by the villain. Murdered by a lethal injection into the IV tubing.

Stop it, Sabrina.

I poured a cup of coffee and sipped thoughtfully as I came up with a game plan.

Aabout, chipper as ever and working in her office, I headed out to see Rita. A young lady at the information desk of Lavender Memorial Hospital cheerfully reported that Rita Colletti had been moved from intensive care to a private room.

"I hope your sister has a speedy recovery," she said after directing me to Rita's assigned room.

"Thanks." I hurried to the elevator feeling guilty about the lie. I'd decided to go with the sister angle just in case Rita wasn't allowed to have anyone except family in to visit her. It struck me as I took the elevator up to the fourth floor that I didn't even know if Rita had any siblings. Odd, but then I may not have ever mentioned my brother to her. She could never be bothered with trivial information, and she'd have filed any personal information about me under "useless."

I reached the door to her room and looked around. No one was in sight. No officer had been sent to guard Rita's door. Had it not occurred to the authorities that a killer might come back to finish the job? I raised my fist and paused. I felt awkward about invading the woman's personal space, but swallowed back my trepidation, knocked, and pushed the door open.

Rita lay against the raised back of the hospital bed with her eyes closed, her hair disheveled, her skin unnaturally pale. Purple bruises covered the left side of her face, and lacerations decorated her forehead. My gaze followed the tubing that trailed from an IV bag to a needle taped to her arm. The bedside monitors appeared to show her vital signs, and I was glad to see them. No villain had come in during the night to do her in. It struck me that I had tried to burn this bridge, but now I needed Rita and I really didn't want her to be hurt.

As I approached the hospital bed slowly, Rita opened her eyes.

"A visitor," she said through dry lips. "Lucky me."

"You *are* lucky," I said. "How are you feeling, Rita?"

"Bad question."

"I know. Sorry."

"Feel like hell. Monster headache. Fractured rib. Separated shoulder. Hurts like a bitch."

I cringed at the thought. "I'm sorry."

"They say I'll live."

"I'm glad you're out of intensive care."

"Lucky me," she said again.

"Any idea who did this to you?"

"None. Cops came. Asked the same thing."

"I'm sure they did."

"Didn't have anything to tell 'em."

"Did they ask about your clients?" I said.

Her eyes narrowed. "Why would they?"

Instead of answering, I said, "Did they question you about Crystal Devlin's death?"

"With me practically on my own deathbed?" The words came out more forcefully. "No."

Having this conversation with Rita in this condition might be taking an unfair advantage, but it was a heck of a lot easier than facing her when she was at a hundred percent.

"I'm trying to find out who hurt you, Rita, so bear with me."

She considered me for a moment before replying. "Okay."

I swallowed, got up my nerve. "Was Lance Devlin planning to divorce Crystal?"

I waited while she thought about my question, and I could almost see the wheels turning behind the cuts and bruises. "That is none of your concern."

"There was a murder here in Lavender, too close for comfort. I'm making it my concern."

"Too bad. I claim the attorney-client privilege."

I blew out a breath. "I used to work for you. You asked me

to work for you again, so let's pretend I said yes and I'm bound by the same rules. Lance Devlin asked you for an opinion—about the separate property."

Rita cocked her head. "How do you know this?"

"My cat brought me some evidence," I said.

"Right."

"We've worked on plenty of cases involving separate property, and I know how it works in a divorce. If Crystal Devlin had a chunk of separate assets, they'd be off the table in the divorce settlement."

Rita stayed silent but her eyes never left my face.

"But if Crystal died, then it's possible that Lance keeps everything."

"You haven't read her will," Rita said.

"Have you?"

She hesitated for a moment before shaking her head.

"He didn't have a copy."

"Do you think Lance would have killed Crystal rather than lose out in a divorce?"

"No," she said.

A monitor started beeping. I scanned the buttons, then studied Rita's face. She didn't appear to be in any sort of physical distress. Maybe mental distress had set something off.

A nurse came into the room and fiddled with the IV. She looked at us. "How are things going in here? Glad to see you looking alert, Rita. How's the pain? Need me to raise the dose a bit?"

Rita shook her head. "I'm tough."

I smiled at the nurse. "She's not lying."

After hanging a new bag of fluid, the nurse told Rita to ring if she needed anything and left the room.

"Lance is innocent," she said after the door closed.

"What if someone else did it for him?" I said, thinking about Ace.

"I don't believe that."

"So if Lance consulted you about a divorce and his wife died, why are you still so busy with him?"

"He needs counsel."

"For criminal reasons?"

Rita squirmed in the bed. "No."

"Why do you have a copy of the family trust? Was Lance doing something with that?"

Rita fumbled at the sheets, then pressed a button to raise her bed. With a soft whir, the back of the mattress brought her into more of a sitting position. She cringed with the effort of moving. The sheet slid down, and I saw her left arm was bound against her body. To keep the shoulder still, I guessed.

"Clearly, you've been snooping in my cottage," she said. "I don't appreciate it."

"Well I don't like the fact that whoever ran you off the road might have been after me."

"What?"

"Deputy Rosales brought up the idea, though I think it's a lot more likely someone is after you. You're working with the richest family in the county. One of them has already been murdered."

"Not by her husband," Rita said.

"That remains to be seen."

Rita's gaze moved to the bedside table and a big cup sitting there. "Could I get a freaking drink of water?"

"Sure." I picked up the cup and held it for Rita as she leaned forward to take the straw into her mouth and drink.

When it seemed like she meant to empty the cup, I said, "Don't overdo it."

Her head dropped to the pillow, and she licked her lips.

"Thanks." She stared at the wall briefly before turning her gaze to me. "Crystal was about to change the terms of the trust."

I placed the water cup back on the table. "How do you know that?"

"Lance told me."

"Why was she changing it?"

"They weren't happy about Cody's plans for his future," she said. "Eighteen's too soon to turn over money like that."

"How much money?" I said.

"A lot."

"Can Lance make a change now that Crystal's gone?"

"Not exactly," she said. "And he doesn't want to."

"Why not?"

"He trusts Cody to make the right decisions." She grimaced. "I think he's wrong."

"Have you told all this to the sheriff?"

"No." Rita shook her head. "That would go against the rules of professional ethics."

"Isn't there some kind of an exception to attorney-client privilege if someone's trying to kill you?"

"I'm not sure," she admitted. "This never came up before."

"Who do you think killed Crystal? You must have a theory."

"I do." Rita paused. "Cody Devlin had the biggest motive of all."

29

IN SPITE OF the things Rita Colletti told me, I couldn't for the life of me imagine Cody Devlin killing his own mother. Then again, I knew next to nothing about the boy. After leaving the hospital I headed straight to Knead to Read, where I hoped to get a teenage perspective on Cody's personality.

The bell over the door jangled as I entered the bookstore. Tyanne looked up from where she knelt next to a box on the floor in front of the "New Arrivals" shelf. She wore purple today, from her headband down to her Crocs. Ethan stood behind the sales counter ringing up purchases for a customer. I detoured by the front window to pat Zelda and Willis on the head and was rewarded with loud purrs.

"Look what the wind blew in," Tyanne said in an uncharacteristically snippy tone.

"Having a bad morning?" I said.

She stood and propped fists on her hips. She glanced toward the checkout and lowered her voice. "When were you going to tell me you almost got yourself shoved off the side of a cliff last night?"

I rolled my eyes. "That's an overly dramatic way to put it. I wasn't even in that car."

"You could have been," she said.

"I wasn't, and I'm thanking my lucky stars. Sorry if you were worried."

"*If?*" she said. "Of course I was worried. Everyone in town is talking about the accident."

"Then you might know more details than I do." That sounded snide, and I didn't want to come across that way. "If you wanted to hear them straight from me, you could have called."

"I *did* call. Where's your phone?"

My shoulders sagged. "Uh, I'm not sure. In a pocket maybe?"

"You used to be more organized." She shook her head, as if mourning my out-of-control state of being, but then a smile broke through. "Sure is good to see you, though."

We exchanged a brief hug, and the tension in the room eased.

I said, "Mind if I borrow Ethan for two minutes? I need a teenage POV."

"You're working on your book?" Tyanne grinned. "That's good to hear. Need his help? Be my guest." She headed for the checkout, stopped to say a few words to Ethan, and greeted a woman coming into the store with a small child.

Ethan looked up and came my way. "Doin' research? I'm your guy."

"Not exactly." I glanced at Tyanne, busy with the customer for the moment, and felt guilty for misleading her. "Maybe we should talk in the back."

Ethan grinned. "Top-secret plotting?"

"Something like that."

"One sec." Ethan pulled some books from the cardboard box Ty had left behind, arranged them on the shelf, then picked up the empty box. We went into the storeroom, where he placed the box with other empties in the corner before turning to me. "Fire when ready."

"This is, um, delicate," I said.

Ethan folded his arms over his chest. "What's goin' on?"

"You're more observant than the average teen." I trusted Ethan had a feel for Cody Devlin if only from observing the other boy around the school.

"Thanks, I think."

"Tell me what you know about Cody. Pretend you're writing a character sketch to describe him. What would it say?"

"Are *you* writing a book about Cody?" Ethan said.

"No, nothing like that. I want to know more about him as a person, his traits, what he likes, what he doesn't. Anything you've observed, even if it doesn't seem important."

Ethan put his head back and looked at the ceiling. "He keeps his feelings locked up. He's sensitive. Opinionated, but doesn't show much of that side. Driven, not in the direction his parents want. Sorta moody. That's not exactly right." He chewed his lower lip, thinking. "I got it, he's smoldering."

"Smoldering?"

"You know, when there's something burning right under the surface, like it has to break free sooner or later, but he keeps holding back."

"That sounds bad," I said.

"Not always." Ethan shrugged.

"You mean sexy?"

"No, well, girls compare him to some kid on TV. Lots of 'em are jealous of Mimi. Cody has the looks, you know? I bet he'll make it big out in California."

"Right. You told me he wants to go into acting."

"That's his plan," Ethan said. "Matter of fact, I'm surprised he's still here in Lavender."

"What do you think he'd do if someone tried to stand in the way of his dream?" I said.

"You mean like would he kill his mom?" Ethan shrugged again. "I dunno, maybe."

Tyanne appeared in the doorway and cleared her throat loudly. "Sabrina Tate. You aren't talking about fiction at all, are you?"

"You assumed. I never said that."

"And why on earth are you trying to pin a murder on that poor boy?"

"Uh, I'll go watch the store." Ethan ducked his head and left the room.

"I'm not pinning anything on anyone," I said. "Rita says he has the best motive. I just came from visiting her in the hospital."

"So now you're throwing Cody under the bus based on what your least favorite person in the world told you?"

"No. I'm more suspicious of the dad. I can't vouch for what Rita will or won't tell the sheriff. Not that she'll tell him anytime soon. She's so banged up it hurts to look at her."

"How long do they think she'll be in the hospital?" Ty said.

"She might be released as early as tomorrow."

"Is that safe?"

"You mean because of her injuries?"

"No, because someone might try to finish what they started. At least in the hospital she has people close by day and night."

"True."

"More important, are *you* safe?"

"Of course." I fidgeted, knowing she was right to be concerned. "So long as I stay away from the rodeo I'll be fine."
Knock on wood.

"Then make sure you stay away," Ty said.

"I will. Lance and his men give me the heebie-jeebies."

"What about your aunt and her friends?"

"After last night, Aunt Rowe knows better than to go over there. Watching that car run off the road—" I paused as gooseflesh rose on my arms.

Tyanne pursed her lips, looking thoughtful. "I don't know who was behind the car accident, but I don't believe Lance or Cody killed Crystal."

"Because she's family?"

"No, because men shoot, stab, strangle. None of this 'let's clunk her over the head with a brick.' Men go for a sure thing."

"You have a point, but everyone close to Crystal was male."

"What about the woman who worked for her?"

"Jordan Meier."

"Right. I hear she's taken charge of the business. Maybe she wanted that all along."

I thought of the things I'd heard about Jordan over the past few days.

"Now that you mention it, Crystal treated Jordan very badly. What if Crystal pushed her over the edge?"

"Does Jordan have an alibi for the time of Crystal's death?"

"I talked to her shortly after Crystal's body was found. She told me she was visiting her mother at the assisted living home. Said she went there every morning."

"Did the sheriff's department check that out?"

"If they haven't already, they need to. This is an important piece of the puzzle."

Tyanne waved an index finger at me. "Leave it alone, Sabrina. You have a book to edit."

"I know, but imagine your daughter's disappointment if Pearl goes to jail for a crime she didn't commit and she never sees her BFF Julie again."

"Now *you're* being overly dramatic," Ty said.

"Maybe so, but I can't sit around and trust Deputy Rosales to do the right thing, 'cause that might never happen."

A N hour after leaving the bookstore, I pulled into the Manor House parking lot and found a nice spot under a shade tree. Tyanne probably thought I meant to ask questions about Jordan at the sheriff's department, but if I checked on her alibi first, I'd be armed with facts when I went to see Sheriff Crawford. If the young woman's alibi panned out, I'd gladly cross her off my suspect list. I wasn't sure yet if Cody Devlin needed to stay on the list or not.

I looked at the home in front of me, a long ranch-style building of red brick with white shutters. The sign in the front yard read, "Manor House, Assisted Living and Memory Care." I didn't know if they allowed pets inside, but I'd soon find out.

"Mrreow," Hitchcock said from the passenger seat.

"Yes, you must wear the harness. I need you to be the model of a well-behaved, perfect pet for a senior citizen—or their families and friends. The more cats we can place in loving homes during our event, the better."

I'd brought flyers for the black cat adoption day to hand out. The perfect disguise for my real purpose in visiting.

A woman behind a window in the vestibule had a phone to one ear while she typed on a computer. She glanced at me briefly, pointed at a spiral notebook on the shelf in front of her window, and motioned for me to sign in. Her attention went straight back to the computer.

If everyone who entered the building had to sign in, then Jordan's signature should be here on the morning Crystal died. Checking up on her might be easier than I thought. From the looks of the book, the place didn't have all that many visitors, a fact I found depressing.

The woman at the computer seemed to have already forgotten my existence. I poised the pen over the book, then "accidentally" pushed the book to the floor and stooped down where the woman couldn't see me. I glanced up at the corners of the ceiling to make sure they didn't have surveillance cameras, and didn't spot any.

Hitchcock pawed at the book as I tried to read the signatures. I scanned and turned pages quickly but I didn't see Jordan Meier's name on any of the recent days. Before I could look farther than two weeks back, I heard a voice above me.

"Excuse me," the woman at the window said. "Do you have a problem?"

"Uh, no." I looked up and saw she'd poked her head out of the window and was looking down at me. "I'm fine."

"Oh," she said brightly, noticing Hitchcock. "You're from the animal place. Why didn't you say so? You can go on in. Folks here love the therapy visits."

My cat sat in his most photogenic pose and looked up at the woman with an adorable and innocent expression. What a suck-up.

I stood and placed the book back on the shelf. The woman was watching me, so I quickly signed my name on the appropriate page and placed the pen next to the book. I pulled a flyer from my tote.

"We're glad to visit," I said. "And here's a flyer about a cat adoption event that's coming up in August. Maybe there's a place you can post this where residents and visitors will see it."

"Sure thing."

She took the flyer from me, then pushed a button to unlock the inner door. I heard a buzz, and she nodded for me to go in.

I pushed through the door into the inner sanctum and took in my surroundings. Hitchcock's nose twitched as he sniffed the air. Unless I missed my guess, the residents were having hot dogs for lunch. Not my idea of a nutritious meal, but if they made the senior citizens happy, why not?

A dozen or so people sat in a dining room off to our right, apparently the lunch early birds since it was barely after eleven. Employees scurried around, some of them assisting people using walkers, others carrying arms full of folded laundry, some coming and going through a swinging door I guessed led to the kitchen.

A young lady with strawberry blond hair worn in a bun on top of her head came over to us.

"Welcome to Manor House," she said in a cheery tone. "I'm Ashley. And what's your name?"

She knelt beside Hitchcock and ignored me, as if the cat would answer her question himself.

"This is Hitchcock," I said.

She looked up, her eyebrows nearly at her hairline. "Hitchcock, the bad luck cat?" she said.

"No, no," I said. "He's not bad luck." I scanned my surroundings to make sure no one was listening. The seniors in view were intent on a woman carrying a tray filled with water glasses and distributing them at the tables.

"My grandma told me a story way back when about the bad luck cat," Ashley said. "Then he showed up in town not long ago. She freaked out when she heard he was back."

"My cat is not the legendary cat you heard about."

I wanted to convince her that no cats were bad luck, but she seemed oblivious to the fact that I'd spoken at all.

"These folks have enough bad luck in their life already," she said. "I don't think it's such a good idea for the bad luck cat to be here at Manor House."

I lowered my voice. "My cat is *not* going to cause anyone bad luck, and I'd rather not continue this line of conversation. I came to visit people and make them feel better."

"Oh, right. Sorry." She glanced around warily as if she expected bad luck to come up and tap her on the shoulder.

"I'd especially like to visit Jordan Meier's mother," I said. "Do you know where I can find her?"

"Irma Meier?" The girl frowned. "Bless her heart, she's holed away in her room as usual. Down that hall in room twelve." She pointed the way.

"Thank you." I stooped and picked up Hitchcock, then turned away from Ashley and headed down the hall.

"Sorry about that, Hitchcock," I whispered to the cat. "The last thing we need is people calling you names. That sure grates on my nerves."

"Mrreow," he said softly.

"You're right. I need to put on a happy face."

I headed for room twelve, holding Hitchcock close, and noted the variety of decorations and drawings on each of the doors. Irma Meier's closed door held a wreath made from strips of fabric, one of them a colorful cat print. A wooden black cat cutout sat in the center of the wreath's yellow bow. I took this as a good omen and knocked on the door.

A gruff voice answered, "Who is it?"

Hitchcock and I exchanged a glance, and I leaned in close to respond. "My name's Sabrina, and I've brought my cat to visit you."

"Come in," she said. "Make it quick."

Sounded like she was in a hurry to get out to the lunch table. I opened the door and stepped inside.

A stern-looking woman with curly gray hair sat in a blue recliner in the corner next to the bed. She wore a heavy black sweater that made me hot just looking at it.

I smiled. "Hi, are you Irma?"

"Quick, quick," she said. "Trash it."

"Excuse me?"

"The door. Don't let her in." She made a shoving motion with her hand.

"Oh, sorry." I closed the door behind me, then looked at Irma. "Is that better?"

"Trash it. No, not trash it. You know what I mean. I can't talk right." She put a thumb and forefinger together and twisted them.

"Oh, you want me to lock the door?"

"*Yes,*" she said emphatically.

I did what she asked and turned around. "This is Hitchcock. We thought you might like to have a visit."

"Oh, yes." She held her arms out and wiggled her fingers in a gesture for us to come closer. I walked over to her, and she patted her lap. "My, he's a big boy."

I leaned down and Hitchcock jumped from me to the arm of the chair. Irma's stern expression softened as she stroked the cat.

"Hope we're not interrupting your lunchtime," I said. "If you need to go to the dining room, just let me know."

"No way," she said. "We pay buckets of money, and they feed us off-brand hot dogs."

"Is that why you wanted me to lock the door? So they won't come and make you go to lunch?"

"Lots of reasons. Lady down the hall comes in, uses my bathroom. Another one steals my pants. People in here are nuts, and I don't belong here."

"Have you lived here long?" I said.

"Since my stroke," she said, "but I don't need this place. I need to go home. Will you take me?"

How to respond?

I knelt by the chair and talked to my cat.

"Hitchcock, isn't Irma a nice lady? She likes you a lot."

The cat took my cue and rubbed his head against Irma's shoulder. The woman cupped a hand around his head and put her cheek next to his.

"I do like the cat," she said, "but don't patronize me. If I don't get out of this place, I'll go insane."

"Have you talked to your family about this?"

"Yes," she said. "My daughter won't listen."

"You mean Jordan?"

"Yes," she said harshly, as if Jordan was a thorn in her side. She didn't question how I knew her daughter's name.

"But Jordan's very nice," I said. "She comes to see you every day."

"That's not true." Irma turned away from Hitchcock to glare at me. "Who told you that?"

"Um, she did," I said. "But if she misses now and then, I'm sure it's because she's very busy with her work."

"Work is a four-letter word." Irma paused, and her watery

blue eyes met mine. "Don't you think she should care more about her mother than that woman she hates?"

"Who does she hate?" I said.

"The fancy one, what's her name? Like a stone, but sparkly."

"Crystal?" I said.

"Yes."

"Why would you say she hated Crystal?"

"She hates me, too," Irma said, her tone growing more agitated. "Used to bring me things I need. Little things. Hairpins. Lotion. Those peanut butter crackers and Life Savers I like. Now I'm too much bother."

"I'll talk to Jordan about those things," I said, "but she was here to see you today, right?"

Irma shook her head. "She was not."

"Yesterday?"

"Nope. That's Bingo, and she missed."

"How about Monday?" I said. "She told me she was here to see you Monday morning."

The old woman shook her head so hard I was afraid she'd get dizzy. "She missed Monday, and that was the most important day of all."

"Why?"

"The 4-H girls came to put on a show. Group she belonged to years ago." Irma's expression grew wistful. "She promised she'd watch the performance with me, but she didn't come."

"I'm sorry. Maybe she'll make it next time."

"No," she shouted, causing Hitchcock to jump off of her lap. "I won't be here next time," she went on. "I'll be at my own place. You tell Jordan I said that."

I agreed to do so, grabbed the end of Hitchcock's leash, and quickly said my good-byes.

We stepped into the hallway and I closed the door, then blew out a breath. "Well, that was an experience."

"Mrreow," Hitchcock said.

A woman in royal blue scrubs and white tennies quick-stepped down the hall toward us. "You're Jordan Meier's sister?"

"Me?" I glanced around and saw no one else.

The woman held a piece of paper out toward me. "We need this bill taken care of posthaste, or we'll have to release your mother before the end of the month."

"I'm not—"

"I've talked with Jordan about this a number of times," she said. "Has she mentioned our conversations?"

I shook my head. "No, she hasn't, but—"

"She said she'd have to talk to her sister. I'm sure you understand we can't allow residents to fall so far behind in their payments."

I thought Jordan didn't have siblings.

"So, will you be making a payment today?" the woman said. "We accept credit cards—"

"Wait." I held up my hand, palm out. "I am *not* related to Jordan Meier, I don't know if she has any relatives aside from her mother, and no, I won't be making any payment."

The woman ran a hand through her curly brown hair. "Oh. Jeez, I'm sorry. Here I go, violating all kinds of privacy laws."

"No one needs to know. You can trust me to keep quiet." I introduced myself and Hitchcock.

The woman stooped to pet the cat and blew out a breath. "Thanks. I'm Connie from accounting." She lowered her voice. "If I don't find a way to collect on the Meier account, my boss will have my head—or Irma Meier will have to be moved—or both."

Irma would be happy to move, so long as it was back home to her own house. I'd be surprised if Connie hadn't already heard that song and dance from Irma.

"Wish this handsome guy worked in my office," she said as she continued to stroke Hitchcock's back. "He'd do wonders to soothe my nerves." She sighed. "The thing with that girl is she slips in and out of here under the radar whenever she can so I don't see her."

"You mean Jordan?"

Connie nodded. "I know she's been here, but I miss her every time. Maybe that's her plan."

"I wouldn't know anything about that," I said.

"When I heard you were here and that you were going to see Irma, well, I made an assumption."

"Don't worry about it," I said, "but I was under the impression Jordan came here every single morning to see her mother."

"Used to," Connie said. "Lately, she's suspiciously absent. I checked the book. Last time she signed in was two weeks ago Wednesday."

"Huh," I said. "Wonder what's up?"

"I realize cleaning out a parent's house can be an arduous chore." Connie chattered on, privacy matters obviously forgotten. "Not to mention the emotions involved since she's selling the home where she spent her whole life."

"She's selling her mother's house?" I whispered for fear Irma Meier would somehow catch wind of what would be quite distressing news.

"Place is already listed," Connie said. "Might sell quickly. Jordan may be planning to pay our bill then. Problem is, the owner of Manor House won't bend his rules for the Meier family or anyone else. If they don't pay soon, like within the week, I don't know what will happen to poor Irma."

30

I MULLED OVER MY conversation with Irma as Hitchcock and I headed back into town. I didn't know with certainty that everything Jordan's mother said was true. The stroke might have affected her memory, but she sounded lucid. Did Jordan hate Crystal to the extent that she'd kill her? Had she believed such a drastic act would somehow cure her financial problems? If so, she wouldn't be selling the family homestead.

I didn't think any of these actions would bring in the quick money Jordan needed to pay the Manor House bill. Irma wouldn't care one bit if they kicked her out, but boy oh boy, I didn't want to be around to witness her reaction when she learned her daughter was selling the house. Hitchcock was sitting up on the passenger seat and had a nervous purr going as if he, too, was concerned about Irma's plight.

So where *was* Jordan on the morning of Crystal's death? I still didn't have an answer to that question.

"Maybe we should give Jordan the benefit of the doubt,"

I said to Hitchcock. "She might have a plan for her mother's ongoing care."

"Mrrrrreoooooow." Hitchcock's meow sounded more like a complaint.

"Guess you're not convinced," I said. "We could go to ask her."

"Mrreow," the cat said with what looked like a nod of his head.

I had to laugh. He seemed to understand exactly what I said, and I was in the mood to confront the young real estate agent on her mother's behalf.

Fifteen minutes later, we arrived at the Devlin Realty office and parked out front. Hitchcock was growing accustomed to the leash and harness, and he stayed by my side as we walked through the office door.

Mimi Trevino looked up from a magazine that lay open on top of a mess of papers. The girl's hair was held back haphazardly in a clip, and her eyes looked red and puffy. I would normally chalk up her appearance to a young person's night on the town. Due to the week's events, though, the poor girl was more likely dealing with Cody and the aftereffects of his mother's death.

"Hi, Mimi," I said. "Is Jordan in?"

"Nope." She looked up at me and glanced at Hitchcock. The cat stood on his back legs with his front paws on the edge of her desk. "He sure is tall."

"That he is."

Hitchcock nosed at the papers surrounding her magazine, and I couldn't help but notice an envelope-sized slip of paper that read, "Insufficient Funds Notice" on top.

I would have liked to get a better look. Instead, I politely averted my gaze and said, "Do you know when Jordan will be back?"

"No idea." Mimi grabbed a tissue from the box on the desk corner and wiped at her nose. "She's out meeting with a client."

"You doing okay?"

"Just great."

"And Cody?"

"He's hangin' in there."

"That's good."

I paused and considered what information the girl might be willing to give me. Her working relationship with Jordan was new. I wondered how much allegiance she felt toward the other woman.

"Have you heard that Jordan's selling her house?"

"Yeah. You interested in buying it?" Mimi lifted her magazine and pushed papers around. "I have a flyer about it here somewhere."

Hitchcock got back on the floor and strained at the leash to walk around to Mimi's side of the desk.

"I'm not in the market right now," I said. "I was thinking about the stress she must be going through. A lot has fallen on her shoulders suddenly."

Mimi shrugged. "I guess."

"She handling it okay?"

Mimi scrunched up her face and put a finger to her nose, holding back a sneeze. After a second, she said, "How would I know?"

"She's probably still in a state of shock about Crystal," I said. "Were they close?"

"Doesn't seem like it."

"I didn't think they were." I checked over my shoulder to make sure we were still alone, then leaned closer. "Does Jordan talk about Crystal at all?"

"Not much. Why?" She paused, and after a few seconds her eyes widened. "Holy sh—, I mean, um, you think Jordan had something to do with it?"

"I don't want to jump to conclusions, but—"

Mimi said, "You know, she acts kind of like she's glad Crystal's gone."

That gave me a jolt. If Jordan was involved with the murder, wouldn't she at least play the part of a grieving friend to throw everyone off? Maybe she didn't realize her behavior looked guilty.

"Has anyone from the sheriff's office come to speak with her?" I said.

Mimi riffled the corners of the magazine. "Haven't seen anyone. They could have talked to her at home."

"I'm sure they're covering all the bases."

"They haven't asked me a thing." Mimi sniffed and swiped at her nose with the tissue again.

"Do you know anything?"

"I have an opinion," she said. "I'm the one who sees the big smile on Jordan's face when the commissions come rolling in."

I wondered how many commissions could have come in within the past few days. "Have you mentioned this to anyone? Mr. Devlin perhaps?"

Mimi grimaced. "Yeah, right. He thinks my opinion's worth squat."

"Who does the accounting for the business?"

"Beats me," Mimi said. "Nobody here but me and Jordan."

Which meant Jordan might be able to siphon money off to herself.

"You happen to know who Jordan's meeting with or where?" I said.

"I think she's at Sweet Stop," Mimi said, "or the building next door. The one that candy-store lady's buying."

Interesting. The woman who might have done away with Crystal meeting with the woman who had been accused of doing the deed.

I called to Hitchcock. The cat materialized from behind a file cabinet, and we said our good-byes. We had barely stepped onto the sidewalk when I heard the lock snick shut behind us. I turned to see Mimi had flipped the Open sign to "Closed—Back in One Hour." Protecting herself from additional questions, maybe? Probably regretting that she'd said too much.

She could have told me from the start that Jordan was only a few doors away from her office, but things worked out for the best. I wouldn't have gotten as much information from her as I had. Whether or not any of the things the girl said would prove valuable was anyone's guess. I didn't like the idea of Pearl spending time with a woman who not only seemed to be neglecting her mother and selling the house out from under her but who also might have murdered her boss.

My imagination flew into overdrive as we hurried down the sidewalk. I paused in front of Sweet Stop and looked through the plate glass window to scan the store. There were two clerks behind the sales counter and half a dozen customers in the aisles perusing the candy displays. No sign of Pearl.

"Let's check next door," I said to Hitchcock, and he was right beside me as I moved on to the adjacent storefront. The two buildings shared a porch roof, and I could see why Pearl was eager to acquire this property to expand her store. If Jordan was selling the place to Pearl, I wondered what had happened to the seller Crystal had lined up to buy the building.

The front door stood open, so I went on in and saw Jordan and Pearl leaning over a sales counter with paperwork in front of them. Pearl held a pen in one hand and was in her candy store apron as if she'd rushed off for a coffee break. She looked up as we walked in.

"Sabrina, I'm getting it," she said, her complexion glowing. "I'm buying the store."

"That's nice, Pearl." I forced a smile as my gaze went to Jordan. "Did Crystal's buyer back out?"

"He had to wait on something before he could buy," Pearl said, "and I'm paying cash, so I'm *in*."

Jordan said, "His purchase was contingent on several factors, and I'm happy to sell to Pearl instead. We might close in less than thirty days."

"Can you afford to wait that long?" I said before my better judgment set in.

Jordan frowned. "What do you mean?"

Pearl watched me with a yeah-Sabrina-what-*do*-you mean expression. The paperwork in front of her appeared to be a contract. She looked perturbed that I was interrupting her deal.

I kept my eyes on Jordan. "I understand your mother has some needs that aren't being met."

The young woman frowned. "Who told you that?"

"She did. We went to visit her at the home a little bit ago."

"You mean you and the cat?" Jordan said.

"That's right. Your mother likes cats. She'd like to get one of her own after she moves back home."

Hitchcock looked up at me as if he knew I embellished the story.

Jordan's complexion paled. "I'll talk with my mom about that."

"Will you tell her you're planning to sell the house and she's not ever moving back home?"

"That's a personal matter."

Pearl said, "Sabrina, we're about to sign the contract so I can buy this property."

"Sorry," I said. "Jordan and I can talk after you're finished. I'll wait outside."

Jordan stared at me. "We have nothing to talk about."

"Tell me where I need to sign," Pearl whined, "and we'll put this baby to bed. Sabrina, why are you bothering us now?"

"You wanted me to clear your name," I said, "and that's what I'm trying to do."

"Clear her name of what?" Jordan said.

"Crystal's murder," I said. "As I see it, now that she's gone, you have an advantage in the business. Money-wise."

"Advantage? That lawyer is advising Mr. Devlin to sell the business. If he does, I'll be out in the cold."

My mental gears churned with this new information.

After a moment, I said, "How angry does that make you?"

Jordan's cheeks had grown rosy-pink. "What are you implying?"

"Things aren't going the way you'd like. You know, the lawyer you mentioned was run off the road last night. She's in the hospital."

Jordan gasped and put a hand to her chest. "No, I hadn't heard." She searched my face. "You think *I* had something to do with that?"

"Did you? I *do* know you weren't really at the nursing home the morning Crystal died."

"I haven't done any—" Jordan's voice cracked, and she bowed her head.

I stepped closer and spoke quietly. "Maybe you didn't mean to kill her."

The young woman looked up with tear-filled eyes. "I did *not* kill her. I would *never* hurt Crystal."

"Was it an accident?"

"No, you don't understand." She buried her face in her hands and collapsed into sobs.

Pearl stepped closer to Jordan and put a hand on the younger woman's arm. "Jordan, honey, it's okay. Of course you didn't do anything wrong." She pinned me with a glare. "Sabrina, that's enough. This girl is innocent."

I guess Pearl didn't appreciate me pinpointing another suspect—at least not this one. She and I exchanged glances and looked at Jordan as her sobs became quiet snuffles. After a minute or so, Jordan looked up.

"I care for Mother the best I can," she said. "You have no idea how hard it is to keep up."

I nodded with what I hoped was an expression that invited her to go on.

"There's no one else to help," she said. "I have to sell the house to make ends meet. I'm out of options."

"I know a good home health care woman," Pearl said. "She works cheap. Bet your mom would rather stay at her own house."

Jordan looked at Pearl and attempted a smile. "Thanks, but my problems run deep."

Hitchcock went to Jordan and rubbed against the woman's legs. I pulled on the leash even though cat hair on her slacks might be the least of Jordan's worries.

"What do you mean deep?" I said. "If you're innocent and you're able to pay the Manor House bill, things will work out."

Jordan blew out a breath. "I wish it were that easy."

"Chin up, girl," Pearl said. "Let's get the papers signed."

"Maybe we can help," I said. "Explain why it's not so easy."

"I don't want to get in trouble," Jordan said, "but the stress over all this is going to kill me if I keep everything all pent up inside."

I waited, pinching myself to keep from telling her to spit it out. Pearl stayed blessedly quiet. Hitchcock kept up the leg rub, but Jordan didn't seem to notice him.

Her gaze flicked from me to Pearl and back. "I borrowed money from Devlin Realty," she finally said, "to pay the Manor House bills."

"But they're not paid," I said, "at least not according to their accountant."

Jordan's jaw dropped. "You got private information about my bill? Why would you do that?"

"There was a simple case of mistaken identity," I said, not wanting to drop Connie in the grease. "Apparently you mentioned something about consulting with your sister about the money owed."

A blush rose on Jordan's cheeks.

"You don't have a sister, do you?" I said.

She shook her head. "You have to understand something."

I waited. Pearl appeared interested in hearing the explanation, too.

"I never made enough money working for Crystal to pay for that home," Jordan said. "Not enough to pay for anyone to come into the house to take care of mom. I barely took home what I needed to keep food on the table."

"So you borrowed from Crystal?" I said.

"Without her knowledge." Jordan's body shook as if a slight earthquake had hit the building. "I took money from the company account when I needed it. Paid it back as I could. But then Crystal died—"

"And you panicked," I said.

"Right."

"And that's why you're selling furniture and antiques," I said, remembering my conversation with Ernie Baxter.

Jordan nodded. "Mom would have a fit if she knew, and now I have to sell the house to put every penny back into the account before—"

Her voice broke.

"We'll help you," Pearl said. "Right, Sabrina?"

"Okay." Though I didn't approve of what Jordan had done, I felt her pain and believed she was telling the truth. "I'm sorry your family is having these problems."

Jordan met my gaze. "I'm not the only one with family issues, and mine aren't the worst. I think someone in Crystal's family killed her, and I'm afraid it was her own son."

31

I THOUGHT ABOUT GOING straight to the sheriff's department after talking with Jordan, but my stomach complained
loudly about that idea. I'd missed lunch a couple of hours
ago. Probably not a good idea to push on without any fuel to
keep me going.

Rather than stopping at a restaurant and risk getting involved in conversation with the town gossips, I bought two
taquitos from Juan's drive-through and parked in the shade
of a pecan tree to eat and think things through. The tree didn't
do much to cut the afternoon heat, so I kept the car and the
air conditioner running.

Hitchcock stretched across the console and propped
his front paws on my leg to get his nose closer to the food
wrapper.

"Hold on. I'm getting you some."

I unwrapped a tortilla, checked to make sure there was no
onion, and dumped a portion of the egg and sausage filling
on a napkin. I tore the bottom part off a paper cup and poured

bottled water into the makeshift bowl, then placed the water and food on the passenger side floorboard for the cat. He was suitably grateful and lapped at the drink before nibbling on a piece of sausage.

I tore open a packet of picante sauce and doused the remainder of the taquito before taking a big bite. Yum. That hit the spot. I settled back in the car seat and reviewed my conversation with Jordan.

She was the second person today who pointed a finger at Cody Devlin. I could hardly ignore him as a viable suspect. While working with Crystal, Jordan heard Crystal's end of many a phone call between mother and son. Conversations in which Crystal insisted Cody attend college in the fall at her alma mater, Texas A&M. She had no tolerance for talk of Cody's dream to become an actor. A week ago Jordan witnessed a shouting match that ended with Cody telling his mother he didn't care what she wanted, he was going to live in California. She could take her money and shove it.

I could envision the boy saying such things in the heat of the moment. Realistically, though, he'd need money to live on.

Hitchcock was back up on the passenger seat and taking a bath, apparently satisfied with the bits of food he'd picked off the napkin. As I reached down to gather his leftovers, I heard a ding that signaled an incoming text. Where the heck was that phone?

Hitchcock twisted around to look at the back of his seat, and I found the device lodged deep in the crease. I pulled it out and smiled at the message from Luke.

Missing you. Hope you're staying safe.

I hesitated for a moment before answering.

Miss you, too. Dinner when you get back.

I slipped the phone into my tote and ate the second taquito, absorbed with thoughts of the man and the promise of a deepening relationship. I hadn't addressed the *safe* topic, but I wasn't planning to do anything that would jeopardize our second attempt at a dinner date.

Back to Jordan. She might be trying to take heat off herself by bringing up Cody's fights with his mother. At the time of the murder, Jordan was allegedly at home packing up things to prepare the house for selling. She had no one to confirm her alibi.

Did I see her as the killer? Nope. An embezzler? Yes. I'd already decided it wasn't my job to report her for stealing money. She intended to turn herself in now that she'd spilled the beans about her wrongdoing to me. I'd wait and give the woman a chance to make things right. That left the big question.

If Jordan wasn't the killer, who was?

I cleaned up my lunch wrappings, shifted into reverse, and looked at Hitchcock.

"Time to see Sheriff Crawford."

The cat glanced up for a moment and went straight back to his bath. Some statements didn't deserve a response, I guessed.

A s Hitchcock and I approached the entrance to the sheriff's department, the dispatcher came barreling out. Laurelle smiled broadly when she saw us.

"Howdy, Sabrina. Hitchcock." She bent to rub the cat's head.

"Where are you going in such a hurry?" I said.

"Quick run to Hot Stuff," she said. "Get you anything?"

"No thanks. Sheriff Crawford in?"

"Yup. He's alone in his office."

"Great."

"Ainsley's here, too." She looked down at Hitchcock.

"He'll give you grief about bringing a cat inside. Just a warning." She took off toward the back parking lot.

Hitchcock looked up at me.

"Well, I hate to leave you in the car, but I have an idea." I picked him up, went back to my car, and punched the button to open the trunk. I set the cat and my tote inside the trunk.

"Mrreow."

"Of course I'm not leaving you in here." I dumped everything out of the tote, then picked Hitchcock up and deposited him into the soft-sided leather pouch. "Will this work?"

He seemed to glare at me, but he made no attempt to leap out when I picked up the tote and hung it from my shoulder.

"I hope this will get us as far as the sheriff's office without having to deal with Deputy Ainsley."

I closed the trunk and walked into the building, my right arm cradling the cat-in-tote. I could see Hitchcock's ears sticking out of the top. Ainsley had never paid much attention to me, and I hoped he wouldn't start now.

I needn't have worried. The deputy was seated at his desk, intent on a man in a cowboy hat across from him. The man made hand motions as he talked and had a harsh and familiar voice, though I couldn't make out his words.

Ace McKinney.

I wanted to know why he was there, but not badly enough to call attention to myself. I waved to Cookie, the dispatcher on duty, and walked straight through toward the sheriff's private office before either of the men noticed us.

Sheriff Crawford looked up from his paperwork when I stepped into his office and quickly closed the door behind me.

"Afternoon, Sabrina." He removed his reading glasses and without missing a beat said, "Hello, Hitchcock."

The cat's head popped through the tote opening. "Mrreow."

The sheriff's brows drew together. "Something wrong, Sabrina? You look worried. Is Rowe okay?"

"She's fine," I said. "Least she was when I left this morning. You know Aunt Rowe. Witness a murder attempt last night, business as usual this morning. Nothing much fazes her."

"You're tellin' me." He sat back in his chair. "Then what has you riled up?"

"The man out there." I pointed at the lobby. "McKinney. Are you investigating him for the murder?"

"He came to report a stolen truck," the sheriff said. "You know something we don't?"

I thought for a moment before responding. "McKinney and that clown guy, Birch, were in town the morning of Crystal's murder."

"A lot of people were in town," he said.

"True, but he's so, so—"

"Rough around the edges?" Sheriff Crawford said.

"He has a nasty personality, and I have a bad feeling about him."

"The jail'd be jam-packed if I arrested everyone who gave me a bad feeling."

"When did his truck go missing?"

"Wasn't his," the sheriff said. "Belonged to the ranch. And it's not missing anymore."

"Any idea who took it?"

He shook his head. "Truck was abandoned behind Krane's Hardware. Middle of the night, I'd guess. Front end's banged up pretty good."

"Is it the one—" I paused as a vision of the car being rammed off the road flitted through my memory.

"Probably. We'll have it checked out."

Hitchcock started squirming, and I knelt down to hold the tote open. The cat slipped out and walked to the sheriff. Crawford patted the corner of the desktop, and Hitchcock jumped up to say hello. As man and cat enjoyed each other's company, I concocted a theory.

"Hypothetically," I said, "Ace McKinney could have used the truck to run Rita off the road, ditched it, got a ride back to the ranch, then come here to report the vehicle stolen to cover his tracks."

"Save that for your next plot," the sheriff said. "We questioned McKinney. He admitted Crystal Devlin wasn't his favorite person. He was in town that morning pickin' up supplies and didn't stay long."

"Anyone back up his story?"

The sheriff nodded. "Both Lance Devlin and the clown guy as you call him."

"Who may also be suspects," I said.

Crawford patted Hitchcock on the head. "Enjoyed the visit, you two, but I have work to do."

"I hope you're narrowing down the suspects." I said, "and that Pearl's name is off your list."

Sheriff Crawford used a thumb and index finger to smooth his mustache. "The investigation is ongoing."

I rolled my eyes. "You know telling me that is going to make me obsess about the murder even more."

"One of the things I like about you." He smiled. "If it makes you feel better, I no longer suspect Pearl."

I brightened. Maybe Ty's daughter and Pearl's granddaughter would have their BFF visit after all.

"Will you make an official statement to that effect?" I said.

"Not yet. Between you and me, and I know I can trust you to keep the info to yourself, right?"

I made a cross on my chest. "Absolutely."

"We're taking a closer look at the husband, the son, and the clown," he said.

"Seriously? The clown?"

He nodded. "He's a more likely suspect than the other two in my opinion."

His statement gave me hope that I could stop worrying about Cody Devlin being the culprit.

"Did you know Lance was consulting with Rita Colletti about a divorce?"

"I heard as much," the sheriff said.

"She has plenty of information about the Devlins."

He nodded. "So she says. I went to visit her today in the hospital."

"Oh, good. Then she filled you in on everything."

"She said *attorney-client privilege* a half dozen times."

"Of course she did," I said. "Why is Birch voted most likely?"

He held up a hand. "That's all I'm saying."

His desk phone rang, and Hitchcock jumped straight up in the air.

The sheriff and I shared a chuckle as he reached for the phone. I gathered my cat and put him back in the tote before we left the office. Tyanne would be glad to know I didn't do or say anything that would jeopardize Cody. Jordan would likely tell the sheriff everything she'd heard when she came and met with him.

Neither McKinney nor Ainsley were in sight as I crossed the lobby and slipped out the front door.

Whew.

"We're home free, Hitchcock," I whispered as I headed to my car. "I'm really curious what the sheriff has on Birch—"

I stopped short when I saw Ace McKinney leaning against a tree in front of the building, smoking a cigar and talking with another man I didn't recognize. I was close enough to hear McKinney loud and clear.

"What's the difference between a dead skunk in the road and a dead lawyer in the road?" he said, repeating the tired old joke.

The second man was already laughing and didn't respond.

"There's skid marks in front of the skunk," McKinney said and burst out laughing.

Really? The day after a lawyer is run off the road? And

the sheriff didn't think McKinney had anything to do with Rita's accident? He was exactly the kind of man I could see causing the wreck and killing Crystal, too. Being a jerk didn't make him guilty, but it made me think of him as a suspect even more.

"Hang on, Hitchcock. I have something to say to this dipwad."

McKinney's back was to me as I approached.

"Gotta run," the other man said, watching me from the corner of his eye as he hurried away.

McKinney turned to face me.

"Well, lookie here. Ain't you a little out of place here at the sheriff's dee-partment?"

"Maybe so, but you're perfectly situated."

His forehead creased. "Say what?"

"Kind of ballsy to bad-mouth lawyers the day after you run one off the road." I wanted to get a rise out of him, and the accusatory statement worked.

His complexion darkened. "You're talkin' crap, lady. I didn't do nothin' to that lawyer."

"But you don't like her."

"Hell, no, I don't. She has Lance wrapped around her little finger. First off tellin' him not to divorce the worst mistake he ever made, then orderin' him how to handle his own business."

"You really didn't like Crystal either, did you?"

"It's no secret. Had no use for that evil witch."

I frowned. "Isn't that a little strong? I mean, she was your boss's wife. Did you help him out by getting rid of Crystal for him?"

"You mean did I kill her?" he said.

I nodded.

"Can't take credit for that. You might wanna ask Birch. He and Crystal fooled around for a while. Heard her threaten more than once to go to Lance with that."

I didn't get why Crystal would have admitted her own

wrongdoing in order to cause trouble for Birch. "What would Lance have done?"

"Fire Birch's butt." McKinney smirked, as if the event would have made his year.

"I don't guess it's all that easy to find clown work," I said, wondering if this was why Sheriff Crawford had Birch high on the suspect list.

"Guy used to work on the highway crew. This is a lot better gig, especially with him chasin' all them barrel racing gals. He has a thing for women, case you hadn't noticed."

I *had* noticed, but I still found Hayden Birch a likeable person.

Which was more than I could say about McKinney.

"You see yourself as Lance Devlin's one loyal employee, don't you?"

McKinney shrugged. "'Cause I am."

"What about the gambling?" I said, going with my instincts. "What does your boss think about that?"

The man's eyes narrowed. He leaned toward me without answering.

"Did Crystal know?" I prodded. "Did she threaten to tell?"

"Where are you gettin' this pile of crap?" McKinney said.

"I know why you didn't like her," I said.

"No, you don't," he said.

"Then why don't you tell me?"

McKinney's arm shot out, and he slapped the tree.

"Fine. You wanna know?"

I nodded as my heart raced. I told myself I was safe here, right in front of the sheriff's department. McKinney wouldn't do anything to hurt me. I kept my arm curled protectively around the tote holding Hitchcock. I could feel the cat's body tensing.

"I knew that woman a loooonnng time," McKinney said in a low voice. "She got my fiancée killed. Sweetest woman ever lived. Ruined my life forever."

My eyes widened. I wasn't sure what I was expecting Mc-Kinney to say, but it wasn't this.

"So you ask me," he went on, "am I sorry that Crystal Devlin is dead?" McKinney's eyes went crazy and his mouth turned up in an obscene smile. "Nosiree. I hope that bitch rots in hell."

32

MCKINNEY THREW HIS partially smoked cigar on the ground and stomped the end. I was too unnerved by his stormy expression to ask the question foremost on my mind. What exactly had happened to his fianceé?

"I'm very sorry for your loss," I said.

He grunted, and I expected him to walk away. He looked toward the parking lot, then back at me.

"Appreciate it," he said, all of his usual bluster gone.

I readjusted the tote on my shoulder, and Hitchcock began to purr. Ace didn't appear to notice the cat sound coming from the tote. Curiosity about the man's fiancée urged me to continue the conversation.

"Did this happen recently?" I said.

He shook his head. "Nineteen years."

"Thinking about my dad's death brings me to tears," I said, "and that was long ago, too. I understand how you feel."

"Was he killed?" McKinney said in a tone that insinuated his grief held more weight than mine did.

"No. Sudden heart attack."

He removed his hat and used a shirt sleeve to mop his perspiring forehead.

"How did Crystal, I mean, how did your fiancée—"

"They were on a boat," he said.

I had a healthy fear of boats and found myself holding my breath. After a few seconds he went on without any prodding.

"Crystal was one of them bridezillas," he said. "Spent money like water. Rented some villa in Mexico for the bachelorette party. Tabby—" He paused, and his whisker-stubbled chin quivered. "Her name was Tabitha."

I felt myself tearing up as I watched the crusty old cowboy talk about the woman he loved.

"Tabby was a bridesmaid. A dozen of 'em total, partying on some fancy-ass boat with a bar, waiters, the whole nine yards. Nothin' too good for ol' Crystal."

His eyes met mine.

"What happened to Tabby?" I said.

"They ain't sure," he said. "She got seasick, but did Crystal give a crap about her friend? Think about turnin' back? No, ma'am. They stayed out there partyin', drinkin', till near midnight."

I waited, dread growing until it felt like a solid lump in my stomach. Sweat trickled down my forehead.

"Got back to the dock," McKinney said in a near whisper, "Tabby wasn't there. Guy who rented them the boat says, 'Hey, where's the other one, you had a dozen women, now you got eleven.'"

"How awful," I said.

"Crystal was too drunk to understand the question."

I rubbed the side of the tote, and Hitchcock's purring sped up. "So no one knows to this day what really happened?"

Ace swallowed visibly. "One of 'em saw Tabby hangin' on the rail, sick as a dog. My Tabby never drank. Didn't like the stuff. Seasickness got her. They think she passed out. Fell over."

"Dear Lord."

"We found her. Brought her back home." He bowed his head.

Tears leaked from my eyes to mix with the sweat on my face. No wonder Ace disliked Crystal so much. If she'd chosen a different location for her party, Tabby would probably still be here. She and Ace could have married, had children.

"I'm really sorry I brought this up," I said.

Not to mention accusing you of murder and attempted murder.

"Wasn't you," he said. "It's everything happened this week."

"It's been a crazy one," I agreed.

"I didn't run nobody off the road," he said, "and as many times as I'd've liked to get my hands around Crystal's neck and squeeze till there wasn't a breath left in her, I didn't kill the woman. That's the God's honest truth."

"Okay." After hearing his tale, I could hardly blame the man for holding a grudge against Crystal even though she'd only done what she set out to do—rent a boat to go out with her friends and party hard. Plenty of brides-to-be did the same sort of thing.

"I ain't perfect," Ace said. "Drink way too much, and I take a few bets at the rodeo. Strictly small-time. Crystal didn't like it, but it wasn't none of her business. Lance don't care, and nobody gets hurt."

I shrugged. "Not a big deal."

He put his hat back on his head. "Better get on back."

"Okay. Sorry I kept you."

He pinned me with a stare. "Talkin' about Tabby ever' so often does me good," he said. "Keeps her memory alive."

We exchanged a smile. The private Ace McKinney sure was the total opposite of the persona he wore for the world to see.

"You enjoy acting like you're a big bad cowboy, is that it?"

"Basically. Got a reputation to uphold."

"What about Remy? What's his story?"

Ace waved a hand. "He's harmless. Spends most of his time watchin' old westerns on TV. Guy's livin' in the age of *Gunsmoke*. We do some playactin' when nobody's around. Just for grins."

Until now I wouldn't have imagined either of these cowboys ever smiled, much less acted like a couple of silly kids.

"I suppose you get to play Marshall Matt Dillon."

"Every time," Ace said. "Remy's a good Festus."

He pointed at me. "You don't need to go tellin' anybody about this or how I went soft and mushy talkin' about Tabby either."

"Not a word," I said.

AFTER Ace McKinney left, I felt emotionally spent and guilty for keeping Hitchcock pent up in the tote for so long. I let the cat out of the proverbial bag and put him on the grass.

"Bet you're ready to stretch your legs," I said and took hold of the end of his leash. "How about a little walk?"

"Mrreow," he said.

We headed down the lawn next to the sidewalk in the direction away from the main drag through town. I turned on a residential street, thinking about all that I'd learned today. Lots of interesting bits and pieces. Nothing to pinpoint the killer.

"Maybe it's time to go home and get to work on that book," I said. "Give up this investigation business."

Which I could do since it looked like Pearl was going to be in the clear soon. Hitchcock gave me a meow that I was pretty sure meant he was ready for his afternoon nap on my deck. The day was slipping by, and if we didn't get home soon, the afternoon would be over. I kept walking anyway, mulling over the secrets people kept, figuring I must be a pretty boring person 'cause I couldn't think of any secrets of my own.

We reached Lavender Square, a small park in the midst of the residential area. I circled the park to head back the way we'd come. Two children were climbing on a play set while a woman I assumed was their mother looked on from a nearby bench. A few people sat at the picnic tables under a grove of trees off to my right.

As we grew closer, I noticed a young woman seated by herself reading a book. Nothing curious about that. A tall man and someone younger—I assumed his son—occupied another table.

I stopped walking and stooped next to Hitchcock. "You doin' okay? Want me to carry you?" I stroked his back a few times, then picked him up. Rather be safe than sorry. Cats weren't accustomed to being walked with a leash, and I didn't want to him to hate me for making him overexert himself.

As I stood, the men at the table stood, too. They hugged each other, and the older man strode toward the street where a pickup truck was parked. The boy sat back down at the table. I squinted and checked each of them out.

"It's the Devlins," I said to the cat. "Huh."

He looked up at me.

"Well, if you insist, I don't mind going over there and saying a few words to Cody."

"Mrreow."

"It'd be rude to ignore him. I wonder what he's doing here."

My feet were already headed that way as if by their own volition. I swear my nosiness was worsening by the day. I wouldn't mind having a talk with the boy, though, if only to assure myself that he had nothing to do with his mother's death. He looked up when I approached his table, and brushed dark bangs from his eyes.

"Mind if we sit here for a minute?" I said.

He looked at the other table where the woman was still by herself, reading.

He shrugged. "No problem."

I slid onto the bench opposite him and put Hitchcock down beside me.

"You doing okay?" I said to Cody.

"Sure." He gave me a palms up with another shrug, then looked at Hitchcock.

"Cool," he said. "Never saw a cat on a leash before."

"It's not his favorite thing." I scratched Hitchcock's head and returned my attention to Cody. "You're kind of far from home. What brings you here?"

"Waitin' on my girlfriend to get off work," he said.

"Oh." Hitchcock tensed, ready to jump on the table. I kept a firm hold on his leash and hoped he'd get the hint.

Don't distract us. Let the boy talk.

"I saw your dad leave just now. Has he made plans yet for a memorial service? I'd like to pay my respects."

"He's workin' on it," Cody said.

"I was thinking about my dad earlier. He passed away years ago. Whenever I think of him, I'm still as sad as the day it happened. People will say things trying to make you feel better. Doesn't really work."

"Yeah, I know."

"Somebody told me you're going into acting."

"Thinkin' about it," he said.

"Sounds interesting. How does your dad feel about the idea?"

"Dad's listening." Cody's complexion seemed to brighten with the change of topic. "Least he's not as freaked as my mom. She was doing everything she could to force me to go to college. Keep me in Texas."

"Lots of mothers have trouble letting their kids go."

"Mine wanted to control every move I made, like from now on."

"And the two of you fought about this?"

"Oh, yeah."

"You realize that might make you a suspect?"

His eyes widened. "No way. I'd never hurt my mom, not

physically. I probably would have gone to California, though. That's what I really wanted."

"Past tense?" I said.

He dipped his head. "I'm kinda rethinking everything. Might get away for a few days with Mimi. She's pushing for that 'cause I'm so stressed."

"You're young," I said. "No need to have a woman start tellin' you what to do already."

Cody smiled. "That's what my dad said."

"Sometimes Father knows best."

"Yeah. I'll probably stay with him and work on the ranch for a while till I figure things out."

"Good plan."

"Dads are kind of like an anchor, you know? I think that's what I need for now."

I smiled at the boy and hoped that his anchor didn't get yanked away and sent to jail for murder.

33

WHEN WE GOT back home a little after five in the afternoon, I noticed a patch of black clouds in the distance. A rainstorm would be welcome—lessen the thousand percent humidity. Give the grass a much-needed drink.

One could hope.

Aunt Rowe's car was parked in her driveway. I'd fill her in over dinner about the ground I covered today. First on the agenda—Hitchcock and I needed water. With the brutal summer heat, staying hydrated seemed like a losing battle.

The cat eagerly leapt out of the car when I parked at the Monte Carlo cottage, and he was up on the porch in three seconds. While unlocking the door, I glanced toward the Paris cottage and wondered how Rita would get home from the hospital now that her car had been wrecked. Best-case scenario, someone would pick her up and take her straight home to Houston.

I scolded myself for the nasty thought and went inside to

feed the cat. With Hitchcock chowing down on his dinner, I decided to check my e-mails and make sure there wasn't anything earth-shattering going on in my world that I didn't know about.

Not that anything would rattle me after today's conversations with a handful of murder suspects. And who stood out as a killer in that group? No one really.

I sighed. Hopefully Sheriff Crawford, or even one of his unlikeable deputies, had the perfect clues that would lead them to solve the murder and Rita's hit-and-run. They'd close the cases, and I would go back to the quiet life of a writer who only dealt with death on the page.

Twenty minutes later I'd deleted what seemed like a thousand junk e-mails and scanned the ones that were halfway important. In spite of my late lunch, I was feeling hungry. I went outside and found Hitchcock curled on a bench cushion on the back deck.

"Hey, I'm going to Aunt Rowe's. You wanna come?"

He lifted his head and gave me his contented slit-eyed look.

"Okay, next time," I said.

I walked up the driveway to the house. Thirty seconds into the short trip, sweat rolled down my back and I wished I had driven. I found Glenda in Aunt Rowe's kitchen making dinner.

She looked up from stuffing bell peppers with a mixture of ground beef, rice, and onion when I walked in. "Where have you been all day? In a sauna?"

"Very funny." I tore a section of paper towel off the holder and used it to dry my face. "Actually, I went to five or six places. Never a dull moment."

"Still investigating instead of writing?" she said.

"I'd rather you didn't put it that way and make me sound so irresponsible."

Glenda grinned. "If the shoe fits."

"I had a good motive," I told her. "Aunt Rowe will be glad to hear her friend Pearl is off the sheriff's suspect list."

"You don't say?" Glenda placed one filled pepper in a

baking dish and picked up another. "Glad to hear it. I never thought Pearl was involved."

"Her only involvement with Crystal, if you can call it that, was planting a black cat in Crystal's office to cause her bad luck."

Glenda froze in mid-pepper-stuff and looked at me. "Did she take Hitchcock?"

"No. I told her she couldn't take him, so she found a substitute black cat."

"Well, that's ridiculous," Glenda said. "Does Pearl believe that bad luck cat hooey?"

I shrugged. "More like she believed Crystal would think she had bad luck coming her way after the cat crossed her path. Turns out she did."

"But not because of any cat." Glenda finished with the second pepper and added it to the dish.

"Absolutely not because of a cat," I said. "Because of a killer. Hey, you have dessert planned for tonight?"

Glenda shook her head. "Hadn't thought that far."

I opened the pantry and perused the contents, my eyes settling on a box of graham cracker crumbs and a can of cherry pie filling. Hmm. I went to the refrigerator and pulled out two packages of cream cheese.

"How about that no-bake cheesecake?" I said.

"Sounds good to me. Rowe will love it."

I took out a nine-by-thirteen pan. As I measured brown sugar and butter with the crumbs to make a crust, I reported on my conversations with Jordan and Ace. Touched briefly on Jordan's financial problems and told her about Ace's history with Crystal Devlin.

"Now that you mention it, I remember hearing about that woman falling overboard. Sad, sad story." Glenda had finished stuffing the peppers and had them sitting in the baking dish, lined up like little green soldiers. She went to the stove and stirred a pot of tomato sauce I knew she'd made from scratch with tomatoes from her garden.

"I saw Cody Devlin, too," I said. "Poor kid is trying his best to hold it together, not sure what to do with his life."

"Bless his heart," Glenda said.

"Talked to Mimi at the real estate office."

"What was she doing there?"

"Working. You didn't know she worked with Jordan?"

"Mimi? In an office?" Glenda looked over her shoulder at me. "She's more of the artsy type."

"Maybe it's a temporary thing," I said. "Crystal had Jordan to help her. It makes sense that Jordan needs some help."

Glenda shrugged. "I'm sure Mimi's glad to spend time away from her parents. Sometimes I can hear them screaming from three doors down. The parents, not Mimi."

"Yeesh. That's no fun. My mom got on my nerves constantly, but at least she wasn't a screamer." I pressed the crumb mixture into the pan and smoothed it out with the back of a spatula.

"So after all this visiting around town, who do you think murdered Crystal?" Glenda said.

"Sheriff Crawford suspects Hayden Birch."

"That's surprising," Glenda said. "I like Hayden."

"So do I, but turns out he was having an affair with Crystal. Maybe things took a bad turn."

"He should have known better than to mess around with a married woman," Glenda said. "Behavior unbecoming to a clown, that's for sure."

I grinned. "Maybe he didn't read the clown manual. Anyway, I have a hard time seeing him as the guilty party."

"Who do you think did it?"

"Well, I think Rita showed Lance how things would look financially if he divorced Crystal. Male clients have a tendency to blow up when they realize how hard a divorce will hit their bank account. I haven't ever known one who killed his wife instead of divorcing her before."

Glenda spun to face me. "You think Lance Devlin killed his wife? Are you serious?"

"I think it's a distinct possibility."

"You know, Rowe said that on the first day."

"I'll bet lots of people said that. The husband's always the number one suspect. This time, it might be true. All I know for sure is I wouldn't trust Lance Devlin for a second."

Glenda turned, her brow creased, a big frown on her face.

"That's really bad news," she said.

"Why? You have some connection with him?"

"I don't, but Rowe is there."

"What do you mean? I thought Aunt Rowe was in her room."

"She's not. She's at the rodeo."

"Are you kidding me?" I dropped the spatula on the counter. "She witnessed Rita being run off the road last night. She knows somebody killed Crystal. She wouldn't go back there."

"She did," Glenda said. "All she talks about is those darn goats. Had some brainstorm about turning the whole performance into a comedy skit instead of the standard rodeo event, so she headed back out there again tonight to work on her new idea."

"But her car's in the driveway." My heart was racing, and taking deep breaths wasn't slowing it down.

"Pearl picked her up," Glenda said. "The two of them are crazy, you ask me, dressed in their new purple shirts with those long sleeves in this heat. I told her I'd fix the stuffed peppers and she could warm 'em up if she's not back in time for dinner."

"I'm going out there," I said. "I won't be able to eat until she's home safe and sound."

"You watch yourself," Glenda called to my back.

I ran to my place. My clothes were nearly dripping with sweat when I got there and went inside to snatch the car key. Outside, I saw Hitchcock sitting on the car hood.

"Sorry, bud, not this time." I picked him up and took him to the porch. "You can't go to the rodeo."

I paused and looked him in the eye. "Do I need to lock you up inside?"

"Mrreow." He jumped up on the porch railing and sat down.

"Good. I'm taking you at your word. I'll return soon with Aunt Rowe in tow."

I kept one eye on the rearview as I drove down the lane. The heat must be getting to the cat, too, because Hitchcock didn't even try to catch up with me.

34

KNEW THE SHORTCUT that would get me to my destination faster, but I couldn't bring myself to take the route over the hills. My fear didn't make logical sense. The killer couldn't know I'd be driving there tonight. He might not feel it necessary to follow me even if he knew exactly where I was headed. All I knew was I had to get to Aunt Rowe, make sure she was okay, and take her home.

Maybe I should call Sheriff Crawford and have him come over, too, to back me up. But he'd ask me what was happening, and I had nothing concrete to tell him. Even though he didn't approve of Aunt Rowe performing in the rodeo, he wasn't likely to ride out with sirens blaring for no good reason.

I didn't need a big reason to show up. I could imagine a dozen problems, beginning with Aunt Rowe running into Hayden Birch, the sheriff's prime suspect. I told myself that the two of them had gotten along fine, even had fun with the goat tying practice. Birch had no reason to hurt my aunt.

Did he?

A chill raced over my body. The combination of sweat-drenched clothes and air-conditioning was a bad one. I flipped the AC switch to low and aimed the vents away from me. The black clouds were multiplying and moving in fast.

Moving to the scenic Hill Country was supposed to relax me compared to my stress-filled city life. Aunt Rowe kept me on my toes, though. Worrying about her, I saw no stress relief in sight. Why did she insist on doing things like this? Was it peer pressure? At her age?

Was she going to be ticked at me for showing up and causing a scene?

Probably.

Okay, then, instead of dragging her to my car, I'd stay and watch the goat tying practice. Make sure nothing happened to her or Pearl. Get them out of there the second they'd had their fill of wrestling goats. This whole situation might be funny if I wasn't so worried.

I reached the rodeo in twenty minutes that felt more like hours and parked in the lot. As soon as I climbed out of the car I spotted Hayden Birch in the corral with the fierce-looking bull. Rambo pawed at the dirt and lowered his head, horns aimed toward Hayden, and I wondered if the man had a screw loose to put himself in mortal danger every time he worked with the animal.

No sign of Aunt Rowe or Pearl out here, so I hurried through the gates and past the concession stands. I stepped into the arena and stopped behind the last row of seats. There they were—Aunt Rowe and Pearl—behind the fence with five goats prancing around them. A red hat with a purple plume lay in the dirt. Aunt Rowe's, since Pearl was still wearing hers.

Laughter rang out. "That's the way, ladies," a man said. "Get your goat."

I scanned the seats and didn't see anyone except for a gray tabby cat walking the top of the arena fence like a tightrope.

"This is priceless," said a voice behind me.

I spun to see Lance Devlin approaching. He looked pretty happy-go-lucky for a man whose wife was recently murdered. His attitude and the fact that my irritation gauge was already hitting the top made me want to wipe the grin off his face.

"Why are you willing to let these ladies fool with dangerous animals?" I said. "They're senior citizens for crying out loud."

"This is an attraction," he said. "People will love it."

"I don't."

"You're in the minority," he said. "Ladies want to be here, that's *their* business. You don't see them complaining, do you?"

I glanced at the arena. Aunt Rowe stood with knees bent, her arms spread wide. She eyed a brown goat that looked smaller than the others. The scene did strike me as comical, but in these circumstances I wasn't laughing. I worried about what her blood pressure would read. Pearl was chasing a white goat, the goat winning by a wide margin. I turned back to Devlin.

"I thought you blamed Pearl for killing your wife. Are you planning to arrange for her to have an accident out there as some sort of retribution?"

His grin disappeared. "I don't think she had anything to do with what happened to Crystal."

"What *do* you think happened?"

"I don't know. The sheriff is handling that."

"Right." I paused, measuring the wisdom of continuing the conversation. Maybe I'd sweated out some of my smarts, 'cause I couldn't keep quiet. "I'm wondering why Rita Colletti's still here in Lavender. Obviously, you don't need a divorce anymore."

"How do you know about my personal business?"

"I keep my eyes and ears open. People talk."

"I didn't kill Crystal if that's what you're thinking," he said.

I shrugged. "I'm thinking it's kind of handy for you that she died. Saved you a ton of money."

He shook his head. "The decision to divorce or not wasn't all about money. You didn't know my wife."

"She wasn't faithful. I get that. Do you suspect anyone in particular?"

He didn't respond.

"You must have some thoughts about it," I pressed. "How could you not?"

"I don't answer to you," he said. "You shouldn't even be here. We're not open to the public tonight."

"I came to pick up my aunt."

"Sounds more like you came to give me the third degree," he said. "You're the one's been poking around town asking questions. Don't you know sticking your nose where it doesn't belong can be dangerous business?"

I should heed that warning bell and get while the getting was good. Instead, I asked, "Is that why Rita was targeted? She asked too many questions?"

He threw his arms up in a frustrated gesture that made me back away.

"How would I know? If you're worried about that, you ought to butt out. Mind your own business."

"Fine. I'll be gone just as soon as my aunt—" I turned back to the arena. Aunt Rowe and Pearl were gone. Only the goats remained.

"Where are—" I spun back to Devlin and saw him heading for the exit.

"Where's my aunt?" I said.

"Probably had her fill for one night."

"Where did she go?" He shrugged and kept walking.

What's happening?

"Aunt Rowe," I yelled at the top of my voice. "Where are you? Aunt Rowe."

I ran down the steps to the perimeter fence and looked both ways. Nothing except for five pairs of beady goat eyes watching me. Something farther down the fence caught their attention and they looked that way.

What do they see?

I climbed over the fence and jumped into the arena, then ran in the direction the goats were looking.

"Aunt Rowe? Pearl?"

This was crazy. The women couldn't disappear into thin air. Maybe they decided to go home before the storm began.

What if someone grabbed them?

I ran along the fence and heard the shuffling of goat hooves behind me. I glanced over my shoulder and saw the little buggers were running after me. Did they think I'd come to feed them or what?

I came to a gate that opened into a hallway, and spotted a Restrooms sign.

That's it, they had to stop here before going home.

Made all the sense in the world. I managed to get myself through the gate without the goats following and closed it behind me. Their little noses pressed up to the fence. The biggest one bleated at me.

"Sorry, guys. If I wasn't so eager to find Aunt Rowe, I'd stay and chat."

Thunder sounded in the distance.

I took two steps toward the ladies' room door and thunder rumbled again. The arena lights flicked off, leaving me in near darkness with only the glow of a red Exit sign beyond the restroom doors to guide me.

My heart thudded. The storm didn't seem near enough to have killed the electricity. Best-case scenario, the rodeo people were closing up for the night and didn't know anyone was inside. Worst case? I'd just accused a man of murder, and here I was. A sitting duck, not willing to leave without knowing Aunt Rowe and Pearl were all right. I moved slowly, feeling my way along the wall to the restroom door, and pushed it open.

"Aunt Rowe?"

Silence.

"Anyone here?"

I blew out a frustrated breath. They were probably well on their way to the car, though I didn't know how they could have gotten so far ahead of me. If I hadn't been so intent on spouting off to Lance Devlin, I wouldn't have lost track of them in the first place.

It's your own fault.

I went to the door under the Exit sign and pushed the bar to open it.

The door wouldn't budge.

I rattled the bar in frustration, then stopped when I heard a noise. Someone might be on the other side. Maybe that cat.

"Hello?" I called. "Is somebody out there? Let me out." I knocked on the door and waited. Repeated.

Nothing.

I thought about the goats. Someone would come to put them up for the night. I couldn't imagine the poor little things sleeping in the dirt arena. I hoped whoever was in charge of the animals showed up soon.

I turned and felt my way back to the gate that I'd taken to come this far. Another faint noise made me stop.

"Hello? Is anyone out there?" Hayden?" I waited, then whispered, "Aunt Rowe?"

My heart rate, already rapid, escalated. Aunt Rowe shouldn't be in danger, but what if I brought danger to her by being here? By frustrating a killer who was already put out with me the night before. The person who may have intended to run me off the road and got Rita instead?

Oh, jeez.

I hurried back to the arena.

"Hey, goats, where are—" I listened carefully, but the noise I heard this time didn't come from the arena in front of me. It came from behind.

And then something collided with my head, and my knees buckled.

My world went dark.

*   *   *

I DREAMT of a storm so powerful that lightning bolts struck my head and thunder sounded like the pounding of a thousand horses' hooves. I should move, go inside, get myself to a safe place. Better yet, wake up and get out of this darn nightmare.

Wait. This is no dream.

My memory began to return, and my eyes fluttered open. There wasn't much to see. Near darkness. I was on the floor. Hot. Something was stuffed in my mouth. Hands bound behind my back. Legs tied together. Thunder boomed. The storm was real.

Something pummeled the wall next to me. Boards rattled. I tried to scream. Couldn't. More thrashing nearby. Animal noises. Snorting.

A bull. Wild. Frightened.

No more frightened than I was at this moment. I prayed whatever separated me from the bull would hold strong. I struggled against the rope that someone, the killer, had used to tie me. I had to get loose. Had to find Aunt Rowe. Who had done this? Hayden Birch? Lance Devlin? My fingers found an end of the rope, and I pulled. No, that tightened the knot. I needed to get out of this, make a call for help. Where was my phone? I searched my memory and remembered dumping my tote into my car trunk.

Never mind that. Get loose.

My head throbbed where the killer had hit me, but I forced myself to keep moving, keep working the rope. My fingers, wet with sweat, ached as I tried to undo a knot. I wished that I truly had the special powers Twila thought I had—I'd be out of here so fast. Before whoever did this came back and—

What? I had no idea what he had planned for me. I hoped Aunt Rowe and Pearl were already headed home.

I shifted my weight and pedaled my feet as I tried to loosen the rope around my ankles. They weren't tied as tight as my hands. Who had done this? Maybe someone I didn't even see tonight, a person lurking around the premises. Had Cody, the actor wannabe, given me the performance of a lifetime? A sob story about how he would never kill his mother. What if the boy planned to collect his trust money, stay in Lavender for a little while to make it look good, then disappear?

I gave up trying to free my feet and went back to my hands. If only I could get this thing out of my mouth and scream for help.

I kept working, thinking about motive. What did the killer want? Did Crystal—or Rita—put up some sort of roadblock between him and his goal? What changed after Crystal's death? Pearl would buy the property she wanted. Lance didn't need a divorce. Birch's job was safe. Cody would get the money.

A flash of lightning illuminated the barn interior and the huge dark figure of Rambo in the stall next to me. The bull walloped the wooden slats, kicking out repeatedly with his back feet. The killer wanted me stomped to death. My heart was beating so hard I thought I might die of a heart attack before that happened. Make things easy for whoever did this.

Thunder crashed, louder than before. Maybe I could get to a standing position. Open the gate and hop out. The bull quieted, and I forced my breathing to slow down.

C'mon Sabrina. You can do it.

I tried to roll. Failed. Took another breath to try again.

And heard a meow.

Not just any meow. It was Hitchcock.

Even as I recognized his voice, I couldn't believe he was here. How could he possibly be here? Then he was at my head and rubbing against me as if telling me that everything was okay. Things would work out. I wanted to talk to him, hug him, in the worst way. The best I could do came out as unintelligible whining.

Hitchcock stood face-to-face with me, and our eyes met. He rubbed his face against my chin, and the gag in my mouth shifted slightly. That gave me an idea. Hitchcock stood aside as I rocked my body, gained momentum, then managed to roll on my side. I dragged the side of my face along the floor until the fabric caught on the rough concrete. I pushed at the gag with my tongue for a full minute, two. Finally, the obstruction popped out, and I stretched my aching mouth.

"Hitchcock, am I ever glad to see you." I panted from the exertion. "Aunt Rowe. We have to get her."

"Mrreow."

I was surprised the cat hadn't been scared off by Rambo. Or the thunder. The rope around my wrists had caught his attention, and he started chewing on it. He was a resourceful cat, but he'd have to chew for a month to get through this rope.

The storm was moving away, but I heard another noise. Not the bull. Footfalls. A person.

The killer?

"Hitchcock," I whispered, but the cat was gone. Hiding, I hoped.

The gate opened. Shock rolled through me when Mimi Trevino walked into the stall. Were she and Cody in cahoots to get the money?

I noticed the girl held a cell phone.

"Had to charge the damn thing before I could send a text," she said.

A text? Is that all young people thought about anymore?

"What text?" I said.

She didn't even look at me. "Why does that woman even bother having a phone if she doesn't keep it charged? Send texts?"

"Who are you talking about?"

The person who doesn't send texts. Pearl. Does she have Pearl's phone?

"What did you do with Aunt Rowe and Pearl?" I said.

"Nuthin'." Mimi's face screwed up. "I didn't need them, just the phone. She never knows where she puts the thing."

As Mimi's thumbs worked the phone, she recited, "Got the last laugh. Crystal wouldn't sell to me. I showed her."

She held an index finger over the phone, then pushed a button with a flourish. "Send. Perfect. Gotcha."

I used all my concentration and forced myself into a sitting position.

"You're trying to frame Pearl?" I said, wiggling my hands. The rope loosened a bit, and I kept working on it.

Mimi grinned at me. "You're a smart one. That's a problem."

"I'm a writer. I know when a plot won't work, and yours is thin. Riddled with holes. No one will ever believe Pearl killed Crystal."

"Shut your mouth." Mimi came toward me with a hand held high as if she meant to swat me, but then she started sneezing.

Once. Twice. Three times.

She wiped her nose on her shirt sleeve.

"I can't believe you're helping Cody with this," I said. "Not a smart move."

"Cody?" Mimi laughed. "That mama's boy would never have gone for this."

Realization dawned. "You thought he was your ticket out of a bad home life. I get that, but killing his mother?"

"The falling bricks killed her," she said.

"Someone conveniently placed her dead body under those bricks. The sheriff knows Crystal was dead before the bricks hit her, Mimi. You've made a huge mistake."

The girl threw her hands out to her sides. "How else was Cody gonna get his money from that witch?"

I swallowed hard. "Cody's not leaving Lavender, you know. He's decided to stay here."

"He is *so* leaving," she screamed, but her voice was cut off by another volley of sneezes.

"You'll never get away with this." The rope around my

hands had loosened more, and I worked it furiously. "I suppose you're planning to kill me, too."

"Won't have to." She tipped her head. "All I have to do is open this gate. Rambo takes care of the rest."

My heart stopped for a second, but I willed myself to stall for more time. "They'll find me tied up," I said. "The sheriff will know it was no accident."

Mimi paused, and I wondered if she was just now realizing she hadn't thought this plan all the way through. Then the sneezing started again.

Hitchcock jumped up on the gate.

"You're allergic to cats, huh?" I pulled my hands free of the rope but kept them hidden behind my back. "Tough break."

She looked at Hitchcock. "That's the bad luck cat," she managed between sneezes. "Do you take him freakin' *everywhere*?"

A second cat jumped up next to Hitchcock. And another. More cats appeared. Hitchcock had rounded up some friends. They jumped into the stall and swarmed around Mimi, rubbing against her legs.

"Get them—" Mimi couldn't talk for the sneezing. "Off. Me."

While she was distracted in her sneezing fit, I untied my legs and jumped up. I took the longest section of rope and looped it over Mimi's torso, then wound it around so her arms were pinned to her body. As I worked to restrain the girl, I heard Aunt Rowe's voice.

"Sabrina?" she called. "Where are you?"

"In the barn," I hollered, then looked at Mimi.

"Hitchcock is *not* bad luck," I said. "Matter of fact, he's the best thing that ever happened to me."

The barn lights flicked on. Seconds later, Aunt Rowe ran up the aisle between the stalls and spotted me. She didn't look especially rattled, and I knew she couldn't see Mimi from where she stood.

"Noticed Hitchcock runnin' around," Aunt Rowe said, "so I figured you were here somewhere." She gave me a once-over from my tangled hair to the grit and straw clinging to my sweat-drenched clothes. She homed in on the piece of rope I held.

"If you wanted in on the goat tying, Sabrina, you should have said so. It's not too late to order you a shirt."

35

GLENDA, TYANNE, AND I sat together, waiting for Lavender's first Senior Pro Rodeo to begin. Tyanne's daughter, Abby, and Pearl's granddaughter, Julie, sat on the bench in front of us, sharing a cotton candy. Seeing the little girls together warmed my heart and reminded me of the fun summer days Tyanne and I spent together when we were their age. I felt more relaxed than I had in a long time. Not only was the murder solved—I'd sent my revised manuscript off to my agent, too.

Advertising for the pro rodeo had announced guest appearances by several famous performers who'd long since retired from their rodeo days. Former pros, which is what I thought when I first heard about the event, even though locals other than Aunt Rowe and her friends were slated to perform, too.

Doc Jensen and I had placed an ad for the black cat adoption event in the program, taking advantage of every opportunity to attract cat lovers far and wide to come and adopt a new fur-ever friend. The program also included a Devlin Realty ad in memory of Crystal. Lance had decided not to press charges against Jordan Meier for her brief "misappropriation" of company funds, and she was still overseeing the business.

A medley of George Strait hits came through the loudspeakers. Off to one side of the arena, Aunt Rowe and friends were on horseback, lined up for the processional that would start off the night. The rodeo regulars—barrel racers, bull riders, and Hayden Birch—were taking part. The clown was busy entertaining the crowd, no doubt relieved that the murder case was solved and he still had his job. Hayden had admitted to me after Mimi's arrest that he feared Lance had murdered his wife. On the day I'd spotted him as he tried to leave the sheriff's office without being noticed, Hayden had reported some things he knew about the couple's doomed relationship. Luckily, their irreconcilable differences would have simply led them to divorce court, not to one of them killing the other.

I turned my attention back to the processional and spotted Luke Griffin, lined up with half a dozen other Texas game wardens in uniform. He noticed me looking and lifted his arm in a wave. I waved back and felt as giddy as a kid under his attention.

"What's the grin for?" Tyanne said, then followed my gaze to see Luke on horseback.

She smiled knowingly. "Oh, I see. What's going on with you two?"

"Nothing," I said, "other than we're enjoying each other's company."

"Uh-huh."

"I'm just glad I lived to see this day and to have the killer behind bars." I shook my head. "Even though I'm so sorry that Mimi ruined her life the way she did."

"She wasn't right in the head," Glenda said. "Had a rough childhood with that daddy of hers. He mistreated those kids from the get-go, and her mother wasn't much better. Not an excuse for what Mimi did, mind you."

"A more rational killer might have succeeded in getting rid of me and framing Pearl for the murder," I said. "Sending a fake text wasn't the brightest idea Mimi had, as if Pearl would incriminate herself in that text to her own son. The girl was smart enough, though, to take the job in Crystal's office so she could rummage through papers and find the details about the trust and when Cody would get his money."

"Why'd she run Rita off the road?" Tyanne said.

"She knew Lance and Rita were working together on legal documents," I said, "and I'm sure she feared that Cody's trust money was in jeopardy. But if the lawyer died and Cody turned eighteen . . ."

"The kids would be home free," Glenda said. "California, here we come."

"Right," I said. "But she went off on a tangent without a foolproof plan."

"Thank goodness for that." Tyanne turned to Glenda. "I must personally thank you for taking Hitchcock to the rodeo to rescue Sabrina."

"He wouldn't have it any other way," Glenda said. "There I was trying to finish dinner and the darn cat's up on the windowsill howling for all he's worth till I let him in, then he was on the kitchen counter between me and the food, gettin' hair in everything. Finally, I figured he was tryin' to tell me something. Had to involve Sabrina. Luckily, I knew where she went, so I called Thomas and asked him to bring us out here."

I laughed. "Bet Thomas loved that. Riding in the same car with the bad luck cat."

"He argued, but I straightened him out right quick," Glenda said. "He still made us sit in the backseat."

Tyanne said, "Poor Thomas. He'll grow to love Hitchcock one of these days."

"Don't count on it," I said. "He feels the same about Hitchcock as I do about *that woman*."

"What woman?" Ty turned to see Rita Colletti coming up the aisle toward us.

The lawyer was decked out in a western bling shirt, with jeans and boots, her arm in a tight sling. The people from the law firm wouldn't even recognize her in that getup.

I leaned closer to Tyanne. "I had such high hopes she'd already gone back to Houston."

"Maybe she stayed for tonight," Ty said. "Rowe's been talkin' her performance up. She and Rita are chummy, you know."

I grimaced. "Yeah, I know."

Rita reached us, and I forced a smile.

"That aunt of yours sure is something," Rita said. "Out there on that horse looking like she does this every day."

"She's something all right," I said.

"I'm looking forward to getting to know her a lot better."

Good grief. Are the two of them BFFs after knowing each other a few days?

I tried not to frown and lost the battle. "I imagine the firm is expecting you back soon, right?"

"Maybe so," Rita said.

"I don't know how they survived without you." She'd said those words to me plenty of times when we worked together.

How would this place ever survive without me?

"They'll have to figure it out," she said. "'Cause I'm not going back."

My heart rate shot up. "What?"

Tyanne and I exchanged a glance.

"That's news," Ty said. "What are your plans?"

"I'm staying right here in Lavender," Rita said. "Already got my office picked out. The county has plenty of work for a family law attorney. All I have to do is find a place to live."

A voice came over the loudspeaker. "Welcome, y'all, to the Lavender Senior Pro Rodeo. Tonight we welcome that star bronc-bustin'—"

"Better get to my seat," Rita said. "Later."

I looked at Tyanne. I tried to say something, but nothing came out except a couple of gasps.

"Don't worry," Ty said. "You probably won't see much of Rita once she gets settled into her own place."

I rapped my knuckles on the bench beside me.

"Knock on wood," I said.

RECIPES

Black Bottom Cupcakes

BATTER
1½ cups flour
1 cup sugar
¼ cup cocoa
1 teaspoon baking soda
½ teaspoon salt
1 cup water
⅓ cup oil
1 teaspoon vinegar
1 teaspoon vanilla
chocolate chips

FILLING
1 (8-ounce) package cream cheese
1 egg
⅓ cup sugar
⅛ teaspoon salt

Preheat oven to 350°F. Combine ingredients for batter and filling in separate bowls. Fill cupcake papers halfway with batter. Drop 1 teaspoon filling into center of each cupcake. Put 6 or 8 chocolate chips on top. Bake for 15 to 18 minutes. Yield 15 to 18 cupcakes.

Texas Cowboy Cookies

1 cup packed brown sugar
½ cup sugar
½ cup shortening
½ cup butter
2 eggs
1 teaspoon vanilla extract
1½ cups all-purpose flour
1 teaspoon baking soda
1 teaspoon salt, optional
3 cups oatmeal (quick or old-fashioned)

Preheat oven to 350°F. Lightly grease cookie sheet. Beat sugars, shortening, and butter until creamy. Add eggs and vanilla; beat well. Combine flour and baking soda (and 1 teaspoon salt, if desired). Add to shortening mixture; mix well. Stir in oats; mix well. Drop by rounded tablespoons 2 inches apart onto prepared cookie sheet. Bake 10 to 12 minutes or until light golden brown. Let stand 1 minute before removing to racks to cool.

Variations: Stir in 1 cup of any of the following with oats: semisweet chocolate chips, raisins, chopped walnuts, chopped dates, or shredded coconut.

No-Bake Cherry Cheesecake

2 (8-ounce) packages cream cheese
1 cup plus 2 tablespoons sugar
1 tablespoon lemon juice
4 cups nondairy whipped topping

2 cups graham cracker crumbs
⅓ cup packed brown sugar
½ cup butter, melted
1 can cherry pie filling

Beat the cream cheese, sugar, and lemon juice until smooth. Beat in whipped topping until smooth.

To make the crust, mix graham cracker crumbs, brown sugar, and butter. Press into a 9 x 13 x 2–inch cake pan. Spread filling over crust and chill. Top with cherry pie filling. Chill until set, and serve.

Also From

KAY FINCH

Black Cat Crossing

A Bad Luck Cat Mystery

Sabrina has never been the superstitious type. Still,
when she moves to Lavender, Texas, to write her first novel
and help her aunt, Rowe, manage her vacation rental
business, Sabrina can't avoid listening to the rumors
that a local black cat is a jinx—especially after the stray
in question leads her directly to the scene of a murder.

The deceased turns out to be none other than her aunt
Rowe's awful cousin Bobby Joe Flowers, a known cheat
and womanizer who had no shortage of enemies. The only
problem is that Aunt Rowe and Bobby Joe had quarreled
just before the cousin turned up dead, leaving Rowe at
the top of the long list of suspects. Now it's up to Sabrina
to clear her aunt's name. Luckily for her, she's got a new
sidekick, Hitchcock the bad luck cat, to help her sniff out
clues and stalk a killer before Aunt Rowe winds up the
victim of even more misfortune…

kayfinch.com
penguin.com